THE
BEACH
PARTY

AMY SHEPPARD

THE
BEACH
PARTY

bookouture

Published by Bookouture in 2022

An imprint of Storyfire Ltd.
Carmelite House
50 Victoria Embankment
London EC4Y 0DZ

www.bookouture.com

ISBN: 978-1-80314-741-3
eBook ISBN: 978-1-80314-740-6

PROLOGUE

Flames licked at the wood stacked high on the dry sand. The loud crackling drowned out the sound of the waves. Waves that lapped against the shore just a few feet away. The moon was a bright white ball. You could see every star in the sky that night.

People sat huddled around the fire, their faces aglow with orange light. Someone was gently strumming a guitar. A man was singing, but his words were swept away on the wind.

Every person there was just a shape. Shapes and shadows and shards of light. Everyone except her. She was in full color. Her long golden hair lifted on the breeze as she spun around, twisting her tiny feet in the sand. Everyone watched as she danced to the sounds of the beach. Nobody had ever looked more alive.

CHAPTER ONE

It was still dark when I turned onto Sophie's road. Neon green numbers flashed the time in the center of the dashboard: 5:22 a.m. I drank the last mouthful of coffee from my travel mug. It tasted strong and metallic. I'd made it in the darkness of my kitchen before I left only ten minutes ago. It seemed like longer.

I hadn't been to Sophie's flat for a while. Maybe weeks. There was a time when we were always at each other's houses. That was before I got a job, before Tom. Tom is Sophie's boyfriend. He was a friend from home; a friend from Cornwall. At least, that's what we used to be. I'm not sure what we are now.

I drove slowly along the tidy Victorian terrace. Sophie's street looked like all the other London roads in this area. Large imposing properties, half brick, half white-painted stucco. All with wide steps, leading to the front door. Most of them had now been divided into small apartments and studio flats.

I stopped outside Sophie's building. No parking spaces. I would just wait in the road. There was no traffic, not at this time. That's why we were leaving so early. I'd told Sophie I would give her a missed call when I arrived. I was a few minutes early. I craned my neck to look at my reflection in the rearview mirror. Pale and angular. Younger than my twenty-four years, but only because my tiredness was hidden by dark shadows that cast arcs across my face. My long dark hair, scraped into a ponytail, looked black. It made my skin look fragile, like porcelain.

I pressed my cold fingers to my eyes and slowly drew them down my face. I was starting to feel more awake. I reached for my phone and scrolled through the call list. I paused on Sophie's name. Was it really only four days ago that we'd spoken? Four days since we'd made plans to go to Cornwall. Back to my hometown, Pengully. It had been over two years since I'd made this journey.

I pressed the call button. It rang twice before she sent me to voicemail. I saw a shadow pass the window. I'll give her time to get her things together. Their things.

"Hi, you've reached Sophie. Sorry I can't take your call..." Sophie's husky voice broke through the silence in the car.

Her voice was perfect for radio. Confident, sexy and just the right amount of "London." Presenting her own radio show was all she'd ever wanted. She'd laughed when she told me she used to talk over music in her bedroom when she was a kid. Using a hairbrush to introduce the next song. It was everything she was working toward. It was why she'd studied journalism. It was why she started the podcast.

Sophie was unflinching in her desire to succeed. She'd moved to London from a small town too. A place similar in size to Pengully in south Gloucestershire. Sophie had moved to London and had vowed to never leave.

Over the last three years she'd built up an enviable social media following. Her online personality had been carefully curated. She'd created an image for herself, an image that had amassed her over 300,000 loyal followers. They loved her.

Sophie was a fashion and beauty blogger. She had established her own marketing platform to promote the latest makeup and clothes. Sophie was a person who turned heads. She was a person you noticed. With her gym-honed body and golden mane of hair, companies were desperate to work with her. They'd paid large sums of money to be part of her world.

Sophie deliberately connected herself with cool, emerging brands and helped them grow. She had shares in at least two of those brands, building on each other's success. That was the thing about Sophie. She was always two steps ahead of everyone else. She didn't need to do the podcast anymore, but she did. It was the only thing that still connected us.

My life since leaving Cornwall has been very different to Sophie's. We'd met at City University in London. We were both studying journalism. I wanted to write. I had *always* wanted to write. I dreamed of working at a newspaper one day. I imagined myself in a buzzing press office, hiding in a corner booth behind a screen, writing stories. I didn't even care what I wrote about: politics, lifestyle... travel. It didn't matter as long as my days were filled with words.

The course had finished two years ago. I felt like I'd only just got into my stride when it ended. It was like starting again. I moved from the comfortable bubble of student halls into my own tiny flat. I thought I would enjoy the quiet more than I did.

I quickly found a job at a newspaper. Not as a writer, but as a junior researcher. The work was menial and the pay low. My parents had to help me out with rent for the first few months. After two years I still hadn't made any close friendships there.

I often thought about going home. Starting again in the safe, comfortable haven of Pengully. But I couldn't. Not after everything.

CHAPTER TWO

It had all started at college. We'd met through mutual acquaintances and were an unlikely fit.

I was quiet. Not really shy, but it took me a long time to find my feet after I'd moved to London. I think some people saw me as standoffish. I suppose I was at first. But what everyone else saw as boring, Sophie saw as calming. She said she loved the stillness of me.

I never used to be this quiet. The move to London had been hard. I'd spent my whole life in a small town, where everybody knew me. I'd never had to learn how to speak to new people, how to make friends. Maybe it was the same for everyone that moved away from home. I had always been terrible at small talk. I found it exhausting. I never seemed to get beyond the initial stages of friendship with anyone. I got stuck in the awkward preliminary, where silence sits heavy, and conversation is work. It was like that with everyone I'd met. Everyone except Sophie.

Her friendship had been coveted by most of the women on our course. Sophie was bold and daring, people were drawn to her confidence. They didn't understand why she'd chosen me as her friend, her closest friend. I could see it in their faces. I never looked too deeply into it; I was just grateful for her.

Me and Sophie began to spend more and more time together. Sophie had always surrounded herself with people that were the same as her; outgoing, extroverts. Until me. I'd listened to her. Listened for hours to her talk about her boyfriends and family, her dilemmas. I asked questions and never got bored. Sophie liked to talk, and I liked to listen.

It wasn't all one-sided. My friendship with her had brought me out of myself. I felt less overwhelmed by London and less scared of the move I'd just made from Cornwall. In a place where everything and everyone seemed gray, Sophie was in color. I wanted to spend all my time with her.

Our courses had gone in different directions. I concentrated on creative writing modules and Sophie opted for new media; social influencing and podcasts. That was the way modern journalism was going she said.

That was how it started. Sophie had come to me with the idea. A true crime podcast. I'd sat crossed-legged on the floor, watching her pace around the flat as she talked. She was so passionate and so convincing. I didn't want to do the podcast. I'd never had any interest in true crime. Not until I met Sophie. She'd made it seem so exciting. She made *everything* seem exciting.

The premise would be simple.

Each week we'd choose a murder and research it. It couldn't be anything high profile she said. Nothing that the other one may have heard of. We would choose unsolved crimes from backwaters, either here or in the U.S. Murders that had led to an arrest usually gained more coverage over time. She said that choosing unsolved crimes would mean there would be more chance that no one had heard the details.

We would take turns, telling each other the gruesome tale of our selected murder. Sticking to the facts and building up intrigue and tension as we went. We would call it *Small Town*.

The idea terrified me. I didn't want to talk about murder. "Could we not do it about films or... student life?" I'd suggested half-heartedly. But Sophie dismissed it. True crime was where the real appetite was. It was where the money was.

I'd smiled and nodded encouragingly as her eyes danced with excitement.

The truth is, looking back, I would have done *anything*, if it was what Sophie wanted.

So that's what we did. *Small Town* took over everything and we loved it. We produced it all ourselves and recorded it in the living area of Sophie's studio flat. We'd sit on the polished hardwood floors, sun streaming through the sash windows. We drank wine from mugs in the middle of the afternoon, surrounded by bright cushions and recording equipment we'd borrowed from college. We would talk for hours, a familiar shorthand between us. Editing could be long and painstaking. The lengthy recording meant that a lot had to be cut out to fit into a neat one-hour podcast.

I was about to call her again, when out of the corner of my eye I saw a light turn on in one of the upstairs windows. It was Sophie's flat.

Sophie had originally rented a small second-floor studio flat in the building. Despite its diminutive size, it had two beautiful, big sash windows, that faced the tree-lined street below. Sophie's social media endeavors were lucrative. Very lucrative at times. An unexpected contract with a makeup brand had meant a deposit for a flat. Sophie didn't want to leave the rented studio. It was light and airy, and she'd made every corner of it perfect.

Sophie convinced the landlord to sell it to her. Two years on and several campaigns later, she'd also managed to convince the owner of the one-bedroom apartment next door to sell to her. She had just begun knocking through to create one huge space. Sophie could be very convincing.

The upstairs light turned off and I moved my gaze down, waiting to see her opening the communal door downstairs.

The door opened and Sophie walked out, carrying a large holdall over her shoulder. Her outline dimly lit by the entrance security light. She paused for a moment to allow her bag to catch the closing door. Holding it open for Tom. It had been even longer since I last saw him. Dark waves of hair fell into his eyes as he carried Sophie's neon pink suitcase down the steps. I felt an unwelcome lurch in my abdomen. I shifted uncomfortably in my seat, annoyed that he could still make me feel this way.

Sophie skipped lightly down the steps to the car, a broad smile on her face. I unclipped my seat belt and got out to meet her. To meet them. Sophie's hug was warm and all encompassing, she held on tightly to me. Nothing she ever did was half-hearted. She looked and smelled shiny and polished. The pastel green hoodie and matching bottoms that she wore had a crisp newness to them. The perks of being a fashion blogger. Her thick honey-colored hair was swept into a topknot and her tanned face was makeup free. Sophie, with very little effort, looked immaculate.

I walked around to the back of the car to open the trunk. Tom stood next to me and put the bags down. We didn't look at one another. A mutual understanding of distance between us.

"Hi." We had a brief and awkward hug.

"Hi," he replied as we pulled swiftly away from one another.

I'd known Tom since I was five. We went to primary and

secondary school together, back in Cornwall. It was two years ago that I'd taken Sophie back home to stay with my parents for New Year's Eve. We'd gone to the pub. Our pub—the Bull. A pub that for many years had turned a blind eye to our underage drinking.

Me and Tom had always been part of the same group of friends. We'd been close once. But that was before the night of the beach party. A lot of us had been close before that night.

Everyone at home had loved Sophie. She had a way of making you feel special. Conversations with her felt like an experience. It was that night she'd met Tom. Tom still lived in Pengully. He'd moved into a small apartment on the main street when we were eighteen and he still lived there.

Me and Sophie were only in Cornwall for a few days over New Year's, but before January was over, Tom had come to stay with her in London for the weekend. It was fine at first, nice even. Tom was someone from home, someone who knew me. We could be an occasional three.

It was clear that wasn't what Tom wanted. Very soon, weekends that Tom was staying, were weekends that I didn't see Sophie. He never did anything obvious, nothing that I could openly accuse him of, but it was evident that he didn't want me around. Tom was a good listener too. Sophie didn't need me as much. The weekly podcast became a monthly one. Despite the long gaps between episodes, our listeners and subscribers had reached an all-time high.

Sophie had always kept *Small Town* separate from her social media endeavors. Her true crime work would have sat uncomfortably on her feed, in between posts about eyeliner and organic cotton bedding. She'd always been apologetic about not promoting the podcast wider, but I understood. For me, it was big enough. The podcast had grown organically. We were starting to get interest from sponsors and podcast networks that would make *Small Town* a viable business. But we were too inconsistent.

We no longer had endless hours to devote to it. Despite my job being dull and poorly paid, it required me to work long hours. Sophie was tied up with so many projects that sometimes weeks would pass without us recording a single episode.

That was until last week. Last week changed everything.

CHAPTER THREE

Sophie climbed into the front passenger seat and Tom in the back. She turned sideways to face us. One of her feet was tucked underneath her and she held on to it at the ankle. Her pristine white pumps had already been discarded and lay in the footwell next to her oversized black leather handbag. Sophie was excited, despite the early hour. Her eyes shone. As she talked about the project ahead of them, she paused several times to touch my arm, emphasizing points. Her tiny hands and slender fingers felt like ice. As Sophie talked, I slowly pulled away from her building. I'd already input the destination into the GPS; four hours and fifty-seven minutes.

Our journey would take us around the outskirts of London. Through a maze of traffic lights and shuttered shops, before joining the motorway. Pengully was on the south coast. An hour away from the sign that announced you were entering Cornwall. A sign that now made my stomach flip with anxiety.

Last week Sophie had been contacted by a radio station. It was a national station that she'd worked with last year. She was hoping that they'd offer her a presenting role, but they didn't think she was quite there yet. They were developing podcasts.

Looking to expand their network and produce more hard-hitting content. Content that could be sold internationally. They'd listened to *Small Town*. They said they loved it, but felt that it needed to go deeper, be more journalistic.

Sophie had phoned me, full of enthusiasm and ideas. They wanted a story. A single story. A murder that we could tell over several episodes. As I thumbed excitedly through my notes from old podcasts, phone balanced between my ear and shoulder, I knew where Sophie's mind was going. I knew that she was barely listening.

Sophie had already made up her mind which story she wanted to do. She was just trying to find a way to tell me.

We were an hour into the journey and the sun had been up for a while. The traffic was still flowing, but the buildup of cars on the road was increasing with every junction. It was early May. The school holidays weren't for another week or so. The roads weren't as busy as they would be, but the weather was good, so they weren't exactly quiet. "Did you bring your sound equipment with you?" I asked Tom, looking at him in the interior mirror. He had positioned himself in the middle of the back seat. Legs spread, earphones in. He looked at me for a few seconds. I wasn't sure if he'd heard. He slowly took the earphones out. I could see his chest rise with annoyance.

"No. It's back at my flat." He deliberately put the earphones back in and looked away. The conversation was over. Tom had come up to stay with Sophie for the weekend. I wasn't sure why, as we were going back to Cornwall for a month. Tom was going to produce the podcast. His remit on production had yet to be discussed. Me and Sophie had always done it by ourselves. We'd never worked as a trio before.

The radio station had commissioned a six-episode podcast, but that was flexible. We were going back to Cornwall to write and record it for a month. A month at the *most*. They were paying us considerably more than I earned as a researcher and

Sophie was looking into sponsorship. Everything had happened so quickly; we hadn't even had a chance to discuss how the new format was going to work.

My boss had been understanding when I told him. As a junior, it was expected that you would take opportunities as they arose. He had agreed to hold my position open until I got back.

That night on the phone, Sophie had a proposal ready for me. It had sounded rehearsed. After the call, I'd wondered whether Tom had been there, next to her. Whether he'd helped her plan it out. I knew it hadn't been his idea. Tom wouldn't want this any more than me.

Sophie wanted to cover a murder that happened in Cornwall. It had happened in the town where I grew up. Where Tom grew up. Her name was Lacey Crew. She was murdered five years ago, a few months before I moved to London.

What happened to Lacey was something that I'd put away. Locked up in my mind, separate from the other crimes we'd researched. I told Sophie about it, of course, not long after we'd first met. Not the details though. You can't talk about how much you hated a person when they're dead.

Me and Lacey had mixed in the same circles, went to all the same things. But we weren't friends. We had never been friends. I was there that night, the night it happened. Tom was too.

It was the summer we'd all been waiting for. Lots of my friendship group had already moved away, starting courses across the country. Those left behind that year had come together to form a new group, a B-team. I'd just turned nineteen. I had six sun-soaked, beach-filled weeks ahead me, before I moved to London.

The night Lacey died changed a lot of things. There were the people that had been there and the people that hadn't. It felt like everyone had drifted apart after that. I wondered if Tom saw it that way too.

Tom still had his earphones in. His head bobbed very slightly with the movement of the car. I glanced at him every now and then. His chin rested on his fist, propped against the window. I could see his brown eyes, flickering against the movement of the oncoming traffic. Every now and then he pushed his hair from his face. I glimpsed the line of tatty leather wristbands he always wore. Twice our eyes had met in the mirror before we quickly looked away. There was no denying he was good-looking. But good-looking isn't everything.

When you dislike someone, when you've decided that someone is against you and that they are a barrier to your happiness, it's easy to see bad in everything they do. I'm very aware of how jealous Tom makes me, or maybe how jealous I make myself. Jealous that I don't have what they have. That I haven't had anyone, a someone, for a long time.

This project should be igniting a spark in me. It should be making me happy. Even the unpaid leave from my mundane job should be enough. But it isn't. I feel nothing but dread.

CHAPTER FOUR

Only an hour before we get there. Sophie is asleep. Curled up, hugging her knees into her chest. Her chin is resting in the crook of her arm, and she looks like a child.

I'd phoned my mum two days ago. I'd been putting it off. She'd been so pleased to hear from me, delighted that I was coming back to Cornwall for a while. Until I told her why. Her voice had been full of concern. After over thirty years of living in Cornwall, she still had her soft Lancashire accent. Nobody would want to talk about Lacey she said. It was such a sad time for everyone. Mum had been gentle. "It affected you, Katie. You never spoke about it."

Mum had agreed that we could stay in the guest house, as it was now called. Red Rock Cottage was the three-bedroom house that I'd grown up in. My father had walked out on me and Mum when I was five. He'd been a violent man.

I could only remember parts of it. Raised voices, thuds from downstairs that made my small heart race. I remember moments, flashes rather than events. Times I would press the duvet against my ears to block out the noise. I don't think I saw much. As you get older it's hard to distinguish what is an actual childhood memory and what are things you've been told. I do remember it was a very unhappy time. Despite the unhappiness, I was still sad to see him leave. I never spoke to Mum about it, but there was a sorrow in her that went on for a long time. The whole town seemed to know what had happened with my dad. There was a sort of protectiveness toward us. Maybe they just felt bad for not doing something sooner.

Two years after my dad left, Mum met Richard. He was kind and interested—in both of us. He'd never made me feel unwelcome or that he'd rather my Mum was on her own. Richard owned the Carmen Club. He still does. An upmarket holiday resort, a ten-minute drive from town. There are self-catering apartments, hotel suites, a bar, restaurant, tennis courts, swimming pools, everything that a middle-class visitor would want from a holiday. It had expanded over the years, but even when I was a child it was making a lot of money. I was aware that Richard was wealthy.

Mum had been with Richard for sixteen years. When him and Mum got together, people in the town started to look at us differently, with less pity. The same way that you might look at someone who's recovered from a serious illness. We were quickly a family and nearly all my memories after he came into our lives were happy ones.

Richard hadn't been with us for long when he decided to buy the land next to Red Rock Cottage. He wanted a new start for us. Not living in the shadow of misery that my father had cast. He wanted to provide for us.

So, he built a house. Next to the old one. Bigger and newer. A glass-fronted beach house with five bedrooms, four bathrooms, a cinema room and terraced gardens. I couldn't remember much of my life before the new house, so I never truly appreciated the lavishness of it. The old cottage sat awkwardly in the grounds of the new one. They named it Red Rock House. A reminder of what had come before. They always had plans to rent the cottage out as a holiday home, but with the success of the Carmen Club it had hardly seemed worth the effort.

Eighteen minutes away now.

The roads were becoming narrower and more familiar. The high Cornish hedges had begun to grow out onto the lanes. Brambles and woody branches tapped the side of the car when we passed other vehicles. They would be cut back in a few weeks. Trimmed into neat curves by passing tractors. Ready to show off to visitors.

I hadn't been at the pitch to the network. I wasn't sure if Tom had. I didn't want to know. I assumed Sophie had researched the murder enough to present it to them as the perfect *Small Town* murder. She'd obviously managed to convince them that there was something to research. That it was unsolved, unfinished. I'd tried to talk to her about it afterward. I wanted to explain some things to her. Things that I hadn't mentioned when I first told her about Lacey's murder. She didn't want to hear it. "Save it for the podcast." She'd laughed. "I want it to sound fresh, new. Not like I've heard it all before." Sophie liked to be authentic.

Two minutes away.

Pengully town looked just the same. You had to drive through the center of it to get to Red Rock House. The high street was unchanged. A little busier than I remembered, but the same. All the shops were contained in one section of the road. Small stone-built fishing cottages, converted to accommodate downstairs shops. There was a bakery, a convenience store, a newsagent, a couple of gift shops and what looked like an interiors shop. That was new. The pub was a little higher up the hill. A large, imposing red brick Victorian building, out of place against the gray stone of the rest of the town.

Shops were sought after in Pengully. They usually stayed within a family, so rarely went on the open market. Rates were low and income during the holiday season was high. The main street ran down to the beach car park at the bottom of the hill. A large concrete area with narrow parking spaces drawn on the ground. The size of the car park was disproportionate to the scale of the small town above it, but Pengully beach was huge. It was over a mile long. Unlike some of the beaches in the area, Pengully wasn't stony. It had fine, soft sand, perfect for families looking for an idyllic holiday.

As I drove down the hill, I counted only a handful of cars in the car park. It was still early. In the next couple of weeks it would be full. Families would be scurrying across the little wooden footbridge that led to the beach, weighed down by windbreaks and novelty inflatables.

To get to Red Rock House you carried on past the car park. Up a narrow lane, toward the cliff top. I'd hated going up there when I'd first started driving. If you met another car, it was a long reverse, down a steep hill, to get to a passing place. As the car rounded the corner, I saw it. Red Rock House, named after the cottage and the burnt-auburn cliffs it looked across to. The house used to be hidden by trees. Tall, crowded Ash trees. You had to creep around them before you got your first glimpse of the house. You could never really see the full scale of the property on the approach. The row of trees had been cut down. It looked huge.

"Jesus!" Sophie laughed. Tom whistled. They'd seen the house before, but not like this. Even I was taken aback by the size of it. The sun bounced off the glass frontage, making it look like a mirrored palace. I swung the car into the wide gravel drive around the back and put the handbrake on. I was home.

CHAPTER FIVE

Nobody could ever accuse my parents of being ostentatious. They were very low key. Not interested in all the trappings that their wealth could offer them. Mum had no interest in designer clothes or expensive interiors. If you'd just met them, the house didn't look like somewhere they'd live. Maybe Richard had been different back then. The front of the house was predominantly glass. There was a large rectangular panel in the center, sat over a pair of light oak-paneled doors. The rest of the frontage was made up of various configurations of glass. As we walked up to the house, I could see right through the front to the stone-tiled hallway. Empty, apart from a wide oak staircase that swept around the middle of the house to a balconied landing at the top. It was impressive to look at.

The doors swung open before we got to them. My mum was hugging herself with joy as they walked toward us. Richard looked shy and boyish. He was carrying our family cat, Juno, like a sort of prop. An overfed, antisocial tortoiseshell who we'd all adored for years, despite her hostile nature. Juno looked uncomfortable. She was pushing her paws against Richard's chest and arching her back to get out of his grip.

They both looked so pleased to see me I felt a lump in my throat. An overwhelming moment of fondness for them. Tom stepped forward with his hand outstretched. Richard released the cat.

"Hello, sir, I'm Tom. I'm not sure if you remember me?" I nearly laughed at his solemnness.

"Of course, welcome... and it's Richard, please." Richard was warm and easy. He pulled Tom toward him and clapped the side of his arm.

"Sophie, so lovely to see you again, darling," Mum said affectionately.

"Wendy, thank you *so* much for this." Mum and Sophie embraced like old friends. Mum and Richard walked toward me with their arms outstretched and enveloped me in a three-way hug. Their happiness was infectious.

We left our bags in the car and followed them into the hallway.

"I'd forgotten how incredible this place is," Sophie gushed. Tom nodded in agreement.

Mum and Richard dismissed the praise. "Oh I don't know... It's getting a bit tired now," Richard replied. They struggled with compliments. Mum opened the kitchen door, releasing Perno and Morti, their two cocker spaniels. The gray and black dogs had been bought as puppies shortly after I moved away. The spaniels launched themselves at us, before being reluctantly sent to their beds. Richard held Mum's hand as we walked into the kitchen. I could feel their contentment.

"Are you sure you don't mind us staying here?" Mum brushed Sophie's question away with a hand movement, but her face was full of concern.

"You're all welcome to stay here as long as you like—Katie knows that." She was hesitating, trying to find the right words. "This isn't London." She put her hands up to stop any interjection that we might have made. Time goes by very slowly here.

People still remember. They remember everything. Sophie put a protective arm around my Mum and laughed.

"That's what we're hoping for Wendy."

Mum had given us the keys to the cottage. We made the short walk across the driveway. The cottage had been repainted. No longer the faded gray building that I remembered. It was brilliant white. The morning sun bounced off the front walls and a large potted wisteria grew up and around the pale blue door. It was beautiful, but it had an unreal quality about it, like a photo. The cottage was a little more sheltered from the onshore wind than the main house. Tucked into the dip of the upper cliff top. Red Rock Cottage had incredible sea views. When we reached the front door, Tom and Sophie turned their bodies to face the sea. The sun was starting to gather strength and made the surface of the distant water twinkle.

"It's incredible," Tom breathed quietly, looking at Sophie. They held each other's gaze for a moment. They looked like a couple arriving on their honeymoon.

"Thanks," I muttered, giving them a watery smile.

As I turned the key in the lock and pushed open the door, I realized Red Rock Cottage was one of the few things that had changed. Changed entirely. The walls were white and fresh. The floors were covered in large slate-gray tiles. A blue and white striped rug lay in the living area, giving the room a relaxed beachy feel. The two sofas were crisp white, expensive looking. Plump gray and yellow pillows, and chunky knitted throws were draped over them. I remembered the cottage being dark and poky. Nothing like it was now. I wondered who they'd decorated for. The cottage hadn't been lived in for years.

"This is perfect. Just perfect," Sophie purred. Her eyes momentarily closed with pleasure. Sophie pulled her phone from her back pocket. Looking for good angles in the room to take photos.

"I'm going to take my stuff upstairs," I told them. Nobody

answered. I kicked off my trainers. A die-hard habit from child-hood. No shoes in the house. I picked up my holdall and walked up the polished wooden staircase. Everything felt so new.

I went to my old bedroom. The middle-sized of the three. The bed was on the opposite wall to how I'd had it. It was now covered in a light gray duvet with a mustard-yellow bedspread. The small window had a little built-in seat in front of it, covered in a matching gray fabric. It was cosy but stylish. Like a seaside boutique hotel.

I dropped my bag on the floor and sat on the edge of the bed. I'd braced myself for a flood of emotions, coming back to the cottage after all these years, but I felt nothing. A wave of tiredness washed over me. I could lie down right here and sleep. I'd sleep for hours. I'd been in the car for too long, the same thoughts bouncing around my head. I opened my bag to retrieve a carrier bag and dragged it out. My wellies. I'd grabbed them on the way out the door this morning. It seemed like such a long time ago. I headed back down the stairs, carrier bag in my hand.

"I'm going out for a walk," I said as I opened the front door. I didn't wait for an answer. There probably wasn't one. I closed the door carefully, using the latch. I didn't want it to sound like I was slamming it, like I was sulking. I used one hand to steady myself on the doorframe outside, balancing on one foot at a time, as I pulled my boots on. It had been a long time since I'd been to the beach this way. Everything had a distant familiarity, like trying to recall a dream.

Just then, I heard a bark, as the two spaniels rounded the corner. Tongues out, intertwined as they leaped about each other. Not expecting to see me, they ran right past and had to double back on themselves. Mum followed. "Ah, darling, just the person." Mum spoke as if she'd been looking for me. Her walking jacket and boots suggested she was heading off down the footpath. "Be a dear and take the boys down to the beach, will you? They're utterly bored with me. They'd be delighted to have someone sprightly walk them for a change." Mum had always been sprightly. She looked considerably younger than her fifty-two years. Tall and athletic, Mum had never been very good at standing still. Despite her confidence, she had a nervous energy. I remember it from when I was little. It's as though she's trying very hard not to apologize.

"Mum," I whined. She smiled, passed me the bag of dog paraphernalia, and was gone. I gave the dogs a shout and headed off down the cliff path. A blur of spaniels.

When I was little and I was feeling sad or upset, Mum would ask me what the worst part was. Somehow, focusing on the worst part of my worry seemed to diffuse it. My head throbbed from tension and tiredness. I thought about the worst part. The worst part about being here, of doing this. It was having to see people again. People that were there that night. It was having to see Jude.

CHAPTER SIX

It had been two years since I'd seen Jude. That News Year's Eve that I came home with Sophie. The New Year's Eve that she'd met Tom. Everyone had been in the pub that night. Me and Sophie had drunk a lot, before we'd even got there. He'd come up and spoken to me—an hour into the party.

I was standing by the bar waiting for a drink. I'd worn a canary-yellow bandage dress. It was tight and uncomfortable, but I stood out. I *wanted* to stand out that night. I leaned over, arms rested on the bar. I watched him walk over in the mirror behind the rows of liquor. I looked good, or at least I thought I did. It might have just been the wine. My arms were resting in the sticky residue of spilled drinks. I pretended not to notice. I stared at the empty glasses lined up on the busy bar. Different shades of lipstick coating the edges, dregs of yellow and brown liquid floating in the bottom. I was ready for him.

He looked so good it made me ache. He'd pushed his sun-bleached hair from his face. He was tanned—even in December. Years of surfing every day. Already, tiny lines creased around his blue eyes. He wore an old Surfers Against Sewage T-shirt. It was one I remembered, a favorite. There was a tear in the front, on the left side of his stomach. I could see a tiny strip of his taught belly. I kept staring at it...

That night, after I'd walked away from Jude, I'd watched him. I couldn't help it. He'd started talking to a woman, the new barmaid possibly. She was dark, pretty, just his type. She leaned into him to hear what he was saying. Her head thrown back in a laugh, hand self-consciously covering her mouth. Our friends had called him a player. I knew he wasn't. This wasn't a game for him. There was no pretense or ruse. It's just who he was.

I'd suddenly felt very stupid, standing there in my tight yellow dress. I'd walked home by myself. A stomach full of cheap wine and a familiar lump in my throat.

The many years I was Jude's girlfriend had hardened me. At the beginning, people used to gently tell me things that he'd done, girls that he'd been with. They stopped when they realized that it didn't change anything. I saw how people looked at me, how sorry they felt for me. I knew they wondered how I could be so weak, so lacking in self-esteem. But Jude had never lied to me. He never promised that he would do anything except love me. He had made me happy and, for a long time, that was enough. I never thought it was weakness that made me stay.

I'd passed out on the sofa when I got home that night. Richard had woken me with tea and marmite toast in the morning. He knew without asking that the night hadn't ended well. Sophie had gone home with Tom and hadn't got back yet...

I could see the beach now. The walk across the fields brought you out at the end farthest away from the main car park. It was usually much quieter. Very few tourists made the half-mile walk, away from the shops and toilets. We'd always joked that this end was our private beach.

I climbed down the rocks that led onto the beach. I hadn't seen the dogs for a while. I couldn't even remember if they'd been ahead of me or behind. I was calling their names, just as I spotted them far down the beach. Floppy ears and sand spray.

The dogs were rarely apart and at times looked like one animal. There was only one other person at this end of the beach. A woman approaching from the town end, looking out to sea. I jogged away from her to catch up with the dogs, the unfamiliar feeling of wellies weighing my feet down.

The top half of the beach was dry. The tide rarely came up this high. I sat down on the sand, feeling its warmth through my jeans. I picked up a handful and felt its softness, letting it run through my fingers before picking up more. The woman on the beach was getting closer, looking down, so I couldn't see her face. The seagulls shrieked overhead. It was a loud obnoxious sound, but I liked it.

The woman was only a few feet away now. As she lifted her head, she noticed the dogs and paused for just a moment, before looking over at me. There was something about her that I recognized. I watched her for a few seconds longer and realized with a jolt who she was. It was Megan, Lacey's sister.

Megan is twenty-six, two years older than me. Two years older than Lacey. Two sisters couldn't have been more different. We'd been in Girl Guides together briefly when I was ten. Megan had been my group leader; Sixers I think they called them. She was a shy, uncomfortable girl. She'd worn glasses for as long as I could remember and spoke with a lisp. I remember people being quite cruel to her.

Megan was kind, in a way that Lacey wasn't. Shortly after I'd joined Guides, we went on a five day "camp." Sleeping on airbeds in a village hall ten miles away. I'd been homesick. It was the first time I had ever been away from Mum. Megan had looked after me. She'd sat with me every night, whispering about the day. Sometimes reading me pages from her book. I left Guides shortly after and only ever saw her around town occasionally. It struck me that Megan was the sort of girl who would have stayed at Guides until she reached the maximum age.

As Megan got closer, it was clear that she recognized me.

What wasn't clear was how I'd been able to recognize her. Megan looked completely different.

"Hey, Katie." She smiled warmly, showing perfect white teeth. Still quietly spoken but with a confidence that I didn't remember her ever having.

Megan had grown into her body. When I'd known her, she'd been small for her age and so skinny that her frame could only be described as bony. She was still small, but now strong and toned. Everything about her radiated health. Her dark sleek bob was parted off center and was tucked smoothly behind her ears. She no longer wore glasses and her makeup had been carefully applied. She wore black wellies and dark blue denim jeans with a T-shirt tucked in at the waist, highlighting her toned middle. A long fawn-colored cardigan hung down to almost the top of her wellies. She was gorgeous.

"Hi, Megan, how are you?" It came out too quickly, like one long word. I made a move to get to my feet, but she was already sitting down beside me.

"What brings you back?" she said, ignoring my question. I was completely unprepared for this. I felt a cold trickle of panic slither down my chest to my stomach.

"Just a visit, you know? See the parents." I could feel myself reddening. I looked at my feet as I continued to sieve the sand through my fingers. "How's your Mum?" I asked, not looking up.

"She's fine, much the same really. It's still hard. Lacey was everything to her." Megan looked sad. I wasn't sure if it was because she missed her sister, or because she wasn't part of her Mum's "everything." Perhaps it was both. I finally looked up at her face. She really was beautiful, very like Lacey. It wasn't something I'd ever noticed when we were kids.

"I'm sorry," I muttered awkwardly. "That must be really hard." It sounded insincere, but I meant it.

"I found hundreds of photos of all of you after Lacey died.

She had them all on her computer. I'll have to see if I can find them for you. It all seems such a long time ago now... You haven't changed at all," she told me. Megan looked at my expression and smiled. "It's meant to be a compliment!"

"I need to get the dogs home," I told her, climbing to my feet and craning my neck to look for them. I rummaged in the bag my Mum had given me until I found a whistle. I could see Megan watching me, her face impassive. I blew the whistle twice and saw the dogs come running from the other end of the beach.

"It was nice to see you again." I started walking slowly away.

"We should meet for a coffee," she called after me.

I turned. "That would be nice," I lied.

"When?" she asked. It wasn't rude, just direct, interested.

"Ummm, well... I'm not sure..." I wasn't ready for this. I wasn't ready for any of it.

"Next week?" she suggested.

"Great. Er, shall we message... arrange something?" I took my phone out of my pocket and started pressing the screen. I was trying to sound relaxed, but my throat felt tight. How could I tell Megan that we were making a podcast about her sister's murder?

"There," she said, handing me back my phone after inputting her number. I did the same with hers. "It can get pretty lonely in Pengully. I don't get out much these days." Megan smiled apologetically. There was something disarming about her candor. "I'll give you a call in a couple of days," she told me.

Guilt crept around my body as I walked away. I could feel her watching me. I didn't look back until I reached the entrance to the cliff path. She was sitting on the sand, in the same place I'd left her.

CHAPTER SEVEN

I dropped the dogs and the bag back to the main house. There was no sign of Mum or Richard, so I left a note. *Brought the boys back—they're crazy! Thanks for having us. It's good to be back*, I wrote, adding a kiss at the end. They'd tried so hard. It really didn't matter that not all the note was true. As I walked toward the cottage, an Ocado delivery van drove past me. The driver raised his hand and smiled as I got out of the way. Sophie must have ordered food. When I opened the door, I saw that she'd been busy. She'd changed her outfit to another new-looking, fitted co-ord. Her blond hair, now loose, was pushed back with a blue and white headband. She looked fresh and clean. Everything about her coordinated with her new surroundings. "Perfect timing! Are you hungry?" She went to the kitchen without waiting for a reply. "We've got food and I've cooked lunch!" she sang excitedly.

I eased my feet out of my wellies and followed her through. Most of the shopping had already been put away. There, on the oak worktops, were two bowls of prawns and spaghetti. One bowl was placed on a chopping board, the other on a pale cloth napkin. Parsley was scattered over the top and larger leaves lay next to the bowls. Sophie had obviously been taking photos of the food. Ocado branding sat in the background. Subtle enough for people to make the link, without it looking like an advert. The food shop was obviously a freebie. It's what she did. "This looks amazing." I was genuinely astounded that she could have got so much done in the time I was out walking. "Tom...?" I asked. Sophie scrunched up her face and shook her head.

"No, he's gone for a run. This is for us!" I was pleased. I was about to ask if Tom knew where to run, before I remembered that this was his town too. His home. I wondered if Tom was planning on staying here in the cottage with Sophie, or whether he'd go back to his apartment. It wasn't something we'd talked about.

Tom was a freelancer. While me and Sophie were at college in London, Tom had studied sound engineering at a college ten miles from Pengully. He now worked in pubs and festivals around Cornwall; making sure the live bands that performed there sounded good. Sophie had tried to forward his career. Introducing him to her London contacts. Sophie was frustrated with his lack of interest. Tom was happy where he was.

Sophie had pushed all the furniture against the walls. Only the large coffee table remained in the middle of the room, surrounded by large and small cushions that she must have collected from around the house.

"Like old times, eh?" She smiled, placing the pasta bowls on the coffee table. "You don't mind, do you?" She bit her bottom lip in hesitation.

"What?" I asked, confused.

"All this..." She waved her hand around the room at the changes she'd made.

"No, of course not." I laughed. We were about to sit down on the cushions when she jumped up and skipped to the kitchen.

"One last thing..." She returned to the room with two

glasses, a bottle of white wine and a dark green folder tucked under her arm. "Ta-da!" Sophie playfully cocked her head to one side. "Now it really is like old times." She laughed, putting the glasses on the table. I stared at the folder. "Open it," she whispered as she poured two large glasses of wine. I lifted the cardboard lip. There were some press cuttings. Not originals, photocopies. A pile of paper an inch thick. I slowly fanned the top sheets out over the table, looking quickly from one to the other, afraid of what I might see.

A black-and-white photo of Lacey stared out at me. Her long blond hair was almost white in the picture. A single lock curled over one eye as she looked up at the camera. I quickly moved the article to the bottom of the pile. I wasn't ready for this.

"Are you OK?" Those three words. The sympathy in her voice, the realization that I was going to do this, relive this. I could feel sobs rising in my chest, tears pricking the backs of my eyes. A week of emotion threatening to be released by just three words. *Are. You. OK.* I took a gulp of wine and swallowed it down. It tasted like acid in my throat.

"I'm fine, honestly." I smiled weakly at her. I took another mouthful of wine to take the taste away. Deep breath. I thumbed through the pieces of paper without looking at the words. Sophie had decided to let me move on, but I could see her watching my expression. "I hadn't realized there would be so much," I said. All the papers were nationals, a mixture of tabloids and broadsheets.

"An unsolved murder in a sleepy Cornish town? The victim a nineteen-year-old blond, with model good looks? The press were all over it," Sophie said. "Well, for a while anyway. It petered out pretty quickly. Journalists don't like being away from London for too long." Sophie was searching at the back of the pile of papers. "Look at this. Fast-forward two years, to when James... you know... and it's hardly even covered. The closing of his case is barely even mentioned," Sophie said, passing me one of the most recent clippings.

There, in the center of the article, was a photo of Lacey and James. James had been Lacey's boyfriend at the time she was killed. They were laughing, really laughing. Lacey was looking directly into the camera, her plump lips wide and her eyes closed. It was another black-and-white photo, but you could see that the ends of her wavy hair were a different color.

"I remember this." I tapped the photo, tracing her hair with my finger. "It must have been only a few months before she died. We'd all gone to a music festival, about twenty miles away. Lacey had turned up with the ends of her hair dyed bright pink. I think she had it like that for a few weeks." I stared back at her carefree face. She was wearing a sequined band across her forehead and glitter face paint around her eyes. I'd wished that I'd made more of an effort that day. Being around Lacey could make you feel like that. You couldn't see much of James's face in the photo. His head was turned to one side, leaning into Lacey, looking right at her. It was a great photo.

At that moment, Tom came through the door. Red faced and sweaty, he had tiny mud splatters up his legs and over his running shorts. Sophie shifted slightly away from me. It was only a couple of inches, but I felt it.

"Just getting up to speed, babe." Sophie smiled brightly at him. "So, when are we going to get started?" She looked from Tom to me.

"How about now?" I said overconfidently. A bit too loud. I hadn't meant it to come out like that. I drained the rest of my wine and stood up awkwardly. Sophie and Tom were looking at me. My bowl of pasta sat on the coffee table untouched. They thought I was drunk. Maybe I was a bit. "Well?" I laughed at their concerned faces. I tried to sound light, breezy. "We need to start this thing sometime... It might as well be now." I looked at Tom. Sounding more confident than I felt.

"Right." He nodded. "I'll get showered and walk over to the flat. I'll grab the stuff and I can drive my car back here. I can have it set up in a couple of hours." He jogged up the stairs two at a time. A wave of irritation washed over me. Why couldn't he shower at his own place? I turned to Sophie, who nodded encouragingly. This was it.

CHAPTER EIGHT

Tom unpacked the last of the equipment bags. It all looked new. It took him the best part of an hour to set it up. Most of it was stacked on one side of the room. Thick black cables snaked across the floor, attached to two microphones and headsets, set down on the coffee table. The room felt small. It was small, but it felt claustrophobic with the equipment and all three of us in it. I was hot and uncomfortable. Sophie had put the folder away. I hadn't seen her do it. I wondered if she'd read through all the press clippings. She seemed to have read at least some of them. It was clear that, from now on, this was going to be my story to tell. For the first episode at least. Sophie would take the roll of interviewer.

I poured myself another glass of wine. It was slightly warm, as the second bottle hadn't had time to chill. The effect of the first glass was fading rapidly and I needed to relax if I was going to do this. Sophie took a seat on one of the nests of cushions she'd arranged on the floor. She put her headphones on and begun talking into the microphone. Some tests for Tom. She changed her volume, tone, even sang. Tom listened, moving

sliders on the deck up and down to get the right levels. They
were professionals.

After a few minutes, Sophie looked up and took her headset
off. "Ready?" she asked. I nodded, not trusting myself to speak
yet. I sat down on the cushions opposite her and cleared my
throat. Trying to make my voice stronger, push away the tremble. I set my wine down within reach and noticed that I'd
already drank half of it. I was feeling calmer. The wine had
taken the edge off. Sophie started the introduction. It was
similar to our usual one, a little longer. There was the obligatory
nod to the network that had commissioned it and, for the first
time, a contact email: LaceyMurder@gmail.com. I frowned at
Sophie, confused. "We need an email address that people can
contact us on... with new information." I nodded. We'd edit that
last bit out. We could edit whatever we wanted, or rather Tom
could.

Sophie introduced us.

"Welcome to *Small Town*." She breathed; her voice smooth.
"Five years ago, Lacey Crew was murdered. Pause. She was
murdered in Cornwall, in a small town by the beach." Pause.
"Nobody was ever arrested, and no official charges were ever
brought." Pause. "Lacey Crew was nineteen years old." Sophie
spoke slowly and quietly, her voice full of feeling. The silence
in podcasts was almost as important as the words. Sophie was
building up tension.

"On that night, the night Lacey died, my co-host, Katie
Chase, was there. This podcast, over the next few weeks, will
investigate the murder. We will talk to witnesses, go over old
evidence and turn up new leads. As with every one of the
unsolved cases that we've covered... someone knows
something."

It was my turn. I took a deep breath and began.

"It was the end of July. Most of us were on a gap year
between sixth form and college. When you grow up in a small

town, friendship groups are wide. Our group was now made up of those that hadn't left the previous September. There were quite a lot of us, around fifteen or so." I was warming up to it. I could feel Tom's eyes on me. He was part of that group. This was his story too. Or maybe it wasn't. Maybe his story was very different to mine.

"It was Danny Read's birthday. He was a couple of years older than us, but we all knew him from the Carmen Club. He was the bar manager over there. Most of us had worked there at some point, either waiting tables or serving drinks. My dad, well, stepdad owns it." I was losing a bit of pace, stumbling a bit. I wanted to tell it in the right order.

"Did Lacey work there?" Sophie asked, helping me back on course.

"Yeah. Lacey had been working there for a couple of years. She'd started off in the kitchens. You know, washing dishes, peeling potatoes... A few months before, she'd been moved to front of house; serving tables, helping behind the bar. Lacey was popular. She had a nice way with the tourists and the regulars. We occasionally did shifts together, but more often than not, she'd have her shift with Danny. He was in charge of the schedule, so I guess he planned it that way. They were friends."

"Would you say Lacey had any problems? Was she happy?" Sophie asked. She had a pen in her hand and had been writing down notes on a piece of paper. I couldn't see what she'd written. Occasionally she'd underline something.

"She always *seemed* happy. We weren't close. We just had a lot of friends in common. Lacey lived with her mum and older sister, Megan. Her mum adored her. She was quite... um... pushy? No, maybe that's not fair..." It was too late now.

"Pushy how?" Sophie jumped on it, writing something on the piece of paper. I hesitated.

"Her mum just seemed very ambitious for her. She got her into modeling when she was a kid. It didn't last long. Just a few children's clothing ads, catalogs, that kind of thing. She was sent to singing lessons, tap dancing, drama... It wasn't just the regular classes that ran at the village hall. Lacey's mum got her private lessons, right into her teens. It must have cost a fortune."

"What about Megan?" Sophie didn't look up from her notes. I paused.

"I always thought Megan had it a bit hard. She was very different from Lacey and was always a bit in her shadow. Megan was quiet, shy. It might have been that the shadows were just where she preferred to be." How could I be talking about her like this? I made a mental note to ask Tom to edit the last bit out. Sophie scribbled something on the notepad. I could tell from the movement of her hand that she'd drawn a question mark.

I needed to get back to the story. I had planned out a route. "Danny had arranged a beach party. We would have them every so often. Pretty relaxed, last-minute sort of thing. Just whoever was around. This one was planned. Somebody must have gone down to the beach during the day and set up a fire. Usually, a few of us would just grab some sticks, bits of driftwood, but this one was huge. Someone had brought down some kegs of lager. I think there were two. There was a sound system. Not a small one either. Danny must have gone to a lot of effort."

I pictured the scene when I arrived. I'd been drinking. I was pissed off and tired. Tired of Jude and pissed off with myself. The Daft Punk song "Get Lucky" was playing. It had been my song of the summer. My happy song. Not that night. That night it just reminded me of how sad I felt. I never liked the song after that. It's funny how that happens sometimes. I took a couple of mouthfuls of wine.

"Are you OK to carry on?" Sophie asked. I appreciated the concern, but it was a redundant question. We wouldn't be stopping, not now.

"When I arrived, there were small groups of people sitting

and standing around the fire. The blaze was so high it was hard to see over the other side of it. You could just make out smoky silhouettes. Glowing shapes of people with drinks in their hands. I'd gone on my own. I wasn't planning on staying... I was looking for someone." I paused. I hadn't planned for this. Sophie waited. "...I was looking for Jude—my boyfriend." I stammered. "We'd had an argument."

We hadn't just had an argument, I thought. We'd broken up.

CHAPTER NINE

I couldn't do it anymore. I'd ended it. It wasn't just his cheating. It was who the cheating had made me. I was done. I'd got used to sharing him. I'd managed to persuade myself that it didn't matter, that the others didn't matter. Then the others became her. I felt a familiar rage return. A rage that I thought had long gone. I couldn't stand by and watch her take everything from me again. So, I let him go.

I wasn't even sure if anyone else knew about us... about them. There was no one to ask.

I looked up at Tom, perched on the arm of the sofa, earphones on. He looked at the floor and shifted uncomfortably. He had every right to look uncomfortable.

"What time was this?" Sophie's question brought me back to the room.

"Erm, about 9 p.m. It was still light. Hot too, well, warm. Most people were wearing shorts and bikini tops. I decided to stay for a bit, wait for Jude. I sat on the sand. I'd done a shift at the Carmen over lunch and hadn't bothered to change. I was still wearing my pale pink Carmen T-shirt and a pair of jeans..."

I'd felt out of place as soon as I got there. I walked around the fire by the sand dunes. Along with the kegs of lager, there were two big buckets full of glass bottles. The ice that they'd been packed in had mostly melted, so the bottles bobbed around in the chilled water. I fished a dripping cold bottle of vodka from the bucket and looked around for a glass. There was nothing. I slowly unscrewed the black metal lid of the cheap Russian brand and poured the clear liquid straight into my mouth. It burned my throat and numbed my lips, but it felt good. I was just about to put the bottle back when I heard a familiar voice behind me.

"Take it." It was Danny. "...Don't worry, it's not from your dad's bar," he'd sneered. I shrugged, said nothing. Showing him that I didn't care where it was from. I sat down with the bottle of vodka and drank. There were some things that Sophie just didn't need to know about that night.

"Did you see anyone you knew at the party?" Sophie was poised with her pen.

"Yeah, I recognized a lot of the people there." Sophie nodded encouragingly, waiting for me to elaborate. "There was Danny, obviously. Friends of Lacey's, Polly Newcoombe and Tara Haywood. There was a crowd of guys from the rowing team, lots of people from the year above us... Tom, Tom was there." My eyes flickered momentarily in his direction. He was still looking at the floor. "Jude finally showed up, although not for long. Then Lacey and James. They arrived late, maybe 10 p.m.?"

I needed a moment to get my thoughts together. My head was starting to swim with the wine, but I was finding my stride. I drained my glass and poured another. I smiled at Sophie and nodded. I was OK. This was OK.

"What was Lacey wearing that night?" Sophie asked.

"She must have come straight from work as well because she was still wearing her Carmen T-shirt. I hadn't seen her at

lunchtime, so she must have done the evening shift." Something
struck Sophie.

"Hang on... you said Lacey and Danny were friends, good
friends. Danny did the schedule. Why was Lacey working on
the night of Danny's birthday party?" she asked. Why hadn't I
thought about this before? Because I hadn't thought about any
of it before. "Could they have been short staffed?" Sophie
pressed.

"No." I shook my head. "That wouldn't have been it. There
was always someone who wanted shifts and Lacey didn't do
anything she didn't want to do." I laughed. It came out bitter
and unnatural. I felt a blush of shame begin to creep up my
neck. "I suppose she might have just needed the money?" I
offered. Sophie was writing again, nodding her head. "Lacey
changed when she got to the beach, well sort of..." I needed to
be careful now. "Lacey had been wearing jeans, but she'd taken
them off," I started.

"What did she change into?" Sophie probably wouldn't
know, even if she'd read the articles.

"That's the thing, she didn't change into anything. Lacey
just wore her knickers. She still had the Carmen T-shirt on, but
she'd tied it in a knot above her belly button. Lots of the girls
were wearing bikinis, so it was no different really." It was different. I'm not sure if it was what she was wearing, or the way she
was wearing it. I couldn't take my eyes off her. Nobody could.

Maybe it had been her body, tanned and lithe, or it could
have been the knickers. Not overly sexy, but crisp white lace,
with a high leg. Or perhaps, perhaps it was just jealousy. I was
wearing a Carmen T-shirt too. Only, I didn't look like that. It
made me feel shit. *She'd* made me feel shit. Again. Shit and
frumpy and alone.

I really needed to focus. I was going down a path, a train of
thought that would be hard to come back from.

"Lacey was talking to James. I think they'd arrived together.

I watched them on and off. I was there on my own, so there wasn't much else to do." Except drink vodka, I thought. *Concentrate.* "They were having an argument. Well, I think they were. James had a serious look on his face. You could see he was upset. He kept leaning into Lacey when he spoke. I think he was trying to get her to leave with him. Lacey didn't look bothered. She was smiling. It used to happen a lot," I told her.

"What used to happen a lot? The arguments?" Sophie probed.

"They were just one of those couples. James was a nice guy, but I don't think he was enough for Lacey, and he knew it. So, he sort of... he held on to her too tight. Not physically exactly. He was scared of losing her. She was a force of nature. You always knew when Lacey was in a room. She made sure of it."

"I know James was a friend of yours and we'll come back to him. Katie, what time did Lacey leave the party?" Sophie asked. This was going to be tricky.

"I'm not sure," I said truthfully. "I must have been there for an hour or two before I fell asleep on the sand." Sophie already knew this. At least I think she did. When I first told her the story, I'd put this into the timeline, my timeline. What Sophie didn't know was that I was drunk. I was so drunk that I'm not sure what time it was when Lacey left, or what time I'd passed out on the sand.

"Jude had arrived about an hour after I got there. He came and sat with me. We talked. Lacey was still there then," I told her. Yes, there was no question that Lacey was there then.

"You know I love you," Jude had told me.

"I know," I'd replied and I meant it. He wasn't angry, just sad, nodding as if he understood. We'd sat in silence for a while. I stared drunkenly at my bare toes digging into the sand, willing myself not to apologize.

We sat by the fire, eyes stinging when the wind changed direction and cloaked us in smoke. I felt empty, used up. I didn't know what I was still doing there. Too drunk to stay and too tired to leave.

"Jude left," I told her. "He'd walked toward the main end of the beach, the car park. I can't remember where he said he was going, but I got the impression he was coming back. I suppose that's why I stayed."

I was waiting for someone, but it wasn't Jude.

"It rained, really poured down, while I'd been asleep. When I woke up, I had my phone in my hand. I pressed the screen to check the time, but it wouldn't turn on. The water must have damaged it." I could remember it now. My cold wet clothes clung to me, and my hair hung in damp sandy rattails around my shoulders. The sand was hard against my body where I lay. It was dark now. The fire was nearly out, but the moon was bright. Some people had flashlights; I could just make them out, their blinking light across the sand.

"It was then I heard the screaming."

CHAPTER TEN

"Maybe it had been the screaming that woke me. Polly Newcoombe, Lacey's best friend, was on the sand dunes above us. I could only see the outline of her. She had her hands in her hair, holding on to her head. She was screaming.

"I looked around at the shapes of the people and everyone was frozen. Nobody moved or made a sound, none that I heard anyway. Nobody except James. James ran toward her. He climbed and fumbled his way up the sliding sand dunes. When he finally reached her, he grabbed her by the shoulders. The wind carried away their words, but you could see they were shouting at each other. Still, none of us moved. James left. He ran up the dunes toward the car park. Polly fell to her knees sobbing."

"What did you do?" Sophie asked quietly.

"I got up. I followed James. At least I went in the direction that James had gone." I took a mouthful of wine.

"Did you speak to Polly?" I shook my head.

"No." It was the obvious thing to do. But I didn't speak to Polly. I didn't ask her what had happened, and I didn't ask her if she was OK. I just ran, as quickly as I could, through the sand

dune craters toward the car park. My body still felt weak from
the alcohol, my legs faltered with every step I took. Why hadn't
I spoken to Polly? It had been so dark on the dunes. Muscle
memory alone must have guided my body toward the town.

"I could see the lights of the car park below me. Reflections
from the streetlights bounced off the black wet floor. It looked
empty. I remember feeling relieved for a moment. The beach
entrance by the old wooden bridge was blocked from view. It
was only when I got to the top of the hill I could see them. A
crowd of people, about ten or so. Some of them were crouched
and some were standing. It was hard to see what was going on.
At first I thought there'd been a fight." I'd been so scared. Not of
the dark or of being up there on my own. I knew something bad
had happened. I knew as soon as I'd heard Polly. I thought
something had happened to Jude.

"I walked down to the car park. Slowly. I think I was
holding my breath," I continued.

"Did you see Lacey's body?" Sophie asked, almost in a
whisper.

"Yes. Only for a moment. She looked really young..." I
stopped. I didn't want to say any more. Nobody needed to
know. They didn't need to know how blue her lips were. They
didn't need to know how dirty she was, or how her wet hair was
draped like string across her face. How yellow her skin had
looked under the garish car park lights. Someone had covered
her upper body with a blanket. James was knelt over her, a quiet
tinny sob coming from him, like a small child. Nobody tried to
comfort him or even look at him. His pain was too bare, too
private. We all looked away.

"...She didn't... I mean she... Lacey had been strangled," I
told her. Sophie rescued me.

"Were the police there by then?"

"No. I was standing a little way from her, and I felt someone pull me away. It was Jude. We stood in the car park for a few minutes before the police arrived."

Relief had flooded my body. Jude was OK. He held me tightly and I'd pressed my head into his chest. His T-shirt was wet and cold, but I could feel the warmth of his body radiating through it. I looked up at his wet face. I wasn't sure if it was tears or rain. Even over the darker side of the car park I could see how pale he was. Maybe I looked the same. It was then that I heard the sirens.

"I don't know how long we stood there," I pre-empted Sophie. She wanted to get a firm timeline in place. "Twenty minutes or so. My mum came to collect me." Jude had carefully lowered me into the front passenger seat of her car, handing me over. "Mum offered to give Jude a lift home. He must have said no because he closed the car door and was gone."

I looked at Sophie, bringing my story to an end.

"Later I felt a pain in my foot. I turned on the car's interior light and saw that it was covered in blood. There was a deep cut on my sole. I was still barefoot. I must have stepped on glass in the dunes."

I'd stared at the blood in the dim light of the car. It must have happened a while ago as it had partially dried around my toes. My mum spoke soothing words, but I didn't hear them. I just stared at my blood-encrusted foot. We drove home but I don't remember it, or much of the days that followed. There was a numbness. I must have taken my shoes off on the beach that night. I never went back to get them. I'm not even sure which ones I was wearing.

"What happened in the days after?" Sophie asked. Her voice was gentle, but I could tell she was shifting up a gear. Getting ready for her big close.

"The police interviewed me, interviewed all of us. Everyone had been drinking, so the timeline and witness statements were fuzzy. We just assumed someone would be caught. Someone from outside."

A memory fluttered around my head. Like a small butterfly landing. A blue jumper. A man's knitted jumper in a deep midnight blue. Had I told the police about it? The memory was blurry, like I was watching it underwater. I could see her putting it on. I tried to remember, tried to catch hold of the memory, and bring it to the front of my mind. I rubbed my forehead and pressed my eyes closed.

"Katie?" Sophie pressed.

"Three months after Lacey's murder, most of us left for college. I moved up to London..." I said. "There were only a few that stuck around. James never started his course. I don't think he could face it. It became clear that they weren't going to arrest anyone." I felt a wave of sadness run through me when I thought about James, about what happened to him.

Sophie sat up and leaned into the microphone.

"Five years, no arrests and no real suspects. A police force under pressure to put the high-profile murder of a young woman in a vibrant holiday community to rest. But there was more to this story. Things that the press didn't cover, and the police failed to investigate. We will look at the early murder investigation and some of the shocking twists in the next episode. This has been Sophie Miller and Katie Chase, and you've been listening... to *Small Town*."

Sophie took her headset off and slumped back on the cushions. She looked elated.

"You were fabulous, Katie!" She sat cross-legged and leaned back on her arms. "Well...?" She was waiting for me to say something.

"Yes... good, I think? I'm not sure if I added enough... background. About who Lacey was." The memory of the last hour, of what I'd said, was dim. A foggy mess of memories and reality, that over time had blended into one.

Over the months, the only memory from that night that kept coming back to me, were Lacey's feet. It was something that had played over and over in my mind. The blanket that covered her body was thick and red with tassels on the end. I'm not sure where it came from or who put it over her. It looked too cheerful, almost jaunty, like a poncho. Just her small feet poking out. I remember wanting to cover them up. They looked so cold.

CHAPTER ELEVEN

"You certainly know how to piss people off, Soph." Tom laughed, shaking his head and unplugging the sound desk. "You can tell you didn't grow up around here." He was smiling, but it didn't quite reach his eyes.

"What?" Sophie smiled coyly, elbows on the coffee table and face cupped in her hands. "Do you mean the police thing? Well, they didn't investigate it properly. If they had, then someone would be in prison for it." To Sophie it was simple.

"We need to be careful. The town didn't have much tolerance for the police when it happened. They wanted them to look outside the town. They didn't want them picking apart the lives of the people that live here. They won't thank us for dragging this whole thing up again." Tom spoke as he packed away the microphones. Winding the cables around his thumb and his elbow.

"Don't worry, I know what I'm doing. I'm hoping to speak to someone senior who was on the case. The police are always reluctant to get involved in these things. A bit of negative press might force their hand. Make them keen to explain themselves on the record." Sophie always had her next move planned. The alcohol had mostly worn off and I was weak with tiredness. My tongue felt thick, and my mouth was dry from the wine. I needed to drink water. I needed sleep.

"Do you mind if I go and lie down? The drive and... this." I waved my hand toward the recording equipment. I tried to smile, but only managed to lift the corners of my mouth.

"Of course, go. Can I get you anything?" Sophie asked. I shook my head. As I walked slowly up the stairs, every part of me felt heavy.

I climbed into bed with all my clothes on. Enveloped in the fresh new duvet cover. Soft and crisp like crepe paper. I pulled it up to my face and rested the cold fabric on my cheek. I closed my eyes. I knew that sleep wasn't far away. I could feel myself sinking into it. Images from that night came back to me. Like clips from a film, creeping into my unguarded conscious.

Someone was playing a guitar. I couldn't see them. I must have already passed out on the sand. I could just hear the words. "No Woman, No Cry" by Bob Marley. I saw my feet, covered in blood. No, it was her feet. Covered in the red blanket with the tassels. The blue jumper being pulled over my head, or her head. It was all one color with a raised knitted looping pattern on the front. The cable knit looked like rope. I couldn't stop staring at the rope. And then I was asleep.

I wasn't sure what time I woke up. I'd left my phone downstairs. The curtains were open. The sun was still bright and strong, so I couldn't have been asleep for long. I heard a noise from the room next door. It was the bigger of the three bedrooms. It had been my mum and dad's room. It was a low, rhythmic banging. Regular and quiet. I lost the noise a couple of times before my ears tuned into the steady beat again. It very slowly dawned on me what I was hearing. It was the sound of the bed next door, gently banging against the dividing wall. Sophie and Tom were having sex.

I wrapped my hand in the end of the duvet and pressed it to

my ear. All I could hear was a loud nothingness. Like when you put a shell to your ear and hear the sea. My own deep breathing and the sound of my heart pumping. It was a familiar feeling, pressing the duvet to my ear. It was, I realized, something that I used to do in this very room.

They must have known I would be able to hear them. The cottage was too small for me not to hear them. I felt a tide of resentment grip me as I lay there. All alone in my room. In *my* house. I could feel the tears rising in my chest again, brought on by waves of anger and self-pity. My ear hurt under the weight of my duvet-clad fist pressing down on it. I felt a tear escape my eye and trickle across the bridge of my nose. It ran quickly toward the pillow. I felt its cold wetness fall into my ear, right before I fell back to sleep.

When I woke up again it was dusk. I could just make out the shape of the trees outside the window. I strained my ears, listening. The house was silent. I lifted the duvet and twisted my body around until I was sitting on the edge of the bed. I felt better, stronger. I pulled out the hairband that held my ponytail. I'd slept with it like that. It felt disheveled and was pulling at my scalp. I ran my hands through my hair and stretched my neck muscles, easing my head slowly from side to side. I must have been asleep for a few hours.

There was a glass of water on the bedside table. I don't remember bringing it up with me. Sophie must have brought it in while I was sleeping. I gulped down several mouthfuls. I realized how hungry I was. When was the last time I'd eaten? It must have been last night. I had a hollow, empty feeling in my stomach. I went downstairs in search of food. The lamp in the living room had been left on, but the cottage was empty. There, on the coffee table was a note from Sophie. *We had dinner at your mum and dad's. We didn't want to wake you. I've put some leftovers in the fridge. Me and Tom have gone to the pub—see you there in a bit. Soph x*

Why did I feel annoyed about them having dinner with my parents? They'd left me to sleep. Sophie had brought me left-overs and asked me to join them. I had no right to feel annoyed. I realized I was beginning to sound bitter, to feel bitter. I walked to the kitchen and opened the fridge. There, on the middle shelf, was one of my mum's bowls, covered in cling film. I took it out of the fridge and saw that it had a yellow Post-it note stuck to it. On it, Sophie had drawn a smiley face. I breathed, shrugging off my annoyance. It looked like risotto. I removed the cling film and placed the bowl in the microwave. Fiddling with the dial for a couple of minutes before working out how to turn it on.

I leaned against the worktop, listening to the low whir of the microwave. I thought about Lacey. I thought about all the reasons I had hated her.

When someone dies, they become perfect. The tragedy eclipses any character flaws or bad memories you have of that person. But as much as I tried, I couldn't forget. Neither the image of her body on the ground nor the sadness of her friends and family could take the place of my anger. They tiptoed around my mind like a guilty secret. I looked down at my hands. They were gripping the worktop so tight they'd turned white.

CHAPTER TWELVE

I'd known Lacey since the first year of primary school. Lacey had a way of making you feel unimportant, irrelevant. I'd seen her do it to other people, but not everyone. Most people saw her as fun-loving, exciting. Not unlike the way people saw Sophie. Except Sophie was kind. Lacey didn't like me. I never found out why. It started with small things. Things that nobody else saw. If I tried to join in a conversation, she would cut me off, turn her back on me.

When we were thirteen, Lacey had a birthday party at her house. She lived on the estate, the other side of town. Distinctive, boxy, 1970s semis with big windows and oddly placed fascia boards. At the time they were probably considered architecturally innovative social housing. A lot of the kids from school lived up there. Most of the homes were ex-council houses. Bought cheaply under the Right to Buy scheme years ago and resold. Lacey's house had been one of the few council-owned houses left.

It was one of the first proper parties our school had seen. No adults, no birthday cake and no party games. Over the course of the next few days, it was all anybody could talk about. I'm not sure if there were actual invitations or whether Lacey just asked people. It seemed like more and more people were added to the guest list. Boys and girls. There were even quite a few kids from the year below going.

I positioned myself near Lacey at break times, hoping my invite was coming. I knew we weren't friends, but still —*everyone* was going. Finally, when my friend, Jess, couldn't take it anymore, she went and asked Lacey outright if I could come. I waited by the drinking fountain, pretending not to hear.

"Can Katie come to your party?" she'd asked nervously.

"No," she replied loudly. When Jess asked her why, she'd said, "Because it's supposed to be *fun*... Katie is *so* boring." Everyone laughed, even Jess had smiled awkwardly. I felt sick. A feeling like pain gripped my stomach as I watched them all talk about me.

It's funny how a single day can change everything. Before that, I had friends, not a lot but I did OK. That day changed how people saw me. It changed how *I* saw me. Lacey's words became a self-fulfilling prophecy. The day I became boring.

I pretended to Jess, to everyone, that it was OK. Conversations about hair and makeup and music connected to the party stopped abruptly when I walked past. The girls who'd laughed now looked at me with sympathy. I wasn't sure which was worse. I think it was partly relief that they hadn't been left out of the party. Relief that they didn't have to walk the school playground alone. I smiled more that week than I'd ever smiled in my entire time at school. It was exhausting, acting like I didn't mind.

The Friday night of the party, I'd stayed up late watching films in my bedroom. I was determined that I wouldn't be earlier to bed than those that were going. My parents had obviously found out about the party and didn't want to say anything to me. They didn't want me to feel worse by acknowledging it. I could see it in their faces though. The pity was worse than the not going.

The party came and went, with only a few days of post-mortem to bear. The girls had evidently got bored of not talking about the party in front of me. I tried to get back into the fold, hanging around the peripheral of the many girl groups. Some were more tolerant of me than others. It was like Lacey's words had somehow tainted me.

I laughed at their stories and listened with interest. I asked questions about what they'd worn, who had been kissed. I smiled until my cheeks hurt. I showed the school there were no hard feelings. Jess was more excited than anyone. I knew she felt guilty, but she needn't have. What else could she have done? I used to fantasize about throwing a huge party. People would be talking about it for weeks. Everyone would be invited. Everyone except Lacey.

Lacey continued to make me feel small and I continued to let her. I would hear her laughing behind my back. She would be unkind about my clothes, my hair, even about my dad leaving. Which was ironic as her dad had left too.

Most of the time I could just keep my head down. I would find a quiet corner and read during break times. Over time I just shrank into the background. That was until the day of the English test.

We'd streamed into the classroom that day. There was a buzz of anticipation in the air as we settled into our chairs. Rows of individual tables. I was rummaging in my pencil case for a pen when I heard a ripple of excitement spread across the room. I looked around. They were all looking at the whiteboard at the front of the room. There, in big capital letters were the words KATIE CHASE WITH THE UGLY FACE.

For a moment I didn't move. I didn't even blink. The words burned my eyes until I had to look away. I turned to see their faces; I couldn't help myself. They covered their shock and amusement with hands over their mouths. Lacey was right behind me. She smiled at me. Her long dark lashes blinking with joy. Then she blew me a kiss. A big full-lipped kiss to let me know it had been her.

Rage surged through my body so fast the room spun. I don't know how they couldn't see it. I imagined people moving their chairs away from me, as they saw the anger pulsing from my body. I pictured my hands around her throat; squeezing until all the air hand gone from her. I sat perfectly still, my eyes fixed on her until the teacher came in and silently wiped the words from the board.

It shouldn't have mattered. It was childish, almost funny really. But when you're thirteen everything matters. After that people avoided me. Even Jess for a while. It was as though my unpopularity was infectious. People were scared that they might fall victim to it next. Lacey didn't do anything to me after that. There was no point. Things could not have been any worse for me.

CHAPTER THIRTEEN

The microwave pinged loudly, breaking my train of thought. I took the risotto out. The rice was sizzling slightly, and the bowl was surrounded by a cloud of steam. I'd overcooked it. I placed the bowl on the chopping board and opened drawers, looking for the cutlery. In the second drawer I opened was what looked like a pile of manuals for the kitchen appliances. On top of them was the green cardboard folder of press clippings. My hand hovered over it, stroking the front flap before closing the drawer. I will read them. I have to read them, but not now.

I found the cutlery drawer and selected a fork. Everything was new and shiny. When the food had cooled down, I started eating. Pea and asparagus risotto. It was good. A soft creamy texture, with a kick of parmesan cheese. Richard must have made it. He was an incredible cook. He would have been in his element making dinner for Tom and Sophie. Me and Mum used to laugh at him when he was in the kitchen. Giggling affectionately behind his back as he chopped and grated and cut. Singing along to his music, as he danced around with utensils. He would catch us laughing and pretend to be embarrassed.

Sometimes, it's only when you start eating that you realize

the extent of your hunger. What began as savoring every mouthful, turned into devouring it. I was surprised to see the bowl nearly empty. I don't think I'd eaten properly in days.

I thought about going to the pub, but I couldn't face it. The sleep and the food had made me feel much better, but I still wasn't ready. I couldn't face drinking any more today. I would pop over to Mum and Richard's. The idea of spending an hour next door was a comforting one. I went to the kitchen to retrieve my phone. The top light blinked blue to indicate that I had a text message. I turned the screen on and saw that there were two. The first was from Sophie.

Where are yoooou? ☺ I dismissed it. She wouldn't look for a reply, so I didn't send one. The second message was from Megan. My insides jumped.

Hi, Katie, do you fancy meeting up tomorrow? I work at the interiors shop on the high street—Grey & Co. Come in for a coffee, 10 a.m.? When you get a text message from someone you don't know very well, or someone unexpected, it seems oddly intimate. Like they're in the room, watching you read it. I answered quickly, reading the words out loud. I wanted to reply with an excuse. Tell Megan that I was too busy to meet her, but I couldn't. A lifetime of doing the right thing would make me go. *Sounds great! See you tomorrow x* I pressed send before I could change my mind.

I slipped my trainers on and put the door on the latch. I wasn't sure if the key was in the house or if Sophie and Tom had taken it with them. It was dark now. As I walked outside a security light clicked on. I could just about hear the waves crashing below, caught on the wind, making the beach sound closer than it was. The gravel drive had a row of solar lights on either side, illuminating the path to the main house. Some of the larger palms on the grassy area next to the track had been lit at their base. It looked like a holiday resort. Now that the sun had gone, the temperature had dropped. I hadn't brought a coat for the short walk, and I felt cold. I folded my arms in front of me, hugging my body, as my feet slowly crunched across the gravel.

As I approached the house, I could see through the dark entrance way to the living room. The lights were on in there and the door was ajar. There was Mum, sitting on the end of the sofa. The television was on. A large screen mounted on the wall. Mum was looking at a magazine. The front door was unlocked, so I let myself in and called out to her, slipping off my shoes. The house felt warm and inviting and I could still smell dinner. Garlic and onion mixed with something sweet, like vanilla. Mum was already in her dressing gown. Her slippered feet were tucked underneath her, crossword resting on the arm of the sofa. "Darling, how are you? Did you sleep OK? Have you eaten? Richard... Katie's here," she called. Her face was anxious.

"I'm fine." I smiled. I really did feel fine, better than I'd felt in a few days.

Mum smiled back; she could see I was telling the truth. She patted the sofa next to her.

"Help me with this blasted crossword." Doing the crossword had been our thing. Mum had taught me what to look for. How to spot an anagram or a word made up of several parts. I could only get some of the cryptic clues by myself. The rest of the time I would help Mum. I'd look up words in the dictionary or write out the letters for an anagram in a circle on the corner of the folded newspaper. My favorite answers were the multiple word phrases. (2,4,2,5) *As Bold as Brass.*

I sat down on the sofa next to her, pulling my knees up. The door to the kitchen opened and Richard came in, both spaniels in tow. He was carrying a tray. He looked pleased with himself, excited to show us what he had. As he rounded the sofa, I smelled it. Jam sponge and custard.

"I gave the other two chocolate cake. Kept the good stuff back for you!" He said, placing the tray down on the sofa next to me and passing me the steaming bowl. He beamed, so glad to be able to do something for me. I suppose I hadn't really let them do very much for me over the last few years. As I took the bowl it was like I'd never left. I felt the same familiar contentment of being at home. The feeling of being loved completely. I could have sat there all night with that bowl in my hands, just breathing in its smell, the warmth of it.

Richard joined us on the sofa. He'd also brought drinks. Ginger wine for us all, in little crystal stemless glasses. I tried to decline the wine, but they wouldn't hear of it. "It's hardly even alcoholic, darling. It's more like medicine." Mum laughed. We spent about an hour doing the crossword together. Me and Mum laughed at Richard's inability to grasp the cryptic puzzles. Despite doing it on and off with us for years, he'd never got a grip on it. It was getting late. I wanted to stay, but I knew Mum and Richard were ready for bed.

"I'm going to head back now," I said, reluctantly standing up from the sofa. I'd been sitting on my foot, and it had gone to sleep. It felt numb and tingling as the blood rushed back into it.

"Are you sure? You know you're welcome to stay here tonight," Richard told me.

"Of course, she knows." Mum brushed off his questions with an affectionate smile. "Why don't you take one of the dogs back with you?" Mum suggested. "They're wonderful company and terribly disloyal, so they won't mind a bit being away from us for the night... or from each other, for that matter." I didn't relish the thought of going back to an empty cottage.

"Are you sure?" I asked. They looked pleased.

"Yes, of course! Just let him outside first thing and he'll make his own way home." They decided that Morti would come with me. He was selected as being the best sleep companion of the two. I said goodnight to them and made my way back along the gravel drive, following the lights. The overexcited spaniel from earlier was now calm. He trotted silently beside me, occasionally glancing up. I couldn't see any light from the cottage. When we got to the front door, Morti sat down obediently. The door was still on the latch. When we walked in, I saw two pairs of shoes strewn at the bottom of the stairs. A pair of men's Converse trainers and a pair of women's brown ankle boots. Fashionably battered, with a Gucci label clearly visible on the inside sole. They must have gone to bed.

I walked through to the kitchen to get myself a glass of water. The light was still on. As I entered the room and rounded the corner, I realized, with a start, that Tom was standing there. He was making a cup of tea, bobbing the teabag with a spoon, staring intently into the mug. I tried to hide my fright. "Good night?" My voice sounded strange, constricted. He looked up at me slowly. Full, solid, eye contact. He looked at the dog but didn't comment.

"You know, the usual. Same old faces," he said, eyes back on his tea. What faces? I wanted to ask. Who had been there? His mood seemed to brighten a little. "You did good today. It was just right for the first episode," he said. Did he think he needed to buoy me along, keep the podcast afloat? I didn't need it, not from him.

"Thanks," I replied coldly. He noticed and we looked at each other for a brief moment. His facial expression slipped, and he paused, looking like he was considering something.

"Why didn't you tell Sophie about Jude?" My body went cold, ice water coursed through my veins.

"What about Jude?" I attempted casually, but I heard a break in my voice. He waited.

"Why didn't you tell her that Jude, your ex-boyfriend, was sleeping with Lacey?" He looked at my face, studying my reaction.

"I didn't... Well, I couldn't... It wasn't something I..." I stuttered, my voice tight. His face was less sure now. I saw him swallow, a lump moving slowly down his neck. I was struggling to read his expression. Was he sorry he'd said it? Tom picked up his cup of tea and went to leave the kitchen. He had to pass close by me. I held my breath for a moment until he'd left. Halfway across the living room he turned.

"Do you ever think about that night?" he asked.

I was confused. "The night of the beach party?"

"No," he replied. Our eyes locked. He looked away, like he couldn't say the words. Before I could reply, he'd turned and walked away.

CHAPTER FOURTEEN

I woke early the next morning. Morti lay heavy on my feet. I sat up and ran my hands through his soft fur. He let out a gentle moan and opened his eyes, but didn't move. I touched the velvety down of his head. The fur was curled, like baby bird feathers. I buried my face in the silky fur around his neck and thought about what Tom had said last night. I knew what night he meant. I thought about it all the time.

I had known about Lacey and Jude. I'd worked it out before then, but that night I saw it. As Jude sat there, next to me on the sand, I watched him looking at her. Everyone was looking at her, but this was different. She'd returned the look. There was an intimacy between them, an understanding. It was in that moment I knew, without a doubt, that they'd slept together.

I rooted around my bag to find some fresh clothes. The case was full, and the clothes were tightly compacted. I grabbed a pair of black jeans from the top and rummaged down the sides for a T-shirt. I took the first one I came across. Red and white horizontal stripes. Not my favorite, but it would do. I held on to the ends of the top and shook it firmly, trying to loosen some of the deep creases. I found my towel, draped over the radiator next to the bed. I was about to carry my things through to the bathroom for a shower, when the dog sat up and whined. I couldn't leave him in here. I'd have to let him out.

I crept downstairs in my pajamas, the dog padding silently behind me, sensing the need for quiet. It was just before 7 a.m. I'd left the keys hanging from the inside of the door after I'd locked up last night. I went to turn them and realized it was already unlocked. Somebody must have already gone out this morning. I gently lifted the latch and let Morti out. A gust of cold sea air hit me; I could smell the salt. The dog ambled past my legs through the gap in the door. I watched him wind his way up the gravel drive, nose to the ground. Not even a backward glance. Mum was right, spaniels were disloyal.

As I closed the door, I felt resistance. There was somebody coming into the house. It was Sophie, back from a run. "Morning!" she trilled loudly, taking her earphones out. She smelled like fabric softener and outdoors. "This place is beautiful, Katie! It must have been incredible growing up here!" Sophie panted, animated from the run. Her face was pink and clammy with sweat.

"What are your plans for today?" I changed the subject. Sophie was stretching, holding on to her ankles and pulling her upper body close to the floor.

"Um... not sure yet... Tom is going to edit the first episode this morning." She arched her arm over her head, leaning into a new stretch. I looked behind me to see if he was in the kitchen. Sophie followed the direction of my gaze. "He's not up yet. Episode one is going out on Friday," Sophie said, switching arms.

"Friday?" I was surprised. It was Tuesday now. I hadn't expected the podcast out for weeks, maybe not until after we'd gone.

"Yep, every week for six weeks... or until it's done. We need to get started on episode two." She grinned. I tried to return her smile, but my face was fixed in a grimace. I left Sophie to her cooldown and headed upstairs to shower.

I went to my room to get a towel. I moved quickly on the balls of my feet. I wanted to get out of the house before Tom was up, before I had to face any awkward acknowledgement of what was said last night. I wondered if he'd tell Sophie about Jude and Lacey. Maybe he already had.

The shower was hot and powerful. I stood there, letting the full blast of the water hit me in the face. I could feel it burning my skin, but I liked it. I hadn't turned the light on, so the bathroom fan hadn't started. Steam filled the room quickly, until I couldn't see the door. I washed my hair and got out, standing on the hard limestone floor, still cold despite the heat of the room. I opened the window above the toilet and watched the steam rush out, cascading in swirls toward the sky. I hadn't picked up the towel yet. I stood there, enjoying the feeling of the draft from the window wrapping warm air around my naked body.

By the time I'd wrapped myself in the towel, most of the steam had escaped. The room was warm and damp, covering everything it touched in a layer of water drops. I pulled on the light switch and the fan set in motion, the loud humming noise breaking through the silence like a hairdryer. As I brushed my teeth, I thought about Megan. I thought about how I was going to tell her about the podcast.

Would I explain that I think we can help with the investigation? That we want to find out the truth about what happened to Lacey, finally put her memory to rest. Is that what we were doing, or is that what we tell ourselves that we're doing, what we tell the listeners? Would Megan think we were sensationalizing Lacey's murder?

I returned to my room and dressed. Still no sign of Tom. I couldn't find my hairdryer, so I raked a brush through my hair

and scrunched the wet ends into loose waves. As I opened my
bedroom door, I heard the shower running. I went downstairs
and found the note Sophie had left me last night. I turned the
paper over and started writing.

Gone for a walk, be back at lunchtime. K xx

CHAPTER FIFTEEN

The sun had burned off the misty morning haze, it was getting warmer. If I walked straight into town along the road, I was going to be early to meet Megan. I decided to walk the beach way, down the cliff path and along the dunes leading to the car park. It had been five years since I'd done that walk. I needed to line up the disconnected images in my head. I set off down the hill through the dewy grass toward the headland. My canvas messenger bag over my shoulder and denim jacket tied around my waist. I strode with a boldness I didn't feel.

I filled my lungs with the cool, clean morning air, breathing deeply, with purpose. I stared down at the sea below. The sun made tiny jewels flicker on the surface. Occasionally dolphins would come into Pengully Bay. I knew people that had seen them. For as long as I could remember I would scan the water. Left and right and back again. I stared so hard it would make my eyes hurt. I looked for breaks in the wide expanse of ocean. I never saw one, not even a glimpse. I would see seals and cormorants, sometimes a gannet, but never dolphins. When I was a kid, I used to think it was unfair that I'd never seen one. Nobody tried harder than I did.

By the time I reached the beach, I was feeling something close to contentment. The tide was on its way out, leaving behind a band of seaweed that ran through the middle of the sand. The beach was empty. I began the mile or so walk into town, pausing to slip off my trainers and socks as the sand seeped into my shoes, with each sinking footstep. I paused occasionally, thinking that I'd arrived at the spot where the beach party had been that night. Each time I would look up at the dunes and across to the shoreline trying to find distinguishing features, points in my mind that I could fit together. When I came across the actual place, I almost laughed it was so obvious, so recognizable. There, almost in the same spot, were the blackened, burned-out remnants of a bonfire. Kids must still be coming here to have parties. Nothing would change the way life carried on in Pengully. Not people, not time, not even murder.

I sat on the pale warm sand, between the firepit and the dunes, just as I had done that night. But then, my fingers had clasped an ice-cold bottle of vodka, the acrid smell of burning wood and cigarettes... A memory crashed into my mind. I remember feeling upset, maybe crying. It was after Jude had left, but before I'd passed out, I think. It could have just been about Jude, but I didn't think so. There was something else, something from that night that I couldn't grab hold of. A memory that was just out of reach. Every time I got close, it scurried just out of sight. If I tried not to look directly at it, it might slowly creep back to me.

I stood up and climbed the dunes behind me. They were so steep I had to put my hands on the ground and dig them into the sand to stop me from sliding back down. I could see James doing it that night, scrabbling on his hands and knees to get to Polly. When I got to the top, I stood in the same place that Polly had stood. It looked a long way down to the scorched remains of the fire. Why hadn't Polly come down to us, why had she waited up there, crying and calling, all alone. She must have come across the dunes from the car park to reach us. Polly had been running away. Running in the dark, all on her own, from the lifeless body of her friend. When she saw us, down there on the sand, she must have realized. Realized that she was at her destination and that it would offer her no kind of escape from what she'd seen. That was when she'd started screaming. I knew exactly how she felt.

I trudged across the dunes toward the town. The seagulls were readying themselves for having young. A chorus of them echoed through the bay. I found their call restful, familiar. I wondered if I would like it as much if I was hearing it for the first time now. Mum hates the sound of them. She never used to. She once told me that during the summer, when the gulls wake early and start cawing, she wakes up thinking that it's the sound of a baby crying, of me crying. Mum says she can't bear the realization that it's not me, that I'm no longer a baby. She'd laughed, but it was the first time I'd realized how hard it had been for her, me leaving.

The dunes were a series of large bowls in the sand, full of clumps of coarse grass and scattered litter, enough to make it feel grotty. The odd piece of litter poking out from the green stems, half-buried plastic bottles, mixed with the usual assortment of materials washed up by the sea. It didn't make for easy walking. You were either walking up or you were walking down, feet drifting on a landslide of sand. How had I found my way through here that night without hurting myself? Then I remembered the cut on my foot. I don't even think it hurt. If it hadn't been for all the blood, I don't think I would have noticed it. But I'd turned the light on. I'd turned the light on in the car to have a look. I must have realized that something wasn't right.

I'd reached the point where I'd got my first glimpse of the deserted car park that night, just before I'd come over the brow of the hill. There were only a handful of cars there now. It was barely 9 a.m. Too early for the tourists and too late for the first of the morning's dog walkers. I trudged through the sand a little farther, as the bank gave way to the long slope down to the ground. It was then that I saw it, the old wooden bridge. Only a couple of meters long, providing a footway over the small stream that ran through the town, ending on the beach. I made my way down, each step sliding into the next, until I reached it. I ran my hand along the wooden rail, made smooth from years of sandy hands and salty wind. Lacey's body had been only a few feet away.

My bare feet left the warm wood of the bridge, covered in a soft dusting of sand. I stepped onto the cold, rough tarmac of the car park. Lacey had lain there. Face up on the hard, wet ground, coarse with sharp stone chippings. A place no person would choose to lie, a place that wasn't even marked. There was no kind of memorial for the girl that had died here only a few years ago. A place that would be walked over every day, by people who would never know her name. It was as though it had never happened.

CHAPTER SIXTEEN

It was 9:20 a.m. I still had forty minutes before I was due to meet Megan. It was a ten-minute walk away. I pulled my phone out of my pocket and there on the screen was a text message from Sophie. *Tom has started the edit. How about episode two this afternoon?? Soph x* Sophie would be narrating the second episode. We needed to cover the last bit of the story, get the listener up to the present time, on the same page as us.

Yep, sounds good. x I texted back. I went back to my messages and found my last text from Megan. I hit reply.

I've come into town a bit early. Are you around now? Katie x The response was almost instant. *I'm at the shop. I'll put the kettle on. M x*

I walked across the car park and turned the corner, away from the lane that led to Red Rock. There were a few people about. A group of women, probably on their way home from the school run. There was a truck parked outside the pub. The hydraulic lift at the rear was down and two men were taking pallets around the back. I stood outside the interiors shop. I can't remember what it used to be, maybe it was never a shop until now. A closed sign hung on the door of Grey & Co. There was no sign of Megan. I looked through the large window.

Thick, sumptuous curtains hung on either side of the display. The labels were visible, names I vaguely recognized. Expensive names. Sanderson, Morris & Co, Osborne & Little. There was a chaise longue in the center, covered in a mustard-yellow fabric and expensive-looking cushions. None of the items seemed to have prices on them. There was a printed card in the window that read, INTERIOR DESIGN SERVICE AVAIL-ABLE. PLEASE CALL IN TO MAKE AN APPOINTMENT. My eyes adjusted away from the window to movement at the back of the shop. It was Megan and she was beckoning me in.

I opened the door, triggering an old-fashioned bell. The shop was dark. The morning sun hadn't moved around to the high street yet and the room was filled with deep colors and dark woods. Even on the brightest of days it probably never got very light. It smelled incredible, like chocolate and spiced fruit. It reminded me of Christmas. Megan stood by an open door at the back of the shop, an electric kettle in her hand. She was dressed in a gray silk wraparound dress. She looked polished, groomed. My eyes fell self-consciously to my own creased clothes.

"Coffee?" I nodded.

"Please, that would be great... just milk, no..." I told Megan how I took my coffee, as she was asking me. We both spoke over each other and laughed a little at our own awkwardness. This felt easier than I thought it would. Megan wasn't at all how I remembered her. She was more poised, more confident than the timid child I'd known. But I suppose I hadn't really known her at all.

Megan disappeared out the back to make the coffee. I looked around the shop. Everything had an opulence to it. There was modern furniture mixed with antique, and the walls were adorned with rugs and fabric charts. It must have been a nice place to come to work every day.

"So, is this place yours?" I called out to the kitchen.

"Yep, all mine." She laughed. "My own personal vanity project."

"No, it's amazing." I meant it. Megan emerged from the kitchen with two mugs of coffee.

"Sit down, sit down." She was warm and easy. "Thank you, but it is vain really. I started an interior business from home, which would have been fine. I usually go to the client's house anyway. But this..." She looked around the room. "This was just to show everyone." There wasn't a hint of bitterness. "It's a bit of a millstone, but the clients seem to like coming here." I nodded, waiting for the right moment.

We talked about London, about my course and the job at the station. Megan seemed genuinely interested. We talked a bit about the old days, the people, the changes there'd been. Conversation was no effort. I felt comfortable. Even the coffee tasted good.

"I saw Tom at the pub last night," she told me. I froze. "He told me about the podcast." I could feel my face coloring with shame. Megan saw it. "It's fine, Katie, really it is." She spoke softly. I didn't understand. "Katie, I already knew. Your mum told me." I couldn't think of a single thing to say. I opened my mouth, and no sound came out. Megan took the empty mug from my hand. "Top up?" she asked. I nodded mutely. She walked back to the kitchen, and I could hear the kettle turning on. "Your mum and dad have been really good to me. I couldn't have done all of this without them. After I did Red Rock Cottage, they—"

I interrupted her. "You decorated Red Rock Cottage?" Why hadn't they told me? I guess we haven't really told each other much lately.

"Didn't they tell you?" Megan stuck her head around the

door with the jar of coffee granules and a teaspoon in her hand. I shook my head and she shrugged, only mildly surprised. "After Red Rock, Richard let me do some of the suites up at the Carmen. I loved it. It was literally a dream job for me. After that, they started recommending me to their friends, regulars up at the Carmen, people with money." She returned with the coffee and sat down.

"Can I tell you something?" Megan bit her lip and tipped her head to the side, unsure if she should carry on. "Your mum asked me to talk to you. Asked me to try and talk you out of doing this podcast. She's worried about you." Megan waited, studying my face.

"Do *you* want me to stop the podcast?" I wasn't sure if I was ready to hear her answer.

"No. I thought I did when your mum first told me. Not now. I'm not exactly thrilled about the whole thing being brought up again, but it needs to be. Lacey died. She was brutally murdered, and this town was more concerned with keeping the tourists coming than catching her killer." There was no resentment, just sadness. "Please don't tell your mum I told you. She only wants what's best." Megan drained the last of her coffee.

"I won't. I'm sorry I didn't tell you on the beach." She shook her head slightly. It didn't matter anymore.

"Megan, who do you..." I didn't finish my sentence. My words were interrupted by the sound of a baby crying. Howling in high-pitched staccato. The sound was coming from the back room.

"Well, that's my coffee break over!" Megan laughed, reaching for my mug.

"Whose um... is...?" I faltered, confused.

"She's mine. Mia. She's seven months old. Not exactly conducive to running a business, but we make it work." The baby's cry was increasing in volume and frustration.

"I'll leave you to it." I paused. "This has been really nice, thank you." It really had been.

"It has. Stop by next time you're in town. There aren't many of the old group still around. It's good to finally see a friendly face." We said our goodbyes and I left the shop. The street outside seemed too bright. I squinted as my eyes adjusted to the light.

Megan had a baby, a seven-month-old baby. How had I not known? Was I really that detached from Pengully now? A lot had happened around here since I'd left. I headed back down the hill toward the beach. This time I'd walk the quick way home, up the lane.

The town was busier now. A steady flow of traffic moved up and down the high street. People who passed me smiled. Strangers taking time to greet me as they went about their day. The way it had always been in this small seaside town, maybe all small towns. As I looked at their faces, I thought about what Megan had said. Why, when she had spent her entire life here, was I the only friendly face she could find?

CHAPTER SEVENTEEN

When I walked in the door of the cottage, I felt it straight away —the atmosphere. Tom sat on one of the sofas. A laptop rested on his knee, headphones covering his ears. Sophie was looking through her notes, cross-legged on the floor. They'd had an argument. The air felt heavy with tension. Sophie looked up. "Nice walk?" She smiled, but her mouth was a tight line. Tom didn't look at me. I knew he'd told her about Megan, told her that we were meeting for coffee. I would usually go to her, try to gently coax her out of her mood. I couldn't today, my head was too full. I could tell she was waiting. Waiting for me to make it better.

"Good, thanks." I skipped lightly up the stairs, the oppressive silence of the room still ringing in my ears. I could feel Sophie's eyes on me as I left. I lay on my bed, my chin resting on the crook of my arm. I looked around the room, the room that Megan had decorated. It didn't have any of the deep sultry colors of her shop, but looking around, her style was evident. My parents, Richard especially, loved championing local business. He always had. He said it was how you built up trust in the community, said he'd be nothing without the support of Pengully. I couldn't understand why they hadn't told me, why Mum had asked Megan to speak to me about the podcast. Were they really that close now?

I could hear talking downstairs. Normal voices, less strained. Sophie had obviously started cooking. I could hear pans being moved and the smell of fried garlic wafting up the stairs. "Katie, I've made lunch," Sophie called up the stairs a little while later. Her voice was lighter. I lifted some of the clothes from my bag to retrieve an old gray wool cardigan from midway down the pile. An old favorite. On cold nights in my flat in London, I sometimes slept with it on. I slung it over my shoulders and headed downstairs. The smell of food made my empty stomach growl.

Sophie had made grilled chicken and salad with some kind of sauce. It looked incredible. There were three meals that Sophie could cook. Simple food that tasted amazing. This was one of them. Sophie handed me and Tom a plate each. It seemed like the storm between them had passed. But maybe they were just being professional because they knew we had a podcast to record. I looked at Sophie, her mind was elsewhere. Whatever it was, she was no longer interested. It was something she did.

After we ate, Tom cleared the plates away in silence and returned with a bottle of white wine and three glasses. Tom never usually drank, not with us anyway. I poured the wine as Sophie set up the cushions and Tom put the microphones and headsets on the coffee table. We all worked silently, arranging the room, until it was ready. Sophie had put the introduction script in front of me. It was typed. There were a couple of changes that had been made in red pen, probably from the network. I also had my own notes this time. This time I wasn't going into the dark, feeling my way through the story. I took a long drink from my wineglass and started reading aloud. I found my radio pitch as soon as I started. It felt easier today. I never really knew where the confidence to talk like this came from. It just seemed to happen. After I'd read the network text, I introduced the podcast.

"Welcome to *Small Town*." I read it slowly, my voice a little lower and a little quieter. "Five years ago, Lacey Crew was murdered." Pause. "She was murdered in Cornwall, in a small town, by the beach." Pause. "Nobody was ever arrested, and no official charges were ever brought." Pause. "Lacey Crew was nineteen years old." I swallowed. "My name... is Katie Chase."

"And my name is Sophie Miller." We'd done this so many times before. We had a pattern, a rhythm between our voices.

"This is episode two... of 'The Lacey Crew Murder.'" I was handing over to Sophie. I could see that she was ready, she was almost tingling with excitement, her wine already half drunk.

"After the murder, the town was in disarray." She started. "Almost everyone who could potentially be a suspect was questioned. Some people more than once." She was setting the scene, building up a picture in the listener's mind.

I thought back to my interview. I remember being surprised they did it at home. I thought they would ask me to go down to the station, but maybe that was just in films. It took two days before they got around to me. They'd sent two police officers, a man and a woman. The man was older, probably around the same age as Mum. He'd taken notes and said very little. I'd assumed he was senior, as the woman was so much younger. She didn't look much older than me. She seemed cross with me as soon as I spoke. But maybe she was like that with everyone.

"The town had wanted the killer caught. They didn't want to see someone go unpunished for a crime; for a murderer to walk among them. But Pengully is a tourist town. It's a town almost entirely dependent on holidaymakers.

"It was mid-July; the town had been full. It was bad enough that the murder was fixed in the minds of the families that had been staying there, without the enquiry dragging on, affecting future families from visiting. This was a town that needed the investigation to be over quickly." Sophie glanced up at Tom. He indicated for her to continue, but his face was expressionless.

I'd never spoken to Richard about how the murder had affected the Carmen Club. I assumed it hadn't affected it at all. Most of the clientele were older. A retired golf-and-spa set. Married couples looking for luxury. Not the sort that would be put off by the murder of a teenage girl in the town. But perhaps it *had* put them off. Since it happened, there was a darkness that hung like a black veil over Pengully. A darkness that I thought only a few of us could see. Maybe I was wrong.

I could tell that this wasn't Sophie's first glass of wine. Her voice was thicker, more relaxed. It wasn't something the listeners would notice, but I'd been doing this with her for a long time. She was repositioning herself on the floor. Chin up, ready. Her chest rose.

"When Lacey was murdered, the only items missing were her mobile phone and a gold, heart-shaped locket that she always wore. Her phone had a broken screen. Lacey had dropped it weeks before her murder and hadn't got around to fixing it. The locket wasn't an expensive one. The sort you'd pick up for less than thirty pounds. It held a photo of her beloved grandad and she'd worn it around her neck since he'd died two years before. It had been a gift from her mother. This wasn't a robbery. This was someone she knew, someone close to her." Sophie's voice was almost a whisper. She looked at her notes and took another mouthful of wine.

The mobile phone and the necklace weren't the only things of Lacey's that were missing. She'd had a backpack with her on the beach. I remember her arriving with it. It was one I'd seen

her with at work. It was a yellow Puma bag, small and scuffed.
I'd mentioned it to the officer that came to the house, and she'd
written it down, nodding. Maybe the police retrieved it after her
body was found. It might not have been missing at all. I never
thought to check later.

CHAPTER EIGHTEEN

Sophie continued, "Five months after Lacey's body had been found, in late November, an early morning dog walker by the name of Susan Lewis found Lacey's necklace. It was hanging from the wooden footbridge, less than six feet from where her body had lain. A bridge that was used every day over the summer. A bridge that had been meticulously searched by police. This wasn't a piece of evidence that had been missed. Someone, possibly the murderer, had returned to the scene of the crime to place that locket carefully at the end of the bridge. Someone who wanted it to be found." Sophie finished. Her part was over. It was my turn.

I cleared my throat and began. "The dog walker who found the necklace was a friend of Lacey's mother, Lorraine Crew. Susan was married to a man named Brian Lewis."

I remembered Brian well. He'd been my driving instructor. A tall, overweight, friendly man. His booming laugh and large body had filled the car during our weekly lessons. He was always kind and patient with me. He made the lessons enjoyable, and I was fond of him. He was obviously a good teacher; I'd passed my driving test the first time.

"Brian taught most of the kids in the village to drive. He was the only instructor in the area, and he'd been doing it for years. Susan and Brian had no children, and despite being in their late sixties, the police quickly identified them as persons of interest. They were brought in for questioning. It was the first time there had been any sort of significant movement on the case," I explained to the listeners. I thought back to when I'd heard. I'd only been in London for a couple of months. I'd phoned home, spoken to Richard. I think he told me they'd been arrested. That was probably what the village were saying. I wasn't shocked. After what had happened to Lacey, nothing else about the case could have shocked me. They could have told me it was any one of the people that I'd grown up with and I wouldn't have been surprised.

I paused, glancing down at my notes.

"The police quickly learned that, along with having an alibi for the time of the murder, Brian had been diagnosed with Stage 4 lung cancer three months earlier. He'd been receiving treatment. Treatment that had left him tired and frail. Even if their alibi *hadn't* been strong, the police didn't believe that either Brian or his wife were physically capable of strangling Lacey. They were released without charge, but the air of suspicion hung over them. Nobody accused them, but there was no support. The town took a collective step back from the couple. Four weeks later Brian died. Susan didn't get over losing her husband or the way that the town had treated them." I reached for my wineglass as Sophie took over.

"Susan was quite vocal about it by all accounts. She'd felt let down and it wasn't the police she blamed; it was Pengully. Shortly after Brian died, Susan sold their house and moved up north to live with her sister."

My memory of Susan was that she was difficult. She used to help at the Carmen Club from time to time. Cleaning, office admin, sometimes bar work, I think. She always seemed dissatisfied either with where she was or who she was talking to. I don't think she worked at the club regularly, just if they were short of money. Susan also ran the Girl Guides. Another reason why I'd left after only a few weeks. I suppose she had every right to feel let down by a town where she'd spent her entire life. But everything changed after Lacey died. The people, the place, everything.

"So, who returned the locket?" I paused, letting the question hang there for a moment. "There was no DNA, no fingerprints. It could have been found by someone who didn't want to be involved in the enquiry. But the police were sure the locket held the key to this enquiry. They were no longer looking for an out-of-county murderer. They were no longer keen to work with other police forces on similar killings in other parts of the country. No, they were now looking for someone much closer to home. They were now looking for someone local, someone connected. This was not a random attack."

"So, who were the main suspects at this time?" Sophie wasn't really asking me. She was asking the listeners. The success of true crime podcasts depends on the engagement of the listeners. We needed them to want to help solve the crime, to be debating it in online forums, spreading the word to other true crime enthusiasts. I drained the last of my wine and leaned back against the base of the sofa. It was time to give them the next piece. It was time to talk about James.

CHAPTER NINETEEN

I started. "Right from the beginning, Lacey's boyfriend, James Penhaligan, was under suspicion. He was there that night. They'd argued at the party. They argued a lot."

"But he was never arrested?" Sophie asked.

"No. James's mum, Claire, was a solicitor. I think she still is. She advised him not to talk to the police. He was interviewed, several times, but always answered 'no comment' to the questions. From what I heard, it angered the police. They felt that if he had nothing to hide, then why not help with their enquiries? Claire saw it differently.

"The police had made him a priority suspect from day one. Claire didn't trust them not to try and pin it on him. She wanted to make sure that he didn't give them anything they could use against him. There was circumstantial evidence that pointed toward James, but there was circumstantial evidence that pointed to a lot of people at the party that night. The police were obviously going to make James their prime suspect. Overbearing teenage boyfriend? It was the first place to start." I knew I shouldn't have said it as soon as the words came out of my mouth.

"Was he overbearing?" Sophie asked. I saw Tom flinch. Just a tiny movement. Tom and James had been friends, best friends. This was going to be hard for him. He was perched on the side of the sofa, headphones on, his hands placed on top of his outstretched legs. I could see one of his knees twitching with impatience or nerves. He looked up and we made eye contact for a moment, a long moment, longer than was comfortable. He was looking at me, really looking, head tilted to one side. My stomach made an unwelcome lurch, and just for a second, I remembered what I'd seen in him. I looked away quickly, clearing my throat. It sounded forced. I carried on, avoiding Sophie's question.

"James was supposed to study law. He was very bright; he could have had his pick of places. His parents were very ambitious for him."

Maybe that had been one of the few things he had in common with Lacey. They weren't an obvious fit.

"James and Lacey had been together for about a year. I don't think either of their families were particularly happy about it. I can't imagine they spent much time at each other's houses."

"Why weren't their families happy about it?" Sophie was genuinely interested. This was new information.

"I could be wrong. They were both just very different." I needed to tread carefully now. "Claire was a solicitor, and her husband, Michael, was the local MP. They were quite... I'm not sure how to put it—highly regarded in the town. They wanted the very best for James and pushed him to strive for it."

They were pompous assholes from what I remember of them. Michael was friends with Richard. They regularly drank together up at the Carmen and he and Claire would sometimes come round for dinner. I'm not sure what Mum thought of them. They only ever seemed to talk about themselves. I would hear their loud voices echoing up the stairs. The more Michael drank, the louder he got. His accent seemed to be fluid, deviating between home counties and brash Cornish, depending on who he was talking to. It had obviously served him well. Everyone loved him, or they certainly loved what he represented—what someone like him being their MP said about their little town. The next part wasn't going to be easy.

"There had been complaints made about Michael up at the Carmen Club." I'm not sure how Richard would feel about me talking about this. "Some of the waitresses and female bar staff had complained about him. They said that when he was drunk, he would make verbal and sometimes physical advances toward them."

He was disgusting. I can picture him now, sitting up at the bar every Friday night with his cronies. Local businessmen who hung on his every arrogant word. Expensive open-necked shirt stretched over his bulging stomach. Perched on a barstool, licking his lips. Leering at whoever had the misfortune to be on the bar that night. He'd never done it to me, but I'd seen it.

I'd spoken to Richard about it. He'd just kept asking for reassurance that Michael had never touched me. I assured him, over and over. I'm not sure if Richard said anything to him. Michael certainly didn't stop. I did notice that Richard no longer came into the bar on a Friday when he was there. It carried on until official complaints were made. I'm not sure what happened, but Michael never drank at the Carmen again after that. I carefully changed the subject.

"I once heard Lacey and James arguing up at the club. She was just about to start her shift and they were in the staff room together. I heard their raised voices from outside. James was begging Lacey not to make a complaint. It was obvious that they were talking about Michael. Lacey said James had no idea what he was like, no idea what he'd done, but James wasn't listening.

"I think his dad scared him. James couldn't have been more different from his parents." I let the words hang there for a moment. I'd always thought James was sensitive and kind. Remembering how he was with Lacey, I was beginning to wonder how different he really was.

"After James left, I went into the staff room. Lacey was crying. I'd never seen her upset before, not like that, not even when were kids." We didn't speak, didn't even look at each other. "When the complaints were made, I'd checked the list of names. Names of the women who had spoken out. Lacey's name wasn't on there."

"So, Lacey never complained about Michael?" Sophie asked. She was writing again.

"No, not that I know of. Lacey and James weren't a good match, not as far as the town was concerned. Lacey lived in a two-bedroom council house. She had a reputation as a bit of a party girl, a bit wild. She wasn't really, no more than anyone else. But she'd got into trouble for shoplifting when she was about thirteen."

The town didn't forget things like that. It was virtually impossible to change the way people saw you around here. You were never allowed to grow or move on, especially if you were someone like Lacey. You were either in or you were out. Lacey was out, and she didn't give a shit.

CHAPTER TWENTY

"James, on the other hand, lived with his parents in an old rectory. A large stone-built house with a big wraparound garden. The house is one of the best in the village, certainly one of the most expensive. I think Claire even managed to get it featured in an interiors magazine once. Everything about it was impressive. It can't have been much fun growing up there though. The place was like a show home." I was losing my thread, talking unguardedly, like it didn't matter what I said. I glanced up at Tom and was surprised to see him nodding, encouraging me to go on.

Sophie wanted to get it back on course.

"How did the town feel about James not assisting the police with their enquiries?" She was looking down at her notes. I could see she'd written down a list of points.

"At the beginning there was definitely an anti-police feeling. After the witch hunt that surrounded poor Brian, the town wanted them to look outside of the community. They didn't want the investigation concentrating on the town, or anyone in it. I don't think anybody really thought James had done it. Not in our circle of friends anyway. No one except Lacey's mum, Lorraine."

"Lorraine, or Lonni as everyone calls her, always blamed James. At first, she just blamed him for not protecting her, but it was only a few weeks before she started telling anyone that would listen that James had killed her."

I thought back to the weeks after Lacey had died. Lonni had been a permanent fixture in the town. I'd see her in the shop, in the pub, sometimes just pacing up and down the street. I felt bad, but I'd avoided her whenever I could.

Lonni had a wide frame and a big pillowy chest. Her long, thick frizzy hair was dyed a deep burgundy color. It was a brash purple, but Lonni always referred to herself as a redhead. She always wore lots of layers. Flowing skirts, dresses, scarves, lots of tassels and falling fabrics. It gave her a bohemian look that I don't think she intended.

Lonni would stand outside the shop, chewing her nails. Pale face and wild eyes, flitting around as though she were looking for someone. She always carried a cotton bag over her shoulder that had KEEP CALM AND CARRY ON PENGULLY printed on it. The primary school had them printed years ago to raise money for their new minibus. It was when I was still a pupil there. The bag was now grubby and faded. It looked almost empty, and she continuously pushed it back onto her shoulder. Anyone could see that Lonni was broken. She might even have needed professional help. She should have been a person to be pitied, protected. For some reason the town had little sympathy for her. Much less than they had for James Penhaligan and his family.

Lonni once cornered me in the street. It was a couple of weeks before I left for London. She'd been agitated, aggressive. She'd asked me what I'd seen that night, what had happened. I'd been vague, embarrassed by her raised voice. Lonni had moved toward me shouting, until my back was pressed up against the newsagent window. Her stale breath was on my face as she spat her words at me.

She had accused me of protecting people, protecting the town and Richard's business. I stood there, my face flushed and my mouth open. Clint, the landlord from the Bull, had stepped in. He'd ushered me away as he tightly gripped Lonni's arm. As I looked back, she sat sobbing on the pavement. Clint had driven me home and spoken to my parents. I don't think anyone offered to drive Lonni home that day.

Sophie retrieved a sheet of paper from the bottom of her pile and placed it in front of her. She studied it for a few seconds. The room was silent with anticipation. I knew what was coming. Tom did too. He was rubbing his forehead with the palm of his hand. Slowly, backward and forward. Pressing so hard it left a visible trail.

"Two years after Lacey was murdered, something happened. It was so tragic and so unexpected nobody could have foreseen it," Sophie read.

Couldn't they? I thought. Could no one have seen it coming? James had been in a bad way. Lots of people had said it. We weren't really friends anymore. We hadn't been for a while. Sophie continued to read.

"James had lived in Pengully since it happened. Six months earlier he'd moved into an old caravan on Tregolls Farm. A run-down mobile home in the middle of a field. It was barely habitable by all accounts. For two years he hadn't worked. He didn't study and he never had another girlfriend."

"The police case had gone cold. It was no longer still an active investigation. Three weeks before the two-year anniversary of Lacey's death, James's body was discovered in the woods at the back of Hogarth Road. He was found less than thirty feet from the back door of the old rectory, his parents' house. His mum found him." I repositioned my headphones. My hands were visibly shaking.

I hadn't gone back for the funeral. I couldn't face it. Mum
had phoned me late one night. She hadn't cried but I could tell
from her voice how upset she was. I remember an overriding
sense of something being over, coming to an end. The happy,
carefree life we'd all had as kids. Bonfires and Christmases.
Carnivals, sports day, late-night swims. Memories so distant and
removed, as though they'd never happened. Or they'd happened
to someone else. That phone call felt like the end. Closing a
book you know you won't read again.

"James had killed himself. He was twenty-two years old. It
wasn't clear how his mum came to find him. His body, while
close to the house, was hidden by a line of sycamore trees that
ran along the bottom end of their garden," said Sophie, still carefully reading words from the page.

I remembered the rectory. Every year, Claire and Michael
would have a big summer barbeque. It was an annual highlight
in Pengully. Most of the town would be invited. It would go on
into the night, long after it got dark. We ran around the garden,
hours past our bedtime. We'd hide from each other, giggling in
the dark corners of the flower beds. The sound of our parents
laughing, glasses clinking. Drinking until it was too cold to be
outside anymore.

We were never allowed to go into the woods. Even though it
was just yards away from the rectory garden. There was no
access from their property. You had to go to the front of the
house and walk down the lane that ran alongside the garden.
The last party I'd gone to, I must have been about fourteen or
fifteen. Too old to come to a party with my parents and too
young to spend the night at home on my own.

Things were hard for me at school then, but there was a
group of us whose parents were friends. Friends by default. Jess
had been there, so had Tom. There were about eight or nine of
us from our year group. We'd been allowed to have a lager that
night. It was the first time I'd ever drank alcohol. A small stubby

French beer in a glass bottle. Boxes and boxes of them, stacked up under the table outside. Brought back from the Penhaligan's last skiing trip.

The beer had tasted like the Carmen Club bar smelled on a Saturday morning. A stale, earthy taste. It made me shudder, but I liked it. I liked how it made me feel. My cheeks were flushed, and I felt brave, like someone else. We'd played hide-and-seek. We knew we were too old to play but were spurred on by the beer and the lack of entertainment.

It was dark. I think Jess had been counting. We all ran in different directions. Me and James looked at each other, daring ourselves to do it. We ran around the front of the house, along the path to the woods. The moon was bright, we could just about see our way. We laughed as we ran, arms jostling, shushing each other. When we reached the woods, panting and excited, James had grabbed my hand. He'd pulled me toward the bushes between the woods and his garden. Somewhere to hide.

"Over here," he'd said in a whisper. We crouched there. Going into the hedge as far as we could before sharp brambles blocked our way. We pretended to listen for footsteps, but we weren't playing anymore. My heart was beating so loudly I was sure James must have been able to hear it. We both sat there, looking straight ahead, into the darkness. It felt like ages. I finally turned my head to face him.

He was already there, kissing me. It took me a moment to respond. To realize that something was happening. The kiss was gentle at first, enquiring, permissive. Our lips barely touching. His breath was warm and sweet. The moments when our mouths weren't touching as exciting as the moments they were. His lips parted, just a fraction, and I felt his tongue. Unfamiliar feelings pulsed through my body. Excitement and fear. I gave in to the kiss, turning my body so I slowly slid to the ground, lying on my back, my head resting on ivy and sticks and dirt. James was on top of me. The kissing became more urgent. I could feel his heart pounding through his T-shirt. It was then we heard it. A twig breaking underfoot and a tiny flashlight sweeping across our faces. It was Tom. I could tell from the outline of his body and his grunt of surprise.

We'd stopped, immediately. Leaping apart as if it weren't too late. Embarrassment and shock coursed through me as we stumbled awkwardly to our feet. No one said a word. We'd walked silently down the lane. The blackness hiding my shaking legs and burning face. Tom walked ahead of me. My eyes were fixed on his back as we returned to the party.

CHAPTER TWENTY-ONE

We never spoke about it again. I'd tried to stay there at the party. I'd tried to be normal. Tom had taken me aside. He'd asked in hushed tones if I was OK. My face burned crimson. "I'm good," I'd snapped, lifting my head, showing him just how fine I was. After a while I told my parents I had a headache and we left. Me and James were fine after that. It wasn't the same, but it was OK. There was a tension between us that I'd not felt before. I still thought about that kiss sometimes. My first kiss. Up until that night in the woods, I'd never thought about James in that way. Not ever. It's funny how feelings can creep up on you.

Sophie continued, "There had been a rope hooked over a high branch of a tree, but James wasn't hanging from it. He was sitting on the ground, a half-empty bottle of bourbon next to him." Tom crossed his arms, tucking his hands under his armpits. It had always been Tom and Jude and James, for as long as I could remember. But it was Tom and James who were the closer of the three. I wondered if they were still in touch—at the end.

"There was an autopsy, but the results had been inconclusive. Toxicology showed that James had high levels of alcohol and drugs in his system. He would have been so out of it that lots of people questioned whether he would have been able to stand up, never mind attach the rope. There were ligature marks around his neck, but the coroner was unable to conclude that this was the cause of death. It was unclear if the marks were pronounced enough to have been caused by complete suspension from the rope, or whether something else had happened that night." Tom visibly winced.

"Nine months later, there was an inquest. 'Owing to the range of factors involved'"—she read from her sheet of paper—"'an open verdict was recorded.' The Penhaligans pursued a case against the police for what they saw as the harassment that ultimately led to James's death. The case went nowhere. The police hadn't spoken to James for over a year when it happened. There was no case to answer.

"A few weeks after the inquest, Detective Sergeant Steven Trainor of Devon & Cornwall Police released a statement: 'Our thoughts are with the family of James Christopher Penhaligan at this difficult time. There has been much speculation around his death and the murder of Lacey Crew. While we do not anticipate a trial, we are no longer looking for anyone in connection with the murder.' It was as close as they dared to go to naming James as the killer." Sophie looked at her watch. She was wrapping this up now.

"There was very little evidence to suggest that James killed Lacey and a question mark remained over whether or not he'd killed himself. So why did the police make such a bold statement? Why were they so keen for this to go away?

"This has been Sophie Miller and Katie Chase and you've been listening... to *Small Town*." Sophie sat back, pleased with herself. Tom sat still, his eyes fixed on a point on the floor. He removed his headset without looking up, and left the room. Sophie pretended not to notice.

"Well, what did you think?" she asked.

"Good... I mean, I think you told it how it needed to be told." I felt uncomfortable, aware that Tom was listening from the kitchen. Aware that he was upset. Sophie wasn't uncomfortable at all. She reached for the wine bottle and filled up both of our glasses. I noticed she didn't pour any into Tom's glass.

"I got an email today... from Detective Rebecca Rush." I nodded, but the name didn't mean anything to me. "I contacted her last week. She worked on the case. She'd only been transferred here about a month before it happened, but she was involved right from the beginning. Rebecca's a detective now and she says she'll talk to us. Off the record, of course. We can't record anything—but still." I could see Sophie's mind racing ahead to the next episode, the next part of the story. "We're meeting her tomorrow afternoon at the Carmen," Sophie said, gathering up her papers.

Tom came back into the room. He looked tired. His long athletic body leaned against the doorframe. He was looking straight at Sophie, his eyes dark and cold. I didn't want to be there anymore. Tom had something to say, and I didn't want to hear it. "I'm going to pop next door for a bit." I smiled at no one in particular. I picked up my full wineglass and got up to leave. My voice was light. I avoided eye contact. Pretended I couldn't feel the strain in the room, the tension between them.

I slipped the latch on the front door and was gone. I stood outside the cottage for a moment, placing my glass down on the ground. As I pulled my cardigan across my body, I heard raised voices. I hurried to the main house.

The wind had picked up. The palm trees were bent against the force. It was cold, much colder than last night. I struggled to keep my hair from blowing across my face as I walked. I jogged the last bit of the gravel path to the front door. I pulled down the large chrome door handle but it was locked. I took a step back and looked up at the house. I couldn't see any lights on. I was about to turn around and reluctantly head back to the cottage when I remembered the door through the garage. If the garage had been left open, I'd be able to get in.

I walked a little way along the line of the house, until I reached the first of the two garages. It had a white sliding door with a push-down handle. It was unlocked. I used my body to slide the heavy door across, until it was open enough for me to slip through. The security light automatically lit up the room as I stepped inside. There were doors at either end, one that led to the double garage next door where Mum kept her car and one that led through to the kitchen. The garage was virtually empty apart from Richard's old E-Type Jag. He'd had it for as long as I'd known him. It was a bright, scarlet convertible. Carmen Red was the name of the color. Richard would tell the middle-aged men that drank up at the bar that the car was the reason he'd called it the Carmen Club. They loved the story. A bachelor's dream, naming your bar after your sports car. But it wasn't true. Richard's mother had been called Carmen.

Richard's father, a wealthy businessman who'd barely stepped foot outside of Yorkshire, had bought his wife the car as a birthday present. From what Richard remembered, she'd never driven it. Not once. It had sat in a garage like this one at their house in Malton for twenty years. Richard's dad had died when he was still a teenager. When he was nineteen, him and his mum sold up and made the move to Cornwall. Richard said it was somewhere she'd always wanted to live. Six months after they'd moved, Carmen died of a heart attack and Richard was left all alone.

CHAPTER TWENTY-TWO

I opened the door that led to the kitchen. There was no sign of anyone, not even the dogs. The light had been left on, but the kitchen couldn't be seen from the front of the house. I drank from my wineglass, a long slow draw. Walking over to the fridge, I ran my hand along the cool black marble worktop. The fridge was fully stocked. Wine and beer, champagne. Lots of little plastic pots, ingredients from the local deli. Meats and cheeses wrapped in brown paper and string. There was an open bottle of white wine in the door, with only a glass or two missing. Chardonnay. I had no idea what type of wine we'd been drinking in the cottage. It didn't matter. I wasn't drinking for the taste. Not tonight. I poured the chardonnay into the wine already in my glass. Filled it almost to the top. I returned the bottle to the fridge, before changing my mind and carrying it through to the living room.

I turned the lamp on and looked around the large, tidy room. I sat on the sofa and placed the wineglass and bottle on the cream carpeted floor in front of me. The coffee table was too far to reach. I could feel the effects of the wine hitting me. My head was tired and swimming. I turned the television on. The volume was turned high. Loud American voices filled the room. I muted it, pulling a thick knitted blanket from the back of the sofa over myself. I wondered if it was one of Megan's. I propped myself up, covering my body in the soft gray fabric. It felt good to be on my own. I reached for my wineglass, spilling a little as I lifted it to my mouth. I thought about James.

I don't think James and Lacey had ever really spoken before we went to college. Going to college had been like pressing a reset button. It didn't matter what had come before, who you'd been friends with, how popular or unpopular you'd been at school. College was a chance to start again. It was when I'd really come into my own, when a lot of people did.

We'd all started drinking at the Bull. If you were at college, you could get served there. Clint, the landlord, turned a blind eye to the small matter of underage drinking. A few of us had gone there together one night. We were a group. Me and Jess, James, Tom, Jude, and a few others. It was just before me and Jude became a couple. Lacey and her friends, Polly and Tara, had been there. I'd been talking to Jude at the bar and turned around to see Lacey sitting on James's lap. It was the strangest thing to see, like a dream where nothing made sense. Where everyone looked just how they should, but acted entirely out of character. Jude had laughed. He'd given me one of his slow lazy winks and said, "Lucky boy."

I'd assumed it was a one-off. A drunken flirt. But I started seeing James and Lacey together more and more. They would hold hands around college. Heads together, talking, laughing. I saw much less of James. Lacey was no more friendly to me than she had been at school. I think she wanted to make it clear that James was hers now. There was a shift, a movement in the group as the boys spent more time with Lacey and her friends. Jess had dropped out of college and started working at her dad's accounting firm, so I found myself on my own again. I think that's one of the reasons that I ended up with Jude. Why I put up with so much from him. He was my way in. It secured my place in the new order of things and there was nothing, absolutely nothing, that Lacey Crew could do about it.

I picked my wine up and drank half of the glass. Big thirsty gulps. The room began to twist and my eyelids felt heavy. I drank some more. I didn't want to think or remember. Not tonight. I wanted the oblivion of sleep to come quickly. The wine knocking me into a deep dreamless rest. I drained the glass. The wine tasted sour and acidic as it trickled down to my empty stomach. I was starting to feel sick. I put the glass down and let my body sink into the sofa, closing my eyes. Sleep was coming fast. I was sinking into the blackness below.

Drunken dreams came rapidly, swirling so quickly I couldn't keep up. I'm kissing Jude. Winding strands of his soft hair around my fingers, touching his stubbled cheek. Twigs and hard ground are pressing into the back of my head. James's heart beating, chest pressed against mine. Kissing and not kissing. Kissing and not kissing. The smell of smoke, of firewood cracking. I can hear the sound of someone playing a guitar. I can't quite catch the tune. People are singing, but it sounds like screaming. They're with Polly and they're all screaming. A blue jumper over soft blond hair. She's smiling at me, laughing. I can see the knots. A snake made of rope and she's talking to me. I can't hear what she's saying. The sea is too loud.

I hate her. I hate her *so* much.

I tried to lift my head, sober myself. My hands hurt. I held up my palms and could see fingernail marks where I'd squeezed my fists so tightly. I needed to steady the thoughts that were racing through my mind.

Did Lacey come and speak to me that night? The night she died. I can't hear what she's saying. I can't remember. It's like trying to catch a thread. I keep missing it. If I could just catch hold of it, the whole thing would unravel. I think I might be missing on purpose. And then I fall into the deepest sleep.

CHAPTER TWENTY-THREE

I woke the next morning with something heavy on my legs, pushing my lower body into the sofa. I was lying on my stomach and had to crane my neck around to see what it was. Morti. The spaniel lay curled on my blanketed body, looking much smaller than his full size. I could hear the radio in the kitchen and Mum humming as she clattered around the cupboards. My mouth felt dry and swollen and my head jarred with searing pain when I tried to lift it. It felt like it was being compressed. I slowly sat up. Waves of nausea washed over me as I tried to lick my dry lips. The dog stirred and reluctantly climbed off the sofa. Mum put her head around the door.

"Morning, darling! How are you feeling?" She was speaking in a mock whisper, laughing at my delicate state. She probably thought that I'd only drunk the half bottle of chardonnay.

"Fine," I croaked, smiling and rubbing my eyes. I was still wearing yesterday's mascara. My eyes burned as I smudged it. I took my phone out of my jeans pocket: 11:32 a.m. I groaned. How could I have slept for so long? I had a text from Sophie.

We're meeting DC Rush at 2 p.m. Can you drive? Tom's

gone to stay at his flat for a bit. The message was received at 2:43 a.m. Sophie had been up late.

Yep. I'll give you a knock at 1.30 p.m. K x Mum came back into the room with a cup of tea. I took it and leaned back into the sofa.

"Didn't fancy the cottage last night?" She was probing, trying to feign indifference as she folded the covers that lay tangled about me.

"Something like that." I blew on my hot tea. I noticed the blanket I'd covered myself in last night had been replaced with a duvet. It was one that I recognized from childhood. Bright yellow with blue lightning flashes, now faded from years of washing.

"Is it OK if I shower here?" I asked.

"Yes, of course. There are fresh towels in the cupboard and some of your clothes are still in your bedroom." I nodded.

"Right," I said, lifting myself off the sofa, tea in hand. I shuffled stiffly out of the living room to the hallway stairs. I climbed them slowly, holding on to the rounded chrome banister with my free hand. The stone floor was cold on my feet. I could feel it through my socks. I reached the upper landing and continued along the corridor to my old bedroom. It was exactly how I'd left it.

Film posters, photos and certificates covered the walls. It smelled just the same, a familiar mixture of incense and cinnamon. I walked over to my bookcase and ran my hand along the spines. There was teen fiction, textbooks from college and a few magazines that I'd kept. Wedged between brightly covered novels and GSCE English texts. Little china animal trinkets were balanced in front of the books. I used to collect them. Some of them were chipped. All of them were dusty.

I looked at the scattered photos on my pinboard. Most of them were from secondary school and college. Me and Jess on a ferry. A school trip to France seven years ago. A night out at the pub. Me and Jude, Jess, Tom, Polly. James and Lacey. All pulling faces at the camera. It must have been a fancy-dress night. Me and Jude had an orange feather boa wrapped around our necks. We all looked happy, really happy.

One end of my room had floor-to-ceiling fitted cupboards. Shelving, rails, shoe racks. I thought I'd taken most of my clothes with me when I left for college, but I'd obviously left a lot here. There was a pile of jeans. They all looked the same, so I grabbed the pair on top. T-shirts hung on one of the rails. I nudged them across the metal bar one at a time. I paused as I saw my pink Carmen Club T-shirt. Perfectly pressed. I fingered the black stitching of the Carmen logo, before moving it along the rail. I pulled a plain gray T-shirt off the hanger and a yellow polo-neck jumper from the shelf and added it to my pile.

I carried my clothes through to the bathroom and locked the door. The room was huge. Nearly as big as the living room in my flat back in London. There was a rolled-top bath and a separate double shower, with twin heads the size of dinner plates attached to the ceiling. The whole room, floor and walls were tiled in a dark gray slate. It made the room feel like a big cave. I sat on the edge of the bath. My head was pulsing, surges of pain pressing into my temples.

I pressed the sides of my head together with the palms of my hands to try and relieve the pressure. I sat up, remembering. Had I really spoken to Lacey that night? Had I dreamed it? I tried to bring it back into focus. What had she said to me? I could feel the color draining from my face. Fear was making my legs feel weak. Had I done something to Lacey? Had I hurt her? I'd been angry, so angry. I shook my head, shaking it away. I can't have done... I would remember, wouldn't I?

I showered and dressed, before going into Mum and Richard's room. The door was open, but I knocked lightly. Richard must already be at work. I dried my hair and sorted out my makeup, checking my reflection in the full-length mirror as I left the room. I looked better. Still pale, but better. The yellow high-necked jumper suited me. I'm not sure why I'd left it behind when I went away. My long dark hair, straight from drying, sat a few inches below my shoulders. I'd used some of my mum's dark eye shadow. It made my eyes look greener. I went downstairs. Mum was in the kitchen. Folding up washing from the tumble dryer. She had her back to me as she spoke.

"Better?" she asked, still folding.

"Much better, thanks." I paused. I needed to ask.

"Mum? Why didn't you tell me that Megan decorated the cottage?" She froze, surprised. Considering her answer, she turned around slowly.

"Honestly? I'm not really sure," she said, biting her lip. "When you went away, there was... well, there was a void. A void in my life. I tried filling it with spaniels and gardening, but it wasn't enough." She smiled at her own foolishness. "Megan has had a very difficult time. What with Lacey and her poor mother... setting up the business—"

I interrupted her. "The baby?" I watched her expression. Mum looked away.

"Yes, of course, the baby. Having Mia hasn't been easy." She waited, looking like she wanted to say more. "Me, well, me and your dad, we wanted to help. We wanted to get her on her feet, make that part a little easier." She tilted her head to one side, waiting for my response, hoping that I understood.

"So, you're friends now?" I was jealous. Jealous of Mum's close relationship with Megan. Jealous that I'd been so disengaged from my family that I'd had no idea. No idea how sad Mum had been.

"Yes, we're friends," Mum said softly, walking over to me. She held my hands, squeezing them a little as she spoke. "I'm so glad you're home." Her eyes filled with tears as she repeated the words. We hugged. Really hugged and I felt some of the pain and confusion fall away.

I walked around to the side of the house, to where I'd parked my car. Sophie was already there, leaning against the passenger door. Her hair shiny and golden in the sun. She wore black oversized sunglasses and a gray blazer over a crisp white T-shirt. She looked smart, styled.

"How was your sleepover?" she said climbing into the car.

"Sorry, I should have texted to say I wasn't coming back," I said, fastening my seat belt.

"It's fine." She shrugged, but she sounded tired. I couldn't see her eyes behind her glasses.

"So, this Rebecca woman was a detective on the case?" I asked as I looked over my shoulder, reversing the car across the gravel drive.

"Rebecca Rush. She wasn't a detective at the time, she was just a constable. She says she met you." I was confused. "She came to the house. She was the one you gave your statement to."

CHAPTER TWENTY-FOUR

The route to the Carmen Club took us through the town and up the hill past the pub. It was only a ten-minute drive, but the narrow back lanes made it seem longer. Already, the sycamore trees that lined the road were covered with large hand-shaped leaves, creating a shaded green tunnel to drive through. I tried to remember the last time I'd been along here. It must have been a couple of months after Lacey died. I'd worked a few shifts there before I moved to London.

Those months before I left were awful. I counted down the days until I was gone. The murder was all anyone in the town could talk about. Unless you'd been there that night. For those of us that were there, it was different. We avoided each other, avoided the beach. Avoided anything that might remind us of Lacey.

The Carmen had been the worst place to be. Regulars sat perched around the bar, every one of them had a theory about what happened, an update on the investigation. Having to work with Danny those last couple of times was painful. The fact that it had happened at his party just added to the grief and shock he felt. I preferred to be at home. I could pretend everything was normal at home. A few months later I'd moved to London, so pretending became easier.

Sophie tugged her notebook out of the black leather bag by her feet. She thumbed through the pages, scanning over her words. "We need to find out why they were so keen to close the case after James died." She pulled the lid off her pen with her teeth. "We need more information about the forensics. The listeners are going to want specifics..." Her voice trailed off as she thought of something else and started scribbling again.

I nodded faintly. I wasn't required to say anything. This was Sophie's process. I drove down the lanes, letting her words wash over me. Dappled light broke through the trees, shining pockets of glowing beams onto the road. As we reached the top of the hill, the high Cornish hedges widened. They revealed the large modern complex. I was struck by how much the design of the buildings looked like Red Rock House. I'm not sure why I'd never noticed it before. Sophie sat up, craning her neck for a better view. "Your dad doesn't do things by halves, does he?" she said. I laughed, turning my head to agree, but she wasn't laughing.

"He's had this place for a long time. He built it up from nothing," I said defensively.

"Sorry, Katie... I'm really tired." She lifted her sunglasses onto her head. Her eyes looked red and swollen and her skin was pale. I wondered if she'd slept at all.

"It's fine. Are you OK?" I glanced at her, before maneuvering the car through the main entrance gate.

"Nothing some sleep and a glass of wine won't fix." She smiled, but it was strained. I followed the palm tree-lined road through the resort to the staff car park. Everything looked smart and clean. New road signs and freshly painted low-level walls bordered the manicured flower beds. The dark glass frontage of the main building bounced shards of sunlight onto the neatly mown grass below.

The staff car park was half full. Mostly cheap hatchbacks like mine. A stark contrast to the guest car park we'd just passed. New shiny BMWs, Audis, a Porsche or two. I reversed into a space, and we left the car in silence. The car park was around the back of the reception. Hidden from view of the paying guests.

I led the way around the side of the building until we reached the main entrance. The tall glass doors slid away as we walked toward them. It was all as I remembered it. A large, cavernous room with sandstone tiles on the floor. Oversized indoor plants and a wide, curved staircase leading to the restaurant and bar upstairs.

We walked past the front reception desk, heading upstairs. Sophie's heeled boots clinked loudly on the stone floor, echoing around the space. Two women busied themselves behind computer screens, both wearing the familiar chalky pink Carmen T-shirt. We were three or four steps up, when one of the women called out to us.

"Hi, excuse me, hi." She scurried out from behind her desk. "Can I take your room number please?" She was short and stocky, and her voice was artificially high. Her dark hair was scraped into a severe ponytail and her face was heavily made up. Dark red lips fixed in a tight smile. A work smile. I was about to answer when Sophie spoke. "Hi. Connie, is it?" she asked, looking down at her name badge.

"Yes, it's, um, I'm the general manager here..." Connie was knocked a little off balance by Sophie's confidence.

"Perfect," Sophie said, cutting her off. Flashing her own work smile. "This is Katie. Katie Chase, Richard's daughter." She waited for the information to sink in. "We have a meeting upstairs in a few minutes. I wonder if you could arrange a table for us and maybe some food and drinks?" Sophie had a way of asking for things that people rarely said no to.

"I... yes, of course... your dad isn't here at the moment.

Would you like me to show you around the..." Connie was eager to please now, but uncertain how to proceed. Sophie made it easy for her.

"No. Thank you so much, Connie. We'll be upstairs." She continued up the steps, before throwing Connie a final smile over her shoulder. Connie beamed. I muttered my thanks before following Sophie. This is what she did. What she'd always done. Not for the first time on this trip, I wondered what I brought to the table. What I offered to the investigation that Sophie and Tom couldn't have done on their own.

Connie must have called ahead to the restaurant because a bearded blond man greeted us halfway across the room. "I've got a table for you over here." He looked at Sophie as he spoke. "Your dad will be sorry he missed you." He told her. Sophie didn't correct him. She just smiled. A rush of irritation shuddered through me.

The reserved table wasn't necessary. The restaurant was almost empty. Only a couple of seats were occupied, out of the hundred or so here. The barman took us to a large four-seater table by the window. There was a view across the terrace, onto the outdoor pool below. "What can I get you?" the barman asked Sophie.

"Surprise me," she smiled flirtatiously. His confusion quickly changed to pleasure as he turned to leave. I had to call him back, to apologetically ask for a cup of coffee.

"Sure," he said, his smile dropping just a fraction before leaving. That was another one of Sophie's superpowers. Men. They were drawn to her. It happened everywhere we went.

CHAPTER TWENTY-FIVE

My chair faced the restaurant and Sophie's was toward the view of the pool. I scanned the room, checking that Rebecca hadn't already arrived. There were only two other tables taken. On one, a man sat alone. A full cup of untouched coffee sat next to the laptop he was poring over. His expensive suit and furrowed brow suggested that this was business not pleasure. An overnight stop between meetings.

The other table was taken up by a middle-aged couple. They seemed to be sitting in silence. His large frame was devouring a plate of food. Hunched over, head down in concentration. His wife was the opposite in size. Thin and wiry. Her short, cropped hair was styled into a smart, wavy quiff. She watched her husband. A look of disgust barely concealed on her face. She had no food in front of her, just a glass of green juice. Whatever was in the glass made her wince every time she lifted her bony wrist to drink from it. I wondered what a stranger would see if they looked over at me and Sophie right now. The barman returned to the table with a filled tray, his face eager.

"A coffee for you." He stretched over the table, placing what looked like a cappuccino down in front of me. I nodded in thanks.

"Aaand"—he was excited as he placed the tray down for Sophie—"a hazelnut latte and some pastries." He hesitated as he unloaded the drink, waiting for his praise.

"You did good, Ben." She smiled, glancing discreetly at his name badge. "Really good." Ben unloaded the contents of the tray onto our table and walked away happy. I took a sip of my hot coffee. My shoulders dropped an inch, relaxing into the caffeine hit. It was then that I saw her. Rebecca Rush, stood at the top of the stairs. She was wearing a smart navy suit with a pair of old trainers, like she'd walked here. I didn't think that I'd recognize her. I'd only ever met her the once, but her face seemed very familiar. I raised my hand a little to signal her over. As she arrived at the table, Sophie stood up, hand outstretched.

"Thanks so much for seeing us, Detective Rush..." Sophie shook her hand enthusiastically.

"Rebecca, please," she replied, extending her hand to me. We'd barely sat down before Ben was at the table again.

"What can I get you?" he asked Rebecca eagerly. She rummaged in her bag and pulled out a plastic-covered file and a half-filled bottle of water before answering Ben.

"I'm fine, thank you." Ben's smile waned and his eyes dropped to the water. He paused, before giving her a tight smile and leaving.

"So, what is it I can help you with?" Rebecca gave little away. It was hard to tell whether she was happy to be here, or if this was just a professional imposition. She was about my age, maybe a couple of years older. Up close, her suit was in the style of someone much older. Coupled with her young, makeup-free face, she looked like she was at her first job interview.

Sophie started. "Would you be able to talk us through the early investigation? We're really trying to understand it from a police point of view." Rebecca nodded slowly, her eyes on

Sophie's phone that lay face down on the table. She looked to her and waited. Hands clasped together like a teacher. Sophie returned her stare, feigning puzzlement.

"Can you stop the recording and turn your phone off, please?" Her voice was calm, and her face was expressionless. Sophie held eye contact for a moment, opening her mouth to say something, before changing her mind. Smiling in mock defeat, she dipped her head in a show of remorse before switching her phone off.

"I'd only moved to this force a month before it happened. I was on duty the night Lacey was murdered. I wasn't a detective then, so my involvement was fairly low level, but I was there from the beginning." Rebecca opened her file. Half open, so the contents were visible only to her. I saw Sophie's eyes burning through the cover, willing the contents to spill out over the table. "Lacey's murder was full of..." She grappled for the right word. "...inconsistencies." There was a pause while she sipped her water.

"We've got this beautiful popular teenager, no obvious enemies, no suspicious past or backstory." Rebecca thought for a second. "In nearly every case like this, other than domestic murders by a partner, there is clear sexual motivation. I don't necessarily mean that they are assaulted, but that they were selected by the killer... that some form of gratification could be..." Rebecca stopped and sighed, rubbing the back of her neck with her hand. "I'm sorry. I've got so used to talking like this... I don't mean to sound insensitive." She was looking at me as she spoke.

"No, it's fine, really." I nodded for a little too long. She watched me, her eyes narrowing a little, trying to be sure.

"Anyway, that wasn't the case with Lacey's murder. As you know, she was strangled. There was no weapon used. In the absence of a weapon, we assume that the murder was most likely unplanned. Either a stranger—an opportunist who saw

Lacey in the car park that night—or someone she knew. Someone without the *desire* to murder. Someone who, for their own reasons, wanted or needed Lacey Crew dead." Sophie was writing as Rebecca spoke, adding to her pages of notes.

"Did you think it was a stranger or someone she knew?" I asked.

Rebecca considered this for a moment. "We never had enough evidence to rule out either. If you're asking what I thought personally...? I think she was murdered by someone she knew."

"Does the fact that she was strangled make that more likely?" Sophie asked, barely looking up.

"Not necessarily," she replied. "Strangulation is an intimate act. It forces the killer to watch the life slip away from their victim. There is no detachment. There's time. Time to change your mind, time to release your grip. I probably considered a stranger more likely back then. But five years have gone by and no other murders in the county? It makes it less likely in my opinion." Rebecca watched Sophie work, waiting for the next question.

"...and the necklace being returned to the scene? Did that support the idea that it was someone she knew?" Sophie chewed her lip, trying to knot the important threads together in her mind.

"Most of the people working on the case thought so. I was never sure of its significance. I always wondered if we made too much of it. It could have been returned by someone wholly unconnected. Someone who was just afraid of being linked to the case..."

"You mean Susan Lewis, the dog walker who found it?" Sophie interrupted.

"No." Rebecca was firm. "Mrs. Lewis found the necklace on the bridge. I'm sure of that. Any connection that was made at the time between Mrs. Lewis and the case was done by the town, not by the police." Rebecca's mouth was set in a grim line. Sophie looked like she wanted to push the subject further but thought better of it.

"What about evidence at the scene? Was anything found that was considered of importance?" Sophie asked, her eyes boring into the file in front of Rebecca.

"No. I don't think there was anything you'd consider significant. There were several factors that caused problems with extracting physical evidence that night. The rain was an issue. For about half an hour, within the window of time that we believed Lacey was murdered, it poured with rain. I mean really poured. There was localized flooding and some of the lanes were impassable." Rebecca stopped and looked at me. An acknowledgement that I had been there that night. This was my story too.

CHAPTER TWENTY-SIX

"The rain meant that a lot of potential trace evidence, like hair and fibers, would have simply been washed away. It also made getting any DNA virtually impossible. There were other retrieval techniques that they could have attempted, but it was decided that there was little point in pursuing it..."

"Why?" Sophie asked, genuinely interested.

"When we arrived that night, there were at least twelve people crowded around Lacey's body. James, her boyfriend, was draped over her. Someone had covered her in a red blanket. I counted three people touching her, and the rest were close enough to have impacted the scene. The only fibers found were those from the red blanket and a significant number of human hairs, all from different people. We resigned ourselves early on to the fact that there was no point in extensive analysis. The scene had been contaminated. We took statements from everyone that night, but..."

"My statement wasn't taken for two days." I don't know why I said it. It sounded petty and confrontational. I could feel myself blushing.

Rebecca watched me closely before she said quietly, "You're

right. There were a lot of things we could have done differently that night. For two days, we didn't have a single police officer that had ever worked on a murder case. That isn't an excuse or a criticism. It's just a fact." Rebecca's voice softened as she added, "Your statement actually helped us to create a timeline for Lacey's death." My shoulders stiffened. This wasn't something that I knew. Sophie's head lifted abruptly, and she stopped writing. I was just thinking of how to answer when Rebecca spoke again.

"You phoned home at 22:24 p.m." She read from the file. The memory began inching back to me. I had phoned to ask for a lift. I don't remember speaking to anyone. I must have left a message. It couldn't have been long before I passed out. I don't recall a single thing I'd said. My stomach clenched at the thought of my parents hearing me in that state.

Rebecca continued, "Phone records showed that you made that call from the beach. In your statement you said..." Rebecca leafed through the first couple of pages and scrolled down the document with her finger. "...Yes here. You said that at the time you made the call you believed Lacey was still on the beach. There were other witnesses that supported this." Rebecca thought for a moment. "That was actually one of the major problems we had with this case. Nearly all the significant witnesses were teenagers. It's not that they were unreliable, just sometimes a little too eager to help, be involved. The rest of the accounts were hazy at best." Rebecca looked at me, her mouth in a sympathetic line. I turned away embarrassed, realizing that mine was one of the hazy accounts.

I'd told the police everything the day they came to the house. At least everything I could remember. I'd told them how drunk I'd been, how I'd passed out and couldn't recall a lot of the night. I don't know what reaction I'd expected when I told them. Maybe understanding? Sympathy, as I walked around the black hole in my memory. There had been none. They were frustrated, even angry with me at times. I knew exactly how they felt.

"The call to the emergency services was made at 23:21 p.m., by a..." Rebecca lifted the top page of the file, searching for a name. "...Jude West." I had no idea Jude had made the call to the police. How could I not have known that? "That meant a fifty-seven-minute window of time, when Lacey was murdered," she added.

"There was actually something I wanted to ask you about my statement. It's probably nothing. I don't want to..." I was already backtracking.

"No, what is it?" Rebecca asked patiently. She pulled my full statement from her file and waited. I got the impression she was the sort of person who would wait for hours if she needed to.

"When I gave my statement, I mentioned a blue jumper that I thought Lacey might have been wearing that night. I'm not sure if it was... relevant... It doesn't really matter now but..." I was rambling. I could see Sophie looking at me out of the corner of my eye, wondering why this was the first she'd heard of a blue jumper. Rebecca was silent as she scanned the document. I watched as her eyes darted from left to right, chewing absently on her thumbnail. I met Sophie's eyes and she raised her eyebrows.

"Yes, here." She tapped a section a third of the way down the page with her index finger. "I thought it sounded familiar. You told us that later in the night, you thought you'd seen Lacey wearing a blue knitted jumper." Rebecca looked like she was trying to recall that night. "It wasn't something I specifically remember. I don't think it was something we retrieved from her backpack that we recovered from the beach." So they *had* found her bag.

"Did anyone else see her in the jumper?" I asked.

Rebecca looked up, considering the question. "I don't think

so. I mean, I can't say for sure without looking through the rest of the statements, but it's definitely something we would have pursued if it had been confirmed by multiple witnesses." I nodded.

Rebecca looked at me enquiringly. "This is obviously something that has played on your mind. Do *you* think that it might have been significant?" Sophie looked from Rebecca to me, poised for my answer.

"Probably not. It's just..." I looked for the right words. "... The jumper seemed familiar. I remember it being baggy on her, like a man's jumper... like maybe it wasn't hers." It sounded so trivial when I said it out loud, but Rebecca was looking at me with interest. She slid my statement back into the file and returned to Sophie.

"With every single cold case investigation—and that's basically what you're both doing with the podcast—the answers are there. They'll be somewhere." She patted the folder. "In the evidence, in the statements, in the timeline. You just need to know what it is that you're searching for." She paused. "A good methodology for reviewing old cases, is the ABC of investigation: Accept nothing. Believe nobody. Check everything." Sophie's hand scrawled quickly across the page, as she wrote Rebecca's words. She loved a tag line.

"Do you mind us investigating this?" I asked.

Rebecca looked amused. "Do you care?" She laughed a little, releasing a small puff of air through her nostrils. "Look. With anything like this, you're going to find an element of... how can I put it? Professional pride? Nobody likes their work being called into question. But this case *needs* looking at. For a number of reasons, I'm sure it won't be up for a review any time soon. The only things that concern *me* about this podcast, is the hurt it might cause to Lacey's family... and your safety."

"Safety? What do you mean?" Sophie asked, confused.

Rebecca pressed her lips together for a moment. Her

considered answers made it clear that she still didn't trust us. "I live in Pengully. I've heard the rumors. All the speculation surrounding James's death—that he'd found out who the killer was or maybe was the killer. There is no evidence to suggest that any of it's true, but..." Rebecca raised her finger as a warning, "...there is a good chance that the person who killed Lacey is someone local, maybe even someone you know." She turned to me and held my gaze for a second. I swallowed hard.

"I was unhappy with the investigation into James's death and I'm fairly sure there was more to it than was brought up at the inquest. All I'm saying to you is be careful."

CHAPTER TWENTY-SEVEN

Sophie waited a quiet moment before asking, "Can we talk about James?"

Rebecca was drinking from her bottle. She nodded briskly, her mouth full of water, before quickly glancing at her watch. It was a cheap plastic one. The sort that a young child might have when they first learn to tell the time. "Yes, but I don't have long, I'm afraid."

"OK." Sophie sat up. A determined look crossed her face as she flipped the page on her notepad and went straight to her list of questions. I looked up to see Richard striding across the restaurant toward the bar. His pace slowed when he spotted me. I hadn't told him we were coming. He grinned. His eyes quickly scanned the table. He made a circular motion with his hands, checking if we had everything we needed. I nodded and smiled. He gave me a swift thumbs-up before moving on.

"Were you surprised that the inquest into James's death recorded an open verdict?" Sophie read from the page. Rebecca tilted her head to the side and looked at Sophie inquiringly. She was surprised by the question.

"You know that there was no cover-up by the police. If

that's a route you're considering exploring, I can tell you now it's a dead end. The inquest reviewed all the evidence that was available. Witnesses, the autopsy, James's frame of mind. The problem is a lot of that evidence was either unclear or conflicting," said Rebecca.

"So why the statement? Why were the police so keen to link James to Lacey's murder and close the case? Lacey had been dead for two years. There couldn't have been the same pressure on them." Sophie spoke quickly. She was keen to get through all the questions before our time ran out.

"Hmm… yes, it was… an unusual course of action." Rebecca rubbed her neck again. Her eyes flashed momentarily to Sophie's phone, checking for signs of life. She leaned in, her voice low. "DS Trainor was the lead detective on the case. He's ex-military. An experienced soldier who'd spent years rising through the ranks of the army. I'm not sure why he left and joined the police force. Steven Trainor is good at his job… but it has frustrated him that the case has remained unsolved. James died, and he saw an opportunity. A chance to present the case as closed. A nice neat ribbon around the whole thing. As far as I know, he never got permission to make that statement to the press.

"I'm not sure whether he truly believed James did it or not," added Rebecca sadly. She lifted her bag onto the table and started to gather her things. "That statement created a narrative of what happened that night. It has molded the investigation ever since. It's the reason this case will never be opened again."

"Thank you," I said. Rebecca twisted her body around as if to leave.

"There was one thing that really bothered me about James's death." She was still for a moment. Her hand rested on the shoulder strap of her bag. "Toxicology tests found high doses of benzodiazepines in James's system. Levels so high that even without the presence of alcohol it would most likely have hospitalized him. It's a prescription drug. Used to treat alcohol with-drawal, anxiety, insomnia... James was struggling in the weeks before he died. He was drinking heavily and was regularly seeing his GP. Now, we checked: He had *never* had a prescription for benzodiazepines or any other prescription drug. So where did the drugs come from? These aren't easy pills to get, not in a place like Pengully. It probably doesn't matter, but it was always something that troubled me." She stood up.

We both thanked her for her time. She nodded. "Best of luck." She looked like she wanted to add one last thing, before changing her mind. She gave us the briefest of smiles and left. Sophie sat there wide-eyed, her eyebrows raised.

"I have no idea where to start," she said, looking down at her paper. She took a sip from the cold coffee in front of her. My cappuccino sat untouched in front of me. The foam top congealing around the edges. "Do you think the whole thing was a cover-up?" she asked.

"That's exactly what she said it wasn't," I replied, trying to keep Sophie focused on the facts.

"Yes, but..." Sophie started, just as Richard came over to our table.

"Hello, what a nice surprise. I wasn't expecting to see you two." He smiled as he leaned over and kissed my cheek. "Do you have everything you need?" he asked, looking to the bar, ready to call Ben back.

"Yes, perfect. Thank you," I said, feeling guilty about the complimentary food and drink. Richard wouldn't have minded in the slightest. He would have insisted. But it wasn't something I did at the Carmen. I never had.

"If you fancy sticking around, we've got a Mexican night this evening. It's mainly for the guests, but there'll be plenty of locals here too." His face was hopeful. I was about to answer, a line of ready excuses slowly queuing up in my mind.

"Yes!!" Sophie squealed. A little too loud for the quiet

empty room. "Oh, Katie, we haven't been out together for ages... please?" She was so enthusiastic.

"Well, if you wanted to make a night of it, you're more than welcome to have one of the suites here. I'd love you to see the new rooms." Sophie clasped her hands together and gave me a pleading look.

"Yes, fine!" I threw my hands up a little in pretend exasperation. Richard was pleased. He felt around in his back pocket and retrieved what looked like a black credit card. He handed it to me. The dark matt finish had the gold Carmen logo in the center.

"This is one of our master cards. You can use it in the shop if you want to buy swimming things or toiletries—save you going home. Use it for dinner and drinks... anything you want."

"You really don't need to..." I said, reluctant to take the card from him.

"Please, Katie... How often do I get to treat you?" He was willing me to have it.

"Thank you." I stood up and gave him a hug. "Are you and Mum coming tonight?" I asked.

"No, not tonight. Not sure if you've noticed, Katie, but your old man has become an old man." He smiled as he started to move away from the table.

"Rubbish!" Sophie laughed, taking another swig of her coffee.

"I'll let them know at reception you'll be taking one of the suites. Just go and pick the key up from them later. Have a wonderful time, girls." And he was gone. Sophie hated the word *girls* being used to describe women, but she didn't appear to notice. She sipped happily on her drink, waiting for her phone to spring back to life. I looked up at the large station-style clock that hung over the bar: 3:15 p.m.

"Do you want to go for a swim?" I asked tentatively.

"Great." She absently scrolled through messages on her phone. I waited patiently.

"Do you want to stay here, and I'll go down to the shop, grab us some bits?"

"Ahh, sorry, would you mind?" She was clearly frustrated by something on the screen.

"Should we message Tom—let him know we won't be coming home tonight?" I suggested.

Sophie was still staring at her phone. "What? Er... no, I'm sure it's fine. He's staying at his flat." She answered distractedly as she continued to scroll.

I bit my lip nervously. "I might message him—just in case," I told her.

"OK," she replied, uninterested. "We will have fun tonight, you know?" She looked up from her screen and smiled.

"Of course, we will," I said brightly. But the words felt devoid of any real feeling. We both knew things had changed. I grabbed one of the pastries from the platter, and left Sophie to her work. I took a bite out of the peach-flavored dough as I made my way back down the twisted staircase. The sickly sweet syrup clung to the roof of my mouth. I hurried past the reception desk, throwing Connie a quick wave as I rushed toward the doors, keen to avoid another awkward offer of a tour. Connie called out to me, but I didn't hear what she said as the sliding doors closed on reception.

I retrieved my phone from my pocket. As I held it in my hand, it occurred to me that Rebecca hadn't checked *my* phone for recording. I scrolled down my contacts until I came to Tom's number. I pressed the message button. The screen was blank. Not a single text between us in the time I'd owned this phone. I wasn't even sure that Tom had my number. *Hi Tom, Me and Soph staying at the Carmen tonight. There's a Mexican night on. You're welcome to join us. x* I deleted the kiss at the end of the message three times, before finally adding it and pressing send.

CHAPTER TWENTY-EIGHT

I followed the path toward the second of the glass buildings. It was the largest of the four and housed the shop, indoor pool and most of the executive suites. The main lobby was very much like the reception that I'd just come from. Same flooring, same staircase, but there was no desk here. Only the open entrance to the shop.

I used to love the shop when I was little. I would go into the changing rooms and try on expensive clothes and shoes. I'd spend hours in front of the mirror. Adult-sized dresses swishing over my toes as I spun around. They'd always had a collection of locally made jewelry on a display at the back of the women's wear. Silver bracelets, bronze necklaces, pearl earrings. I would run my tiny fingers over their smooth preciousness. Choosing which ones I would buy for myself when I was grown up.

I walked into the shop. There were no customers. Just a member of staff sitting quietly behind the till, her head down, reading a magazine. There was less stock than I remembered there being. In my mind it had been filled floor to ceiling with treasures. Not just clothes. Books, beautifully packaged food, handmade gifts and expensive toiletries. Now it looked like it just carried the essentials. The basics needed to fill in the gaps of a hotel stay. A fridge filled with drinks and homemade deli-style sandwiches. A few clothes still, but not many. Swimsuits and T-shirts mainly. I wandered to the back of the shop, to the jewelry stand. It was still here. Handcrafted local pendants and bracelets. Only now the charms weren't on silver bands; they were on simple leather straps. Everything a cheaper version of what had been before.

I lifted one of the bracelets. A pale tan leather strap. Small shiny shells threaded around it in the palest of pink. I rubbed my thumb over it, feeling the soft layer of dust that had accumu-lated. I looked down at the table and saw that everything had a layer of dust over it. As I glanced around at the empty shop and thought about the empty restaurant, I wondered if the Carmen Club was struggling. I don't remember it ever being this quiet.

I went back to where I'd entered the shop and grabbed one of the baskets, a woven willow box with a thin metal handle. I took the basket over to the clothes area to choose swimming costumes for us. I selected a bright pink bikini with a bandeau top for Sophie. It was similar to things I'd seen her wear before. I chose a plain black swimsuit for myself and placed them both in the basket. I headed in the direction of the till, pausing to get some toiletries. Shampoo, toothpaste, toothbrushes, deodorant. I was nearly at the counter before I remembered we needed towels.

"Do you mind if I leave this stuff here?" I said, lifting the basket onto the counter. "I need some towels..." The woman behind the till was looking straight at me. She wasn't surprised to see me. Not like I was to see her. It was Tara Haywood. One of the trio of girls that had made up Lacey's inner circle.

"Hi, Tara," I managed. "How are you?" Tara was frowning, her top lip curled into a sneer. She said nothing. I tried again. "I didn't know you worked here." I pretended I couldn't see how hostile she was being. Tara folded her arms. She looked very different. Her hair, once long and auburn with a natural curl at the end, was now straight. It sat at her jawbone, a precise line along the ends. Her highlights hung in thick unnatural stripes. Her face was rounder, fuller than before, but mine probably was too.

"I hear you're doing a podcast thing about Lacey," she said sulkily.

"I... yes... we're investigating what happened that night," I replied stiffly. Smiling through gritted teeth.

"Don't you think it's... disrespectful... to her family and stuff?" She spoke in a thick Cornish accent. Her eyes bore into mine accusingly, daring me to answer. I got the impression she was regurgitating words she'd heard someone else speak.

"Hopefully the family will feel that we're handling it respectfully and that it's time the case was looked at again... Wouldn't you like to see someone finally arrested for it?" I spoke the lines that had run through my head many times. I wasn't even sure I believed them myself. Tara looked confused, unsure of how to answer.

"I got married!" Tara suddenly thrust her ring finger excitedly toward me. The aggressive questioning was over for now.

"Wow, Tara, congratulations! Who's the lucky guy?" I asked, my voice thick with enthusiasm.

"Oh, you won't know him. He's not from round here." She beamed. Tara seemed proud to have married someone from out of town. I fawned over the ring, relieved by the distraction. She hugged herself in delight with her free arm. After a few seconds there fell a long awkward silence.

"Did you say you needed towels?" Tara asked, turning around and lifting two white folded towels from the shelf.

"Thanks," I said, searching for the black Carmen card in my pocket. Tara slowly scanned the items in my basket, placing them in a hessian bag that she'd retrieved from under the till. She carefully removed the tags from the swimsuits, I saw her glance up at me a couple of times, a small smile slowly forming on her lips.

"Did you hear about Megan?" she asked. I focused my attention on one of the towels, stroking the bouncy fabric. I ran my thumb along the stitching. I knew something was coming. I could see it in her face.

"Hmm? No." I feigned disinterest, not looking up from the towel.

"She's had a baby!" Relief flowed through my body and my chest relaxed, just a fraction.

"Yes, I know—Mia. I met Megan for coffee," I said, joining in the game of information one-upmanship.

"Oh, so you know then?" She watched me as she folded the flimsy swimsuit material into a Lycra ball. I ignored her question. It was then that she realized. Realized that I had absolutely no idea what I was supposed to know.

Tara said nothing for a moment. She pushed the bag slowly across the counter toward me. I handed over the Carmen card. A look of annoyance passed her face. I wasn't sure whether she was irritated by having to process the card or just the sheer privilege of it. She leaned on the counter holding the card between her index and middle finger. As I went to take it from her, she lifted it just out of my reach.

"You know the baby's Jude's, don't you?" Her eyes danced. If she'd run this scene over in her head a hundred times, it would never have played out as perfectly as this. I froze. I could feel my legs faltering. I took the bag from the counter and walked away. I needed to get out of here, away from Tara.

"Katie?" Tara called when I was halfway across the shop.

"Hmm?" I turned back. I could feel a lump forming in my throat.

"Your card?" She smirked, holding it a little closer to me. I marched quickly over and snatched the card with a shaking hand. I didn't mean to do it with so much force. I attempted an apology. As I turned to leave, I caught the look of delight on her face.

I needed to sit down. I looked around for somewhere, but there was nothing. My head was spinning. Why didn't Megan tell me? Why would she let me find out like this? I leaned against the wall by the automatic doors and closed my eyes. I breathed slowly, trying to relax. It had triggered something in me. I felt my throat constrict, and tears that had been threatening now came quickly. Hot tears spilling down my face. A gasping sob escaped my chest. Loud enough to make me bury my face in the crook of my elbow.

It wasn't because Jude and Megan had a baby together. It had been a shock, but that wasn't why I was crying. Why my legs shook and my heart pounded. No. It was because I realized in that moment that part of me still felt like Jude's girlfriend. I had been on hold. A bit of me left behind in Cornwall. Nineteen-year-old me, back here just waiting. I began to feel calmer. The mist in my head started to clear. Me and Megan weren't friends. She didn't owe me an explanation. And Jude. Well, Jude wasn't mine. Not since the day of the beach party. Not for five years.

CHAPTER TWENTY-NINE

I wiped my tears on the sleeve of my jumper, pulling myself up from sitting position. I felt tired. Tired and drained from all the emotion. My phone buzzed in my back pocket. I pulled it out and looked at the screen. Sophie. I pressed cancel. As my phone went dark, I caught my reflection. My hair looked wild. Untamed static from burying my face in my jumper. My mascara had smeared under my eyes and created a thin trail through my foundation. I reached into the hessian bag and pulled out one of the towels. Using my phone as a mirror, I did my best to wipe away the worst of the stray makeup with the soft material corner. I still looked like I'd been crying, but it was passable. Sophie rang again.

"Hi," I answered, my voice an octave higher.

"Hey, where are you?" Sophie sounded like she was walking. I could hear heels on tiles.

"Um, I'm just outside the shop. It's the next building, in front of the..."

"I can see you!" she yelled into the phone and hung up. I braced myself for questions.

She bounced toward me, swinging her black shoulder bag.

"There you are. Are we swimming?" She didn't notice that I'd been crying.

"Yes, I've got everything we need." Sophie linked her arm through mine as I led her back to the lobby and the direction of the indoor pool. My eyes were fixed straight ahead as we walked past the shop. I willed Tara not to see us. Not to come out and talk to me.

The changing rooms were empty. White unisex cubicles lined one of the walls, with floor-to-ceiling lockers facing the doors. The room felt uncomfortably warm and damp. A glowing light came from twinkling recessed bulbs in the ceiling. The smell of chlorine from the next-door pool reminded me of swimming lessons.

I rummaged through the bag and pulled out the neon pink bikini I'd picked for Sophie.

"I love it!" she cried as I handed it to her. I pulled my own plain black swimsuit from the bag, trying to cover it with my towel. "Show me," she said. I reluctantly lifted the costume up, dangling it from the shoulder straps by my fingers for her to see. Sophie tilted her head to the side and rolled her eyes. She'd tried for as long as I'd known her to make me more adventurous. Dress more boldly, take more risks. But I didn't want to stand out, to go off course. Not anymore.

We quickly changed and I took two white Carmen dressing gowns from an open cupboard. The pool room was dimly lit. Music played quietly, a relaxing background sound. White plastic sun loungers were arranged along each side of the pool. We lay our towels on two chairs farthest from the changing rooms and sat down. Sophie's toned brown limbs looked amazing against the bright pink fabric. My own costume was more revealing than I'd realized. The legs were cut perilously high, leaving little fabric at the back to cover my bum. I draped the robe self-consciously over my lower half as I lay back.

Sophie had just returned to her phone when the staff door

to the left of us opened. A dark-haired male in his late teens walked toward us.

"Can I get you anything to eat or drink?" He was pleasant, but his voice wobbled a little with nerves.

"Yes!! Liam, your timing could not be better," Sophie said with a laugh, squinting at his name badge. I automatically read it too. His tag said Leon. But Leon was too shy to correct her.

"Liam, can we get a bottle of white wine please? Pinot?" He nodded at the floor before leaving.

"I left the card thingy in the changing rooms," I said after Leon had left. I went to stand up before Sophie stopped me.

"Kate, this is your dad's place. You don't need to be running around looking for cards or money or whatever. Just enjoy it." She lay back, her long legs outstretched, her hands resting on her tight midriff. We lay like that in silence for a few minutes. The only noise was the low bubbling of the pool filters. I could feel myself falling asleep. Leon brought through a tray. A bottle of white wine in an iced cooler and two large glasses. He poured the wine for us and walked quickly away. We both lifted our drinks. "Cheers," we said at the same time, giggling a little. Sophie looked like she wanted to say something. I tried to help.

"Are you and Tom OK?" I asked. Her stare was fixed on her legs. She idly stroked them, brushing away imaginary specks.

"Not really. We haven't been for a while..." She rested her head on the back of the lounger. Slowly twisting her neck around until she was facing me.

"It's this place." She laughed, but her heart wasn't in it.

"What do you mean?"

"It's hard to explain... something about this town, seeing him here. It makes me realize just how different we are. It makes me miss London." I nodded, trying to understand.

I wondered if that's how Sophie felt about our relationship too.

CHAPTER THIRTY

"What are you going to do?" I asked her gently.

"Can we talk about something else?" she pleaded, before adding more quietly, "...I don't know. I have absolutely no idea what I'm going to do." She drained the remainder of her wine and reached for the bottle. I didn't know what to say, how I could make it better. We sat there in silence for what felt like several minutes.

"Did you go to her funeral?" Sophie's voice was even again as she changed the subject. I was confused.

"Lacey's funeral," she clarified, peering at me over the top of her wineglass.

I hesitated. Wrong-footed by the sudden change of subject. "I did. I mean, everyone did. You had to. It was the first time I'd ever been to a funeral," I told her.

I thought back to that hot day in August. It was a few days before the bank holiday weekend. It was sweltering. There'd been no rain for a fortnight. The air had been dry and hazy. Mourners stood around at the front of the crematorium, a brown 1960s building set in the middle of lush green grounds.

On a clear day you could see over the hills out to sea. Everyone waited for the coffin to arrive.

The older people in the congregation wore black. They shifted uncomfortably in the heat. None of the clothes worn were suitable for summer. Smart black slip-on shoes and heeled leather boots. Their very best funeral clothes. In stark contrast, the young people had worn bright summer dresses and shirts with oversized dark glasses. Pinks, yellows, oranges. A sad festival of color.

Even here at her funeral a hierarchy had formed. A pyramid of mourners. At the top were the saddest and closest of her friends, led by Tara and Polly. They were the stage managers of the grief that day. Of course, her friends were upset. They were there to say goodbye, but it was more than that. There was a buzz of excitement. I could feel it. I think everybody could. As the doors to the crematorium opened, people flooded in. Keen to get a good seat. The right seat. A seat that indicated where on the pyramid they were.

There was a morbid curiosity to it all. A sort of hysteria. I remembered what Rebecca had said. How difficult it had been getting reliable statements from teenagers. How eager they'd been to help. And then it dawned on me. It was the same morbid fascination that made listeners tune into our podcast.

It's about the unthinkable. The unimaginable. The nights you walk home by yourself, scared of the shadows. A shape behind the bin or a figure hiding next to a parked car. All in your imagination. Until one day it isn't. One day the shape steps out from behind the parked car and that shape is a man. It might never happen to you, but it's happened to someone. An interest in murder is our way of connecting with the horror in the world. It makes us feel alive.

Lonni sat at the front of the crematorium with Megan. She wept loudly. The people who sat farther back pretended not to hear. There was a collective embarrassment. Even in grief, the most pronounced grief of losing a child, the town expected an element of decorum. Polly and Tara had sat at the front with them. Neither had ever been friends with Megan. Yet, there they were like members of the family, offering her hollow comfort.

When it was all over, the people at the front had left first. Filtering through the middle aisle, past the spectators at the back. I saw Polly reach for Megan's hand. She'd snatched it away, a cold hard expression on her face. Megan didn't look like she'd been crying. Her eyes were focused on the double doors at the back of the room. Lonni's crying had become a loud wailing. People caught each other's eye. They wouldn't say anything. Not today. But when a little time had passed, they'd talk about her. And just like that, any sympathy that the town might have had for Lonni would come to an end.

"I'm going for a swim." Sophie jumped up and made her way over to the side of the pool. She dived in. The loud splash echoed around the empty room. Sophie squealed with pleasure. I edged my way toward the pool, reluctantly leaving the protective cover of the robe. I climbed down the metal steps, expecting the temperature change to hit me as my limbs entered the water. It was hot. Not warm like most swimming pools, but actually hot, like a bath. As soon as my feet touched the floor, I used both hands to gather my thick hair into a messy bun. I swam over to Sophie, who was trying to do an underwater handstand. After a couple of attempts she came to the surface laughing. That's how we spent the next hour. Laughing and swimming. Pushing each other under the water. Racing up and down the pool. It felt like how things used to be. Like when we first met and there had been an easiness between us.

My hair, which I hadn't managed to keep dry, hung in wet tendrils around my face. My fingertips were wrinkled, eyes stinging from the chlorine. As I climbed out of the pool, heading over to grab a towel, I heard someone walk into the pool area. It was Tara. Exposed in my swimming costume I reached for the robe and held it up to my body. Tara was not here for a swim.

She was still dressed in her uniform. She wore a thick black parka and had one of the Carmen hessian bags over her shoulder. She already looked uncomfortable in the heat of the balmy room.

"Hi," I said.

"This podcast thing..." Her eyes flitted to the door before resting on Sophie. She clung to the edge of the pool, watching Tara with interest. "I know stuff." She spoke in a whisper.

"Sorry, what?" I frowned, wondering if I'd heard her correctly.

"I know stuff," she repeated. "Stuff about Lacey." I almost laughed. I would have if Tara hadn't looked so scared. I heard a rush of water beside me. Sophie had lifted herself out of the pool.

"Stuff that might be useful for the podcast?" Sophie asked. Tara looked her up and down but didn't ask who she was. She nodded, looking at her feet. We all waited.

"Would you be happy to come and talk to us, to be recorded?" Sophie pressed.

"Maybe..." Tara looked from Sophie to me. She looked embarrassed.

"Tara, if you're worried about how sensitive we'll be, you needn't..." I said. Sophie took over.

"Are you looking to get paid?" Sophie was direct, unblinking.

Tara shifted her bulky frame from one foot to the other. I saw it now. Money was exactly what Tara was looking for. "I'm not sure if..." she stuttered.

"It's fine. The network is happy to pay. Do you have a pen? I'll give you my number and we can talk." Tara nodded obediently and dug around in her bag for a pen. She handed her what looked like an old receipt and a ballpoint. Sophie returned to the low table and scribbled down her details. Tara took the paper quickly, stuffing it in her pocket, the shame she felt evident on her face. Gone was the spiteful bravado from earlier. The snide looks and the nasty tone. Tara looked lost. Torn between loyalty to her dead friend and making a few quid. I felt sorry for her; I really did. Standing there sweating in her fleece-lined coat, her bottom lip quivering. She nodded her red face and walked away. When she was halfway across the room, she stopped and turned to me. Scrunching her face like a child.

"I'm sorry, you know, about earlier." I didn't have a chance to reply as she scurried back into the changing rooms.

CHAPTER THIRTY-ONE

I stood there open-mouthed. Sophie laughed. "What the fuck was all that about?"

I shrugged. "Will the network really pay?" I was surprised. I wondered if it was just one of Sophie's games. A strategy.

"Of course. If the information's good enough," Sophie said, distracted by a message on her phone. "The network has listened to the first episode. It's definitely going out on Friday. They love it!" She looked relieved and happy. I was pleased for her, but I still felt uneasy. The thought of people listening to it, people in the town. It made my stomach turn.

We gathered our things and headed for the changing room. Once we were dressed, we made our way to reception to get the key for our room. The front desk had been abandoned. There was no sign of Connie. We waited a couple of minutes before Sophie went upstairs to try and find someone. She returned a little while later with barman Ben. He trailed behind her, smiling. Happy to be in Sophie's company again.

"I haven't really had training on the computer system down here." Ben looked anxiously at the screen, tapping keys. He ran his hands through his hair, looking at the line of numbers behind him. Numbers that indicated the available rooms. "Did you say you wanted a suite?" Ben had no idea what he was doing. We smiled patiently.

"OK, here we go. I think this one has two rooms." He handed each of us a room card. We thanked him and returned to the building we'd just come from, crossing the lobby toward the lift. I pressed the arrow button for up and waited for it to arrive.

"Why didn't you tell me about Jude and Lacey?" Sophie asked in a quiet voice. She didn't sound angry. Her words were said carefully, like she'd been wanting to say something for a while.

"I don't know," I answered honestly. "Because I was ashamed."

"Ashamed? I don't understand."

"It wasn't the first time he'd done it to me—slept with someone behind my back. It's something that used to happen a lot..." I watched for Sophie's reaction. The lift doors opened, and we stepped inside. I pressed the button for the Ocean Suite.

"You know that's a reflection on him, not you," Sophie said firmly, protectively. She was being kind, but it didn't mean anything. Empty wisdom torn from the pages of every women's magazine I'd ever bought.

"To be honest, I think it was probably a reflection on both of us. I put up with it for too long. At the time, it felt normal. I felt loved. He made me feel like the rest of the stuff didn't matter, that it was all just background noise. But I think it was me too. I think I made *him* feel like what he was doing was normal." It all seemed like such a long time ago now.

"Was it you that ended it?" Sophie asked. The automated speaker in the lift told them they had arrived at their floor. The doors opened.

I nodded. "I had to." I thought about Tom. I thought about that night we had five years ago. The night everything changed between us. I had no idea then that three years later Tom would be with my best friend. I looked sideways at Sophie, checking for any signs that she might know. She pushed the card into the black box attached to the door. A green light clicked on, and we entered the room. Sophie walked around the suite, admiring the décor and the furnishings. Talk of me and Jude was over. She'd moved on to something else.

I'd confronted Jude about Lacey a couple of weeks after her funeral. Even after what had happened, I couldn't let it go. I don't know why. It didn't matter anymore. Lacey was dead. I was leaving. It was the only time I had ever spoken to Jude about a woman, any woman he'd been with.

I knew before I'd even left the house that night I was going to do it. I'd gone to the pub on my own, knowing he'd be there. He looked up and caught my eye as soon as I'd walked through the door. It was as though he was waiting for someone. I shook the thought from my head as I strode confidently over to him. "Can we talk?" I'd asked him. I saw his hesitation as he looked over my shoulder to the door. He glanced at his watch, and it was then that I saw it. His disinterest. He'd switched off from me. In those few short weeks that we'd been apart, weeks I'd spent crying, hurting, remembering. Just like that, he'd moved on.

I wanted to beat my fists on his chest, scream at him. But I couldn't *make* him care. I couldn't *make* him feel the pain and sadness that I felt. I breathed deeply, willing my dignity to rise to the surface and take control of my rage. He nodded to the area at the side of the bar. A hallway that connected the pub to the toilets and pool room. "Did you sleep with Lacey?" I'd asked. My voice wobbled, threatening to break mid-sentence. He rubbed his hand across his chin, making a scratching noise against his stubble. The noise had made my toes curl.

He'd looked at me sadly, his brown eyes full of pity. "Does it matter?" he asked. I nodded, my eyes brimming with tears.

"Yeah once. Just once," he told me, impatience prickling his words. I'd turned to leave. I hadn't wanted to hear any more. I felt like I was going to be sick. He grabbed my arm. "Kate," he said in low voice, his face now full of remorse. "It didn't mean anything." His eyes locked with mine.

"Of course it did, Jude—otherwise what was the point? What was the point of any of it?" The words caught in my throat. I left before the crushing weight in my chest turned to tears. It was then that I felt it. The foreverness of it all. The love, the pain, the desire. All wrapped up in a parcel. A parcel of my memories: Pengully, Lacey's murder, Jude... Tom. A parcel I'd be carrying always.

I'd felt young and stupid as I walked down the hill from the pub. The town blurred ahead of me as tears coursed down my cheeks. I didn't even attempt to wipe them away. It was all so pointless now. Three years would pass before I saw Jude again. The New Year's Eve party at the pub. He was interested then. I saw a light turn back on as he spoke to me. But by then I was new to him again. I'd left Pengully, started a life for myself in London. I was new and shiny and interesting.

CHAPTER THIRTY-TWO

"Shall we order some food?" Sophie asked, looking at both sides of the menu card she'd picked up from the dressing table.

"Yeah, if you like... You choose." I placed the bags on the floor and wandered across the room. The suite was beautiful, there was no question. But it lacked the deep sumptuous colors and contrasting fabrics that Megan made work so well in her shop. The look here was both expensive and bland.

They were standing in the lounge. Two large cream sofas dominated one half of the room, with a dark wood oval coffee table in the middle. The curtains were an oatmeal color. Long, thick, expensive and dull. I went through to one of the bedrooms. The same unremarkable theme. A crisp duvet with a champagne-colored throw covered the large comfortable-looking bed.

I looked at the clock on the bedside table. It was 5:15 p.m. Plenty of time to eat and get ready. The Mexican night started at 6:30 p.m. The earlier we arrived, the earlier I could leave. I returned to the living room to find Sophie emptying the contents of her handbag onto the dressing table. Two big makeup bags, curling tongs, hair grips.

"Ta-da," she sang, her arms outstretched.

"You don't exactly travel light, do you?" I laughed.

"Can I please do your hair and makeup tonight?" she asked in a small hopeful voice. I groaned dramatically, closing my eyes and throwing my head back. Already defeated. There was no point in arguing with Sophie. She clapped her hands and pulled the dressing table stool out, indicating for me to sit down.

I sat down and pulled out my hairband, looking at my reflection. My hair collapsed around my face. A kinked halo crowned my head where it had been tied up. Sophie plugged the tongs into the socket next to me. She ran her slender fingers through my hair, gently teasing out the knots. Her fingernails lightly scraped my scalp and made my nerves tingle. She reached for the tongs and section by section began carefully straightening my hair. Just as she finished, there was a knock at the door. Sophie opened it to an older-looking man with graying dark hair. His eyes were focused on the tray he pushed in front of him. There were three plates covered in plastic lids next to a bottle of champagne on ice and two flutes. I looked from the expensive bottle to Sophie and frowned.

"What? We're celebrating!" she whined. The man had wheeled the trolley over to the coffee table and was laying the plates out, carefully removing the lids. He placed the bottle and glasses on the table and discreetly left the room. I went over to see what Sophie had ordered. A plate of fruit—watermelon, kiwi, grapes—a few crackers on the side. There was one covered in cold meats—ham, salted beef, pastrami. The third was a selection of different breads and cheeses. Enough food to feed about six people, but it looked incredible. I sat down and began picking, while Sophie popped the cork on the champagne. She expertly poured two glasses and handed one to me. "To *Small Town*." She raised her drink.

"*Small Town*," I replied tilting my glass until it clinked on the side of hers. We smiled, enjoying the moment of achievement.

We finished getting ready. The offer of Sophie to do my makeup had thankfully been forgotten. We shared the mirror, giggling as we tried to paint our faces. Music played from Sophie's phone, muffled and tinny. We danced to the distorted sounds of our favorite songs. Sophie quietly and regularly refilled my glass, until the bottle sat empty on the table. I felt good. Like an old version of myself, a knot of excitement and anticipation fluttering from my core. Something I hadn't felt for a long time.

Made up, perfumed and giddy from champagne, we made our way back down to the lobby. Sophie smiled at me. She took my hand as we walked over to the restaurant. As soon as we reached the reception, we heard it: a mariachi band playing loudly in the room above. Disco lights twinkling out of the darkened room at the top of the stairs.

There were about fifty people here and, by the looks of it, most of them were local. Casually dressed, not like the suited and bloused look of a Carmen resident. Bowls of nachos and guacamole sat in the center of each of the tables. The band was turned up high. Two guitarists, a trumpet player, and a man with maracas all stood with a microphone in front of them. There were a few people standing around the makeshift dance floor at the front of the stage, but most people were eating. Despite the advanced age of most of the guests, the room had a teenage disco feel to it.

We sat at the bar. Ben, the barman, had obviously finished his shift and had been replaced by a fair-haired bearded man who looked remarkably similar. Sophie leaned over and spoke to him. I didn't hear what was said, but they both laughed. A couple of minutes later he returned with two bright orange cocktails, complete with stirrers and umbrellas.

I sipped the sugary drink, scanning the room for anyone

that I recognized. I felt exposed sitting up at the bar, sitting high on the tall chair, front and center. There was nowhere to hide. Huge black drapes had been pulled across the tall windows. They blocked all the outside light and made it feel later than it was. Faces were briefly illuminated by the sweeping beams of multicolored light coming from the stage.

Two cocktails and about an hour later I saw him. I think deep down I knew that I would. Jude was standing there at the other side of the room, lit up by the prism of daylight from the lobby below. We locked eyes almost as soon as he stepped off the stairs. It was as though he'd been expecting to see me too. He was with another man. As they approached us, I could see that the other man was Danny.

Danny had always been on the peripheral of the group. He was two years older than us. Not much, but when you're in sixth form it seems like a lot. His friendship with Lacey was what had eventually brought him into the fold. Jude and Danny were one of the last ones of the group still in Pengully. I wasn't surprised to see them together.

I was shocked at how much Danny had changed, physically anyway. His once athletic body was much larger. He wore a yellow faded T-shirt. It stretched tightly over his bloated stomach. Too short to be comfortable and only just meeting the line of his low-slung jeans. His puffy face had several days of stubble. Black circles hung underneath each wild, sunken eye. Lack of sleep, drink or drugs. Maybe all of them. Whatever it was, Danny looked like he was in serious trouble.

CHAPTER THIRTY-THREE

As soon as they arrived at the bar, Danny lunged toward me, pulling my body into a rough hug that lifted me from my seat.

"Kitty Kat," he sang loudly. A brief nickname from school that had quickly disappeared. He smelled awful, like stale sweat and beer. As I half hugged him, I felt the dampness of his body. I saw Jude's face over his shoulder, smiling apologetically. Sophie, who had been chatting to the new barman, turned to watch. Jude gently tugged on Danny's arm until he released me.

"Easy, Dan." He laughed. At that moment Danny noticed Sophie sitting there. His eyes lit up as he lurched toward her with his hand outstretched.

"How do you do... I'm Danny," he slurred, his large body swaying. Sophie glanced over to me to confirm that this was *the* Danny. The Danny who'd organized the beach party. The Danny she wanted to speak to.

"I'm Sophie. Nice to meet you," she answered, looking up at him from under her eyelashes. Danny tried to say something, but his jaw just moved up and down as he drunkenly gawped at Sophie's face.

Jude laughed. Danny's attention was suddenly caught by a

group of women sitting a few yards away from us. Their laughing could be heard clearly, even above the noise of the music. Danny licked his lips and started dancing over to their table. The women shrieked with delight. Sophie looked from me to Jude, before grabbing her bag and heading toward the toilet.

"I heard you were back. How are you?" he asked. Jude took Sophie's barstool and dragged it closer to me. As he sat down our knees touched. I felt a familiar jolt of electricity pass through my body.

"Good. Really good," I lied. My mouth had gone dry, and adrenaline was working its way down my legs. "I heard you have a baby." I cocked my head to the side. It was supposed to be flirty, affectionate, but the words just sounded accusing. I studied his face, trying to see if I'd thrown him off guard. He returned my look, silently connected for a few seconds.

He nodded. "The rumor mill is in full working order, I see." He looked over his shoulder to a table tucked around the side of the bar. I followed his stare. Sitting with their heads bent close together were Tara Haywood and Polly Newcoombe. Watching us. Whispering in the darkest corner of the room. I had no idea they were there. Jude turned back to face me. "If you mean Mia, then yes, she's mine." He was calm, not at all off balance. I was lost for a reply, so I focused my attention on stirring the cocktail in front of me.

"If you mean are me and Meg together, then no." He moved his face a fraction toward mine. I could see him out of the corner of my eye as I gently stabbed at a wedge of orange. Jude turned toward the bar and raised his hand slightly to get the barman's attention. He ordered a lager and reached into his back pocket for some money. I watched him as he fumbled with a handful of change. His body was still as tight and lean as it had ever been. He was wearing a blue and white short-sleeved shirt. It was still his style, young and relaxed, but he looked more grown up than I had ever seen him.

"You look good," he said. "Really good." His stare dropped below my face for a moment. I could feel myself coloring. He saw it. The beginnings of a smile twitched around the corners of his mouth. My stomach clenched. An unwelcome flood of desire rushed through me. I looked over my shoulder, trying to spot Sophie, but there was no sign of her. As I turned my head back, I saw a man walking in our direction. I thought it was Danny until I took in his height and slim build. A beam of light from the stage crossed his face and I saw it was Tom. Jude had seen him too.

"Shit," I muttered. Jude looked at me but didn't say anything. Instead, he stood up from his seat to welcome Tom as he joined us. The two men grasped each other's hand in a high sideways shake and hugged. They looked pleased to see each other, comfortable, like they saw each other regularly.

"All right?" Tom asked me. I nodded, the tension between us was evident. Jude sat watching. Taking it all in.

"What you drinking, buddy?" Jude asked, slapping him on the back.

"Ah... beer please, mate." Tom's eyes scanned the room.

"She went over there, I think." I pointed in the direction of the toilets. Tom nodded. He gave Jude's shoulder a quick squeeze of thanks and left in the direction Sophie had gone. Tom's drink arrived and Jude paid the barman.

"Things aren't as friendly between you two anymore?" He ran his tongue playfully across his bottom lip, his face so close to mine I could smell his musky scent and feel the warmth that radiated from his body.

"What?" I answered weakly. "Tom?" I could feel my breathing getting faster. I tried to find words, but my head was swimming.

"Katie, come on..." he probed, tipping his head toward me and holding my gaze. He knew. Or at least he thought he knew.

"Jude, I'm not doing this..." I could feel panic rising in my chest. I jumped down from the stool to leave. He grabbed my hand.

"Don't go, Katie. I'm sorry..." He was full of remorse. He really didn't want me to go. We both sat back down, not saying a word. He was still holding my hand and I didn't take it away. He moved his thumb so it was resting on top, his fingers inter-locking mine. I felt sick.

"Well, this is cosy." It was Polly. Her sharp tone and sudden entrance brought me back into the room with a thud. She stood close, her face flushed with anger. "I think it's disgusting what you're doing to Lacey's family. It's disrespectful... bringing it all up again," she spat at me. Her words mirrored Tara's accusa-tions from earlier. Almost word for word. Her indignation was gaining momentum. I looked over her shoulder. Tara was standing about a meter behind her, a sheepish expression on her face as she nervously wrung her hands together.

"Always a pleasure, Polly," Jude sniped sarcastically, casu-ally taking a sip of his drink.

"Oh, fuck off, Jude," Polly hissed, looking pointedly at our hands. I slid mine self-consciously back to my own lap. She watched with satisfaction.

"Polly, we really didn't mean to..." I stuttered, still shocked by her sudden appearance.

"How do you think they must feel, eh?" She was on a roll now, wildly gesticulating as she spoke. "It's not bad enough that they've lost a daughter and a sister? You have to go and make a podcast thing about it?" I tried to answer her, but she wasn't interested. This wasn't a debate; it was a monolog, one she could tell people about for weeks to come. Part of the story would no doubt include me and Jude holding hands.

"You should feel ashamed of yourselves," she shouted as her

finale, before stomping back to her table. I sat for a moment, speechless. I looked over at them, checking that they were sitting down, that it was over. Tara shot me a look of gratitude. Thanking me for not exposing her, I suppose.

"Come on," Jude said, taking my hand again and pulling me to my feet.

"Where are we going?" I asked. Thinking for one awful moment that he might have been walking me down to the dance floor. He ignored my question. Instead, he led me to the top of the stairs. I could feel people staring as we walked by their tables. Shadowed faces, hidden by bright backlighting.

We skipped quickly down the steps and outside. Relieved to be out of the stuffy restaurant. It was still early, but the evening sun had started to dim and the air felt colder. I followed Jude along an unfamiliar path around the back of the building. As we rounded a corner, I saw a set of wide concrete steps that led down to the outdoor pool area. Like the indoor swimming pool, the water was surrounded by white plastic loungers. Tall palm trees bordered the terrace, sheltering the area from the wind and the view of the surrounding buildings. The furniture had been laid out in perfect symmetrical lines. It looked like nobody had been down here for a while.

I turned around and looked up at the building we'd just come from. The top windows of the restaurant were black. The heavy drapes separated us from the view of the band and the disco lights. I could still hear the faint high-pitch rasp of the trumpet, but not loud enough to be able to make out the tune. We walked down the stone steps and Jude sat down on the floor, his back against a low wall that rose just above his head height. If anyone were to look out of the window of the bar, they wouldn't see him. They would just see me. My arms folded, rocking nervously on one hip. Wondering how the hell I was back here again.

CHAPTER THIRTY-FOUR

"What's going on with Danny?" I said. It wasn't the question I wanted to ask him. Jude looked up at me. His face set. He held it for a few seconds before answering.

"The same thing that's been wrong with Danny for the past five years—Lacey." He reached into his back pocket. I looked down at his hand. In it was an old travel sweets tin that he used to keep his marbles in when we were kids. The same tin he'd kept his tobacco in when we started college. It's so strange when you see a familiar object from your past. Something so ordinary and nondescript that at the time I paid no attention to. An object that now jabbed me with sharp pinpricks of nostalgia. Jude began carefully rolling a cigarette. His attention focused on the paper between his fingers.

"Why has Lacey's murder made Danny like this?" I asked. Jude lifted his head to look at me.

"Grief, loneliness... guilt. I hadn't realized how close they were until she died." I said nothing. Just watched him as he tapped the cigarette gently on his leg.

"You've been gone a long time, Katie. You've done things, you've moved on. A lot of people are still stuck back there. They haven't been able to move on from that night." I wondered if Jude had moved on. I nodded. It would be pointless telling him that I understood.

Jude took a lighter from the tin. The comforting ping of thin metal scraping across thin metal. A noise ingrained from the past. He lit the cigarette and nodded his head toward the space on the floor next to him. I thought for a second, before sitting down on the cold hard ground. Our shoulders touched lightly. My arms rested on my bent knees.

I noticed it was getting dark quickly. The old-fashioned black iron streetlights were beginning to switch themselves on. Jude put his arm around my shoulder and pulled me in toward him. It was sudden and unexpected. I wasn't ready for it. I reluctantly rested my head on a spot between his chest and his shoulder. A spot I knew well. But I didn't relax. My body was rigid, wary and uncomfortable. I know he could feel it. I breathed him in. An earthiness mingled with the smell of his cigarette smoke. He placed his chin on top of my head for a moment and spoke into my hair.

"Of all the unsolved murders you could have chosen, why Lacey's? Why now, after all this time?" He sounded sad. He moved his head away and took another long drag of his cigarette. I sighed. I couldn't go into this again. I felt a weariness I don't remember ever feeling before. Tired of explaining myself. Tired of thinking back to what happened. Bone-tired, my mum would call it.

"Because someone needed to," I replied with more spirit and force than I felt. He nodded, unaffected by my tone. Smoke curled from the corner of his mouth. He looked like he was trying to remember something. I looked at his profile. Skin soft and tanned. Virtually unchanged after all these years, except for a few lines around his eyes. I thought back to when we'd first got together.

Pengully Parade took place every September. A long-standing town tradition that dated back to the forties. A celebration of the end of season. Most of the holidaymakers had left by then, so it always felt very local. A chance for the town's businesses to relax, have some fun after the busy summer. Each company had its own decorated carnival truck. Kids and adults dressed up in whatever that year's theme was. Music from the trucks created a wall of sound as they passed through the narrow roads.

As I'd grown up, the carnival had changed. Not the procession. That had always stayed the same, an antiquated formula put in motion every year by a town committee. When I was about ten, an evening element had been added to the celebrations. A fun fair set up on the land opposite the school playing field. The town organizers had hated it, but there was very little they could do. I remember the first year I'd gone to the fair. Walking up the hill after dark, to the beat of distant pop music, I held on tightly to Mum's hand. As we walked across the uneven dusty ground, I took in the rides, the lights, the smell of doughnuts and candy floss. I felt a tingling anticipation that I would come to feel every year that I walked through those gates on carnival night.

By the time we'd started college, carnival night meant something different. Drinking cider and smoking cigarettes in the far corners of the field. Groups of us watching the night from a distance. I still felt the tingle. It was different, but I still felt it.

It was the September I'd started my first year at sixth form. Even though autumn was looming, the weather was still warm. Most of us were in T-shirts. Everyone except Lacey. Lacey had been in the procession that day. Star of the Gordon's Building Supplies float, a big trade warehouse on the outskirts of town. Lacey wore a powder-blue princess dress. Covered in lace and off the shoulder, it was the sort of outfit you'd find in a children's dressing-up box. It was perilously low cut and clung to her curves in a way that I'm not sure the organizers had intended.

Nobody had been able to take their eyes off her as she'd come down the street, waving and smiling from her decorated throne.

We'd sat in a little circle on the grass, behind some of the fairground trucks, our faces only dimly lit by the distant flood-lights. We were all drinking from a big bottle of cheap cider, sweet, fizzy and strong. Jess had been there. I'd not seen her for ages. Lacey was there with James. They were a couple now, fingers intertwined and bodies rarely apart. Tom and Jude had arrived late with an extra bottle of cider. Everyone was happy.

I remembered how excited I'd been to see Tom that night. How good he'd looked. We played truth or dare. It was mostly just downing mouthfuls of the sharp cider to a chorus of drunken screams. Until it was Lacey's turn. Jess leaned back on her arms, more drunk than I'd ever seen her. She'd pointed at Lacey. Each word slurred into the next as she spoke.

"I've got one for yooou, Lacey Crew." She giggled when she noticed the words rhymed. We laughed with her. "Yooou need to kiss Tom. Not just a kiss. A *proper* kiss." Her voice was thick, and her eyes blinked slowly, struggling to focus. I could tell she was close to being sick. Lacey had looked at James and then Tom. A playful smile danced across her face. She began crawling seductively across the middle of the circle. Jess cack-led, falling backward onto the grass. Lacey crept slowly toward him, her breasts threatening to burst from her dress as she leaned over. Tom sat there frozen, looking around to the rest of the group for help. She got so close there were only centimeters separating their lips.

"What the fuck is wrong with you?" James had suddenly shouted, jumping to his feet. He reached down and grabbed Lacey by her arm, yanking her violently off the floor. She looked scared. He continued to threaten her, screaming close to her face. Every third or fourth word made her flinch. We all looked on in horror as his rage escalated. "Who the hell do you think you are?"

Lacey had stood there silently taking it. After a couple of minutes, he stormed off, still shouting. "What the fuck is *his* problem?" She'd laughed when he was out of earshot, but we could all see she was upset. Looking back now, I wonder why none of us did anything. Why we hadn't tried to stop him. I suppose it was because it was James. Our friend. He was supposed to be a *good* guy.

We'd sat there. An awkward confused silence hung in the air. Tom had asked Lacey if she was OK. He helped Jess to her feet and put his arm around her, propping her up as we headed back toward the fair.

Jude was next to me. We walked companionably a few feet behind Tom and Jess. The lights from the fair were getting closer. The loud bass from the music pulsed through my chest. Jude suddenly put his arm across my path. I stopped, surprised as he moved toward me. His body slowly pressed against mine. He ran his hands gently down my bare arms. My body responded almost instantly. He slid his hands confidently up to my face, his thumbs tracing my jawline. He kissed me. Firmly, assuredly.

The moment our lips met he took a deep breath through his nose. Like he was breathing me in. Like he'd wanted to do it for a long time. I'd looked over Jude's shoulder and saw Tom there, holding up Jess. Her head flopping in front of her like a rag doll. He was watching us. I couldn't read his face. I'd gently pushed Jude away and we'd carried on walking.

But that was the beginning for me and Jude. The start of it all.

CHAPTER THIRTY-FIVE

Jude raised his hand slightly, offering me a drag of his cigarette. I shook my head, shuffling my body a little along the wall, creating space between us until Jude finally had to remove his arm from around my shoulder. There was something I needed to ask him, but I couldn't arrange the sentence properly in my head. Each time I tried to speak, the words died in my mouth.

"Jude?" He raised his chin. His face still so close. I looked down, concentrating on one of the laces of my trainer. The plastic end that held the lace tight and neat had split, leaving the end frayed. I pulled at the thread. "Where did you go that night, the night Lacey died?" I asked. He waited. He waited for so long that I didn't think he was going to answer me.

"After I left you on the beach?" I nodded, still staring at my shoe. He rubbed the hair at the back of his head and sighed. "I walked into town. I'd got a message from James. We arranged to head over to the pub. Drown our sorrows..." I assumed Jude was drowning his sorrows because of me. "Why did James need to drown his sorrows?" I asked.

"I walked over the dunes to the car park. James and Lacey

were there, arguing. They'd broken up earlier that day and James was in pieces..." he explained.

"James and Lacey broke up?" This was not something that I'd ever heard.

"Yeah, I thought you knew. I thought everyone knew. They used to break up all the time, but I think it was for real this time. Lacey seemed pretty adamant... Oh, man, it was awful." Jude stroked the stubble on his chin, thinking back to that night. "I mean, James could get angry with her, we'd all seen it, but this was different." I could feel my heart beating faster. "He just lost it. You know how she used to just take it when he got like that? Well, she didn't this time. This time she laughed at him. She was saying all this stuff. That he was weak and pathetic... I'd never seen her that angry. I had to pull him away. I don't know what he would have done if..." Jude stopped talking as he remembered. Remembered what had been done to Lacey later that night. He looked upset.

"Did you tell the police?" I asked. I knew the answer. Jude tilted his head to the side and raised his eyebrows a fraction.

"What do you think? That would have been it for him. He would have been arrested for sure," Jude said.

"Maybe he should have been," I replied angrily, finally raising my head to look at him. I reached over for his cigarette, taking a long drag of the nearly burned-out roll-up. I inhaled deeply, holding the smoke in my chest for a moment. The rush of nicotine made me feel light-headed. I let the smoke wisp from my mouth, before taking another puff and passing it back.

"I dragged James away," Jude continued. "He was still raging. Polly and Tara had turned up in the car park toward the end of the fight. They'd tried to get Lacey to leave too, but she wouldn't. The four of us went to the pub and left her in the car park on her own. I can still see her, sitting on the wall, looking at her phone." Jude looked like he was going to cry.

"So, James was with you when Lacey was murdered? He

couldn't have done it?" Jude didn't answer. He sat quietly, before opening the sweet tin and taking another cigarette paper out.

"Kate, he didn't do it. I know he didn't..."

"Was James with you or not?" I shouted. I scrambled my legs around until I was on my knees, eyes blazing. Jude didn't flinch. He spread a thin line of tobacco along his paper.

He spoke quietly. "We went into the Bull and bought a drink. Polly was all over me as soon as we got in there." He gave me a sideways look. I tried to hold my expression, but I felt the muscles in my cheek twitch. "She pulled me into that area just outside the toilets." It was the same place I'd confronted Jude about Lacey, just a few weeks later. "I didn't do anything with her, not then. Me and you had only just broken up." He seemed keen for me to believe him. But the words "not then" hung in the air like an echo.

"What do you want, Jude, a medal?" I snapped. I couldn't help it.

"I didn't mean... Oh, Christ, Kate, you know that's not what I meant." He looked agitated. I didn't say anything. "After a few minutes, we went back to the bar to find James and Tara, but they'd gone. We checked in the pool room, the beer garden... They definitely weren't there." He looked upward, recalling the series of events.

"What did you do?"

"Me and Polly finished our drinks and left. It was pouring with rain when we got outside, really hammering down. We went back down to the car park to look for them. That's when we found her... Lacey." I saw his Adam's apple slide up his throat as he swallowed. "She was just there on the ground... We thought she'd fallen at first... or drunk... Fuck, I don't know... As we got closer... it was obvious." He tapped the ash from the end of his cigarette and wiped his eyes on the inside of his arm. I gave him a minute. "Then Polly just took off, screaming, up in the dunes. I tried to stop her, but she was running... She was just so fast... and my legs..." He looked sadly at his feet. "They just wouldn't move." He took a final drag of the cigarette before pressing the remains into the concrete next to him.

"I called the police on my mobile. As I was talking to them, a crowd of people came into the car park. It all happened really quickly. I felt like I wasn't there, you know? Like I was watching a film. The next thing I knew, James came running down from the dunes... Kate, you should have seen his face. There's no way he could have done it." He pushed both hands into his hair and left them there. "And then you came..."

A silence fell between us. Jude turned to face me. He put his hand on my neck and pulled me toward him. We leaned in until our foreheads were almost touching and then we kissed. It happened so quickly, so naturally, I almost didn't notice the change. I pushed him away. Not hard. Just hard enough to make him stop.

"Jude, I can't..." My hands were on his chest. I could hear his heart and my breath.

"I know..." he muttered into my hair, leaning in and trying again.

"No." I struggled to my feet. Steadying myself against the wall, I stood there waiting for him to say something. Waiting for the empty, useless desire coursing around my body to cease. I looked down. He was staring at the swimming pool ahead of him. I suddenly thought of something.

"Jude, when you found Lacey, was she wearing a blue jumper?" Her upper body had been covered in the red blanket by the time I got to the car park. I could only see her face. Her face and her feet. It took him ages to answer.

"No," he replied at last. "Why?" I didn't answer him.

I must have imagined it. I must have been so drunk my memories from that night had got confused. I felt relief.

"She was wearing a blue jumper earlier though. In the car park, when she was arguing with James..."

I watched Jude, waiting for the implications of what he was saying to hit him. "Do you know what this means?" He shrugged, waiting for me to explain.

"Jude, they never found the jumper... Whoever killed her must have taken it."

CHAPTER THIRTY-SIX

I left Jude down by the pool and walked back to the restaurant. The number of people in the room had doubled since I'd been gone. Most of the guests had finished eating and had moved on to the drinking portion of the evening. There was a livelier more raucous atmosphere. The volume of the band had crept up. Several people were now dancing in the area in front of them. I headed over to the bar, looking for Sophie. There was no sign of her or Tom. I perched on a stool and ordered a large glass of white wine. I saw that Polly and Tara were still here. A fresh bottle of red between them. Polly looked over, before whispering something in Tara's ear. They both threw their heads back, laughing hysterically. I looked away.

Danny was still over at the table with the group of women. A lot more had been drunk, judging by the empty glasses and bottles. One of the women was standing up, doing an impression of a flamenco dancer. Her friends screamed and clapped with pleasure. Danny was sitting down. His legs were spread, and he'd slipped slightly down the chair. It was obvious, even from a distance, how drunk he was. I watched him run a hand through his greasy hair. Beads of sweat clung to his blotchy forehead. He looked like he was having trouble focusing. The dancing woman tried to grab Danny's hand. He snatched it away without looking at her. "Come on," she kept saying. I couldn't hear the words, but I could see them on her lips. She was getting close to his face now, begging him to get on his feet.

Danny leaned over, placing his head in his hands. The woman laughed and carried on dancing. I looked around for Jude, for anyone that could help him. Danny was slowly sliding down the chair.

Out of nowhere, Tom was there, leaning down, speaking close to Danny's ear. His hands flopped uselessly to his sides. Tom's mouth was pressed so close to his ear it was hard to tell if he was saying anything. A moment later Danny was crying. His head hung down, until his chin was almost touching his chest. The only sign that he was still awake was the rhythmic up-and-down movement of his shoulders, as heaving sobs shook his chest.

I returned to the bar, but my stool had been taken by a large middle-aged man dressed in a bright green Hawaiian shirt. He was regaling the two men standing in front of him with a long story about his day on the golf course. They ignored me as I leaned behind them to retrieve my wineglass. I stood awkwardly in the small gap between seats, sipping slowly on my drink. Tom was now crouched in front of Danny. He was trying to convince him to go home. He didn't look like he was going anywhere.

I drained the last of my wine and placed the empty glass on the bar. I had one last look in the direction of the toilets, before leaving the restaurant. I walked down the stairs and outside into the cold night air. It was dark now. I glanced at the path that led back to the swimming pool. All those years ago, when we'd broken up, it had been a struggle to not be with Jude. Not to call him. To wake up every day and not try to see him. It felt like work. After all that work and all those years, here I was, like a teenager, thinking about going to find him. Reliving some long-gone time of happiness.

I felt in my pocket for the room card and forced myself back to the suite. As I stood in the lift, I caught my reflection on the mirrored wall. I looked tired. The makeup that I'd applied so carefully earlier had faded. The mascara had smudged into a thin line under my eyes. I ran my fingers through my hair, thick and knotted from too much hairspray. My yellow jumper hung long over my fingers. The lift doors opened and I walked wearily through them. Stepping onto the private, carpeted hallway by the entrance, I clicked my card into the lock and walked in. There was no noise. Sophie's bedroom door was wide open. Her room was empty and her bed unused. I went to my bedroom and quickly stripped to my underwear, climbing between the cool soft covers. I closed my eyes and thought about what Jude had said.

James and Lacey had broken up the night she died. How many people knew and hadn't mentioned it to the police? Could James have hurt her? Jude was adamant that he hadn't. Even if he didn't kill her, Tara and James must have been in the car park around the time it happened. I didn't understand why everyone had protected him. We'd all seen him try to control Lacey, his outbursts, the anger. Why had we all been so sure that he didn't do it?

I started to drift. Thinking about Jude. About how he used to be. For years he'd worn a tatty old red hoodie, always with the hood pulled up covering most of his face. He'd been shy and self-conscious. He hated having to speak in class. I'd been taller than him all the way through primary school. He was the shortest of all the boys in his year. Toward the end of secondary school, everything had changed for Jude. He shot up to nearly six feet and grew his hair out. He developed a new confidence, a way about him, that had made everyone sit up. The changes in

Jude came as quite a surprise to the girls in Pengully. An even bigger surprise was that he'd chosen me.

I think I'd done my own sort of blossoming as school ended. For two years I'd worn braces, thick metal braces that forced my lips out when I closed my mouth. I never smiled and I never got used to them. A few months before school ended, I had them taken off. I felt like an entirely different person. I put my hand up in class and smiled when people spoke to me. I felt a confidence I'd never felt before. I finally stopped hiding. That's when the boys began to notice me. That's when Jude noticed me.

I woke up with a start. The main door to the suite closed loudly and I could hear voices. I couldn't make out who they belonged to or what they were saying. "For fuck's sake, Danny." Louder that time. Maybe Tom's voice. Sophie laughing. I looked at the clock beside the bed. It was 1:23 a.m. I lay there for a couple of minutes, listening. The handle on my bedroom door began to turn. I saw it just in time to close my eyes and pretend to be asleep. A triangle of light from the living room swept over the bed.

"What are you doing?" Tom hissed. "She's sleeping. Let her sleep." More urgent whispering. The door remained open for a moment. I could see the light, even with my eyes closed.

"I need to speak to her..." It was Jude, pleading with Tom. My limbs tightened. I peeked out between the narrowest of gaps through my eyelids to see them standing in the doorway. I could hear Sophie laughing again with Danny somewhere in the background.

"Don't be a prick, Jude. Haven't you done enough to her?" Tom said, before reaching over and pulling the door closed. I lay there for what seemed like hours. Ears straining to hear the conversation next door. I caught only the odd word or ripple of laughter. I must have eventually fallen asleep.

The next thing I knew, the sun was streaming through the

uncovered window. It was 6:15 a.m. I listened for noise, but all seemed quiet outside the room. I crept over to the door, pulling it silently toward me, hiding my undressed body behind it. There, asleep on one of the sofas, was Danny. He was fully clothed, lying on his back, his mouth open. I stretched to see around the doorframe. Jude was asleep on the other sofa. He'd taken his shirt off and lay with his arm across his face, guarding his eyes from the sun. I gently closed the door and got dressed, stuffing my yellow jumper into the hessian bag I'd been given yesterday.

I gathered my things together and tiptoed out of the room. As I crossed the lounge, Danny's eyes sprung open for a second. He looked right at me, his expression wild and confused. I'm not sure he even registered that I was there before he fell back to sleep.

CHAPTER THIRTY-SEVEN

I left the suite and headed back down in the lift. When I entered the lobby, a woman came through the automatic doors, pushing a cleaning trolley. The white wires of her earphones hung around her neck. We nodded at each other as I passed. I walked round to the staff car park. My car was now one of only four other cars here. I sat in the driver's seat and texted Sophie. *Gone back to the cottage. Let me know when you need picking up and I'll come and get you. X*

I didn't see a single car as I drove back along the lanes. I opened my window, breathing in the cool air that billowed through. The only noise was the loud chirping of birds waking up and my tires crunching along the uneven road.

When I arrived at Red Rock, I slowly drove the car all the way down the driveway and parked outside the cottage. I didn't want to wake Mum and Richard by pulling up outside the main house. I was relieved to find the door had been left on the latch. I still didn't have a key. The cottage looked tidy. Like someone had made an effort to square everything away. I went to the kitchen and put the kettle on. My body ached for caffeine. As I stood there, listening to the low, slow rumble of the water boil-

ing, I remembered the folder. The green cardboard folder of
press clippings that Sophie had tucked away that first night. I
opened the drawer. It was still there, on top of the manual for
the microwave. I pulled it out and placed it on the side next to
my mug. I stared at it until the noise of the kettle clicking off
broke me out of my daze. I finished making my tea and
rummaged in the cupboard for food. I managed to find half a
bag of salted popcorn and an opened box of crackers.

I carried my mug and food upstairs, tucking the green folder
under my arm. I climbed into bed and spread the pile of papers
out onto the duvet. I sipped the scalding tea, before unraveling
the bag of popcorn and scooping out a large handful. Little
brown kernels dropped onto the white covers beside me.

I stared at the articles in front of me. Lacey and James's
broad carefree smiles beamed from the black-and-white page on
top. I spread the papers around the bed. I wasn't even sure what
I was looking for. Some mention of the blue jumper? I wanted
to be wrong about the jumper. But if the killer had taken it,
there must have been a reason. If I'm right, I needed to tell the
police.

It would have been much easier if I were mistaken. But now
it was real. Now I had no choice but to try and unpick the
wasp's nest of memories from that night, fleeting recollections
and darting images, just slipping from my grasp. I thought again
about talking to Lacey on the beach that night, how angry I'd
felt. I squeezed my eyes closed and clenched my fists. I tried to
grab hold of it, to creep around the picture in my head, before it
shriveled up and crawled away. I groaned with tiredness and
exasperation. Time and pain had muddied the water, water that
I should have swam through years ago. I randomly plucked a
couple of sheets of paper from the pile. I needed something,
anything, to trigger a memory. I needed to know what happened
that night. I couldn't hide from it anymore.

The first article I picked was from *The Times*. I checked the date on the top. It was December 2016. Six months after James died. The headline read, UNEXPLAINED DEATH IN SEASIDE TOWN. I skimmed through the article, taking in relevant sections and sources. The journalist who wrote it had obviously been to Pengully. There was a lot of research and background. Derek Cummings was the name at the top of the page. It didn't mean anything to me, but a quick internet search on my phone told me that he was usually the paper's political correspondent. An unusual article for someone who wrote almost entirely about UK politics. Then it occurred to me what the connection was. Michael, James's dad, had been an MP.

I reread the story. Properly this time.

It was well written. The words gave a fond insight into a shy boy from a small Cornish village: "James Penhaligan was a quiet, studious child, a boy who loved riding his bike and nature, and who at the age of nine had built himself a beautiful wooden dovecote. It was not for collared or white doves, but for the wood pigeons that lived in the trees behind his house." The journalist painted a picture of rural innocence. I'd forgotten how much James loved animals.

The dovecote was amazing. The first time I saw it I couldn't believe he'd made it all by himself. I told him as well, but he'd brushed the praise aside. He was only interested in showing us the pigeons. A pair had moved into the cote almost immediately and just a few months later they had chicks. I remember how happy it had made him. That was the James I knew.

The article went on. "James was an accomplished sportsman, playing both cricket and rugby at county level. He had secured a place at Cambridge University and was due to start a law degree." The article had skewed the timeline. The author made it seem like he was just about to take his place at college. James had been due to start Cambridge two years before he died.

There was barely any mention of Lacey.

Derek Cummings wrote: "Two years prior to his death, James's girlfriend, Lacey Crew, was tragically murdered. Her death sent James on a downward path and triggered a series of events that would lead to his demise." He didn't talk about Lacey or their relationship, just that her murder had been the ruin of him. "James leaves behind a loving family: his mother, a respected solicitor, and father, Michael Penhaligan, an MP known for his staunch defense of rural communities, both pillars of the small seaside town where they reside and philanthropists in their own way." The bias of the writer was breathtaking.

Then the story shifted to the police. A dark cloud of vague aspersions and well-timed questions. Questions that lay in the text unanswered, leaving the reader to assume the worst of the investigating officers. There were no accusations, no hard evidence of police misconduct, just a sad ending to a story about a shy little boy from Cornwall.

Nobody likes to believe that lives fall apart for no reason. Because if that's true, it could happen to anyone. Blame is comforting. Derek Cummings had made sure that the path of blame had led directly to the Devon & Cornwall Police.

The article must have been written about the time that Claire and Michael Penhaligan were pursuing a case for police harassment. They were building their own narrative. A PR exercise, it hadn't worked of course. The courts had ruled the police had no case to answer. So why did they even try? Did they really think that the police were to blame for his death, or were they just distracting themselves? A pointless crusade to cushion themselves from the grief and guilt? I leaned back against the headboard. All of it was such a waste. Lacey, James, their families. That summer had started with so much joy and hope.

CHAPTER THIRTY-EIGHT

The year that Lacey died, it had been hot since May. Really hot. It was all anybody talked about. It had taken us all by surprise. Would there be a watering ban? Would it mean last-minute bookings on some of the empty holiday cottages? All of this was up for discussion at the pub every night. The temperature went above ninety degrees Fahrenheit for three days in a row. One more and they were going to close the school.

One weekend, a few of us had decided to go camping. It was still quite early in the season, so there were empty pitches at all the local campsites. We'd chosen Tregolls Farm, mainly because it was cheap, but also because it was pretty basic. We were unlikely to cause much trouble there.

The night we camped at Tregolls was one of the best nights I've ever had. There were about twenty of us, set up in a circle of tents at the far end of the site. The only other people staying were a few seasonal farmworkers, who were pleased to see a bit of life in the place. Danny had set up music and we all grabbed kindling for the fire. It wasn't anything special, no different really to other nights we'd had. But as I danced by the fire, a bottle of beer in my hand and Jude's arm around my waist, I felt complete happiness, like my heart was brimming over. I remember looking around at the faces beside me, faces that I'd known my whole life. It was the first time I felt like I ever really belonged.

Only six weeks later, Lacey would be dead, and nothing would ever be the same again. Eventually, James would see out the last few months of his life in a run-down caravan at the farthest end of the very same campsite.

I'd drifted off for a few minutes. Sitting up, I'd heard the faint sound of tires on gravel outside the cottage. I climbed out of bed and went over to the small window. I could see an old blue Golf parked right behind my car. It was so far over I could only see the very front of it, and even then I had to crouch on the window seat to see. I held my breath. I heard a car door slam and a woman's voice say something. The driver's door opened, and I watched Jude get out. He slowly eased himself upright, as though his body ached. His arms rested on the roof of the car as he looked over at the cottage. I flinched, slinking my body back into the wall.

I crept back, eyes cautiously pressed to the very edge of the window recess. Tom was talking to Jude, leaning on the far-side door. I couldn't hear what he was saying, but he kept shaking his head. Jude looked upset. The cottage door banged open downstairs. I tiptoed across the room, legs bent and body braced, to silently close my bedroom door. I didn't want to talk, not to anyone. I returned to the window just in time to see Jude's car reversing out of sight with Tom in the passenger seat.

I climbed quietly back into bed. My legs ached with tension and my head throbbed with tiredness. I lay still for a few minutes, listening for sounds from downstairs. There was nothing. I was in an uncomfortable position, half on my back and half on my side, pressing my eyes closed. I waited, waited for the darkness to drop me into sleep, but I knew it wasn't coming. Thoughts rippled around my mind, leaving a trail of unanswered questions. I could feel my eyes flitting behind my eyelids, trying to catch hold of threads. I blinked, giving up on sleep, looking instead at the papers scattered across the bed and the floor.

I pulled out some of the sheets near the bottom of the pile. The top half of a photo of Lacey was poking out from beneath some other articles. I'd never seen the photo before. At first, I didn't even think it was Lacey. Her pale blond hair was pinned up, spiraled curls escaping down either side of her face. Her eyeshadow was heavy and dark, and her thick false lashes curled upward to almost her eyebrows. Lacey's mouth was painted a bright glossy scarlet and the very tip of her tongue rested on the top corner of her lip. There was something about the photo that looked quite dated. It had a sort of eighties feel to it. I pulled the page out to reveal the rest of the photo.

Lacey's head was facing forward, but the rest of her body was turned sideways. A profile view of her long naked body. The arm closest to the camera was placed over her chest. The elbow dropped away slightly, revealing the rounded curve of one of her breasts, her forearm only just covering her nipple. Lacey's right leg was forward of the other, hiding her pubic area. Her back was arched, accentuating the curve of her bum. She looked beautiful.

Looking back at her face, I saw something missing. Beyond the suggestive pout and the coy way she looked up at the camera, Lacey looked uncomfortable. It was more than that. She looked scared.

My concentration was broken by the text alert on my phone. It was from Richard. *Hi, darling. Dinner at ours tonight? 7 p.m.? Sophie and Tom welcome too. Dad x* I quickly tapped out a reply. *Yes, sounds good. Sophie and Tom can't make it.* The guilt hit me the second I pressed send. I never used to lie. When I was little I used to tell Mum that lying made my stomach hurt.

I seem to find myself doing it more and more lately. I've found that the more you do it, the less it seems to hurt.

I went back to the photo. I'd never heard of Lacey doing any glamour modeling. It certainly hadn't been common knowledge. I wondered who'd taken it. Reading the tiny letters of the photo credit below, it said Starry Night Studios. I looked across to the article accompanying the picture. The headline read, NO NEW LEADS ON MODEL MURDERED IN SLEEPY CORNISH TOWN. I read the short piece. There was nothing new here. The pointless article had been just an excuse to print the naked photo of Lacey.

I thumbed through the papers to see if the tabloids had run any other glamour photos of her. I couldn't find any. I noticed that every photo of James seemed to be him wearing his school uniform or dressed in a suit for a wedding or special event. They gave the impression of a reliable, naive young man. There were no photos of Lacey in her school uniform. The photos of Lacey showed her partying. They had her in few clothes, looking like she was on a wild night out. You couldn't really criticize the press for the photos. After all, most of them had been lifted right from James and Lacey's own social media accounts. But the contrast was stark and unfair.

CHAPTER THIRTY-NINE

There was a gentle tap on the door. I paused for a second, deciding what to do. "Come in." I hadn't spoken to anyone for so long my voice croaked. Sophie slowly pushed open the door with her foot. A steaming mug of tea in one hand and a plate of crumpets in the other.

"Can I come in?" she spoke quietly. I could hear the nerves in her voice. This wasn't a side of Sophie I saw very often. I nodded. She edged her way around the bed and placed the plate on top of the covers, handing me the hot tea. "I'm so sorry about last night." I opened my mouth to speak, but no words came out. "I made you go. We were supposed to be out together, and I ended up... well, I ended up bringing your past back, drunk to our hotel room." She seemed genuinely sorry.

"Soph, it's fine..." I paved the way for her to come back.

"No, it's not." She was firm. "I've been preoccupied. I haven't been there for you. This whole thing must have been really hard." She climbed onto the bed next to me. I could feel tears beginning to prickle behind my tired eyes. We were both silent for a minute, neither of us knowing how to move forward. Sophie looked down at the photo of Lacey.

"Did you know she'd done glamour modeling?" she asked. I shook my head.

"I've never seen this photo. It wasn't something I heard talked about. If these photos had been published *anywhere* when she was alive, people would definitely have talked about it," I said.

"Have you heard of Starry Night Studios?" She didn't wait for me to reply. "I called them yesterday. They're a photographic place about an hour away. I spoke to the woman who runs it. She's called Debbie. Nice, friendly woman. She used to run it with her husband before they split up. They mainly photographed babies, family portraits, that type of thing. Occasionally they did glamour shots."

"Did she remember Lacey?" I asked.

"Yeah, she did as it happens. The photos were taken only a few months before she died. Debbie saw this..." Sophie tapped the news article. "She'd expected a call from the police, but they never contacted her. In fact, nobody did, until I called yesterday."

"What did Lacey want the photos for?" I asked.

"Debbie couldn't remember if Lacey had told them why she wanted them. She did remember that she got upset halfway through the shoot though. Apparently, she came in full of confidence, stripped off in front of Debbie and her husband almost immediately. They took a few photos. It all seemed to be going well and then Lacey started crying. Debbie said she was hysterical. She'd tried to talk to her, but Lacey told her she'd changed her mind. She got dressed and ran from the studio. Debbie said she called her a few days later to see if she was OK. Lacey told her it had all been a big mistake." Sophie shrugged.

"So how did the photos get into a national tabloid?" I wondered.

"Good question..."

"Debbie's husband?" I asked.

Sophie shook her head. "That's exactly what I thought at first. Debbie can't stand him. He left her a few years ago. Took everything, the house, the kids, the money. Left her with nothing. Even she can't fault his professionalism though. I asked her outright and she said he would never have sold those photos." Sophie thought for a moment. "Debbie said she'd felt guilty about taking Lacey's money. She'd paid them up-front for the shoot. So, after a month or so, Debbie emailed her a selection of the best ones they took that day. She thought Lacey wouldn't have to look at them if she didn't want to, but Debbie felt like she'd done her bit. She never heard back from her." I nodded slowly, my thoughts running ahead.

"If the studio didn't release the photos and Lacey never released them, who gave them to the press?" Neither of us spoke for a minute or two, both deep in our own thoughts.

"Episode one of *Small Town* is up now. We should have the initial download figures this evening. The network has gone hard on promotion this week." Sophie hesitated. "Do you want to listen to it?"

"Have you heard it already?" I asked. Sophie shook her head shyly. She looked worried. "OK," I replied. She climbed under the covers, giggling like a child about to play her favorite game. She arched her hips up and pulled her phone from her back pocket. Scrolling and tapping for a few seconds, she pressed play. Her voice chimed through the phone, sharp and clear. The sound quality was incredible, much better than our old recordings. Tom had done a good job. Sophie gnawed at the edges of her fingers, staring at a coastal painting on the opposite wall. I had never really seen her like this before, unsure and wavering. I'd never really seen her anything but strong and confident. Except when her dad died.

I'd known Sophie for only a few years, when she got the phone call she'd been dreading. The pancreatic cancer that had plagued her dad for eight years had recently become untreatable. Sophie's stepmother had been the one to tell her that he'd died. Her parents had separated when she was little. Sophie had a complicated relationship with her dad. He'd never shown much interest in her, but she was devastated when she got the news. Small and broken in a way I'd never seen a person be before. It was the only time in our friendship that I had ever seen her vulnerable.

I'd gone to the funeral with Sophie. It was hard. Harder than I think even she knew it would be. Her dad's family had treated her like an outsider. Her stepmother, convinced she was there for his money, could not have ushered her away from the house any quicker. The Sophie I knew would have fought back, demanded her place at the table, but she was broken.

We went home to London, and Sophie began to put herself back together. It took months before she returned to her bold, confident self. Tom had helped with that. I always wondered if Sophie and Tom would have got together if her dad hadn't died. When you feel lost and unsafe you search for something to cling to. Tom was her port in a storm.

Our friendship was stronger than ever. We were connected by our past. An unspoken understanding between us. Both from broken families. Both having difficult relationships with our complicated fathers. We were bonded in so many ways. Until we went back to Cornwall that New Year's Eve. Then everything started to change. I hadn't lied. I never told her things that hadn't happened, but maybe I'd left stuff out. Good stuff. She knew about Richard of course, that he'd come into our lives and made things better. I don't think she knew *how* much better. That was my fault. I'd emphasized the terrible years with my dad. The shouting, the fear, it was all true, but maybe not as significant a part of my life as I'd made it out to be.

I saw it on Sophie's face as we'd pulled into the driveway of Red Rock House for the first time. Her confusion when she met Richard, when she saw how much he cared for me, the tight family unit that we had. I hadn't realized until I saw how it must look through her eyes. She never said anything. There was nothing really to say. But I think some of the trust between us went, that closeness. I think she felt let down. Sophie thought my life had been like hers, difficult and lonely. Then she came to Cornwall and all she saw was a warm loving home with two parents who adored me. It had been like watching a shutter go down inside her.

CHAPTER FORTY

We leaned back on the pillows. Sophie's bent duvet-covered legs created a stand for her phone. A few minutes in and I heard my voice. It didn't sound like me. It sounded like a strange distant version of me. My tone was duller, flatter than the voice that I heard in my head. I detected a slight Cornish accent that I never realized I had. I tried to detach myself from the self-analysis and just listen to the words. I rested back on the cushioned headboard and closed my eyes. It sounded good. It was interesting, slick, professional. I looked at Sophie. She was still chewing her finger, her expression glazed and removed.

"Sophie? Soph, it's great..." I placed a comforting hand on her knee and waited.

"Huh? Oh, do you think?" She was distracted, her face lined with worry.

"Yes," I said gently, nodding my encouragement. Sophie's eyes narrowed as she listened to the story. A story we'd told to each other only a few days ago, but one I already had very little memory of telling. "OK?" I added.

"OK," she replied with a smile. Her anxious frown began to slide away. She took one of the crumpets from the plate and began pulling off little pieces from around the side to nibble on. I did the same, only I took a big bite from mine. The melted butter dripped down my chin and I tried to catch it with my spare hand. We both laughed into our food. We listened to the rest of the podcast in silence, occasionally catching the other's eye if there was something we liked, or something we might need to add to in later episodes. We worked our way through the plate of crumpets until there was nothing left but an oily yellow smear of butter.

When the episode ended, Sophie climbed reluctantly out of bed. "Tara emailed me this morning. Seems she's less enthusiastic about talking to us than she was yesterday," Sophie said on her way to the door. "But I've managed to convince her... or rather the studio's money managed to convince her. I think it was a lot more than she was expecting," she added.

"When's she coming?"

"Tomorrow morning. We need to put together episode three at some point, but that shouldn't be too difficult. It's basically going to be all the forensic stuff. The things Rebecca told us." I nodded. "OK, I'll leave you to it," Sophie said, opening the door.

"I'm, um... I'm having dinner at Mum and Richard's tonight," I told her.

"Well, we can go through everything tomorrow then." She smiled. I felt bad. I knew she would have loved to come. To have a distraction.

At six o'clock I went for a shower. I hadn't changed my clothes since last night and I could still smell the faint waft of cigarette smoke. I left the bathroom, my hair and body wrapped in towels. Tom was walking upstairs. He paused when he saw me. His eyes darted to the wall beside him for a moment. "Sorry," he muttered. "I'm just here to pick up some stuff." I nodded. The fine hairs on my arms stood on end, gripped by an unwanted feeling of anticipation. He cleared his throat awkwardly as he went by, our smells colliding as we passed each other. Shower gel and coconut shampoo mingled with his sweet musky body spray.

I closed the bedroom door behind me, pressing my hot back against the cold hard wood for a moment. I dressed quickly in jeans and a T-shirt, throwing my old gray cardigan over my clothes. I perched on the edge of the bed and thought about the photos of Lacey.

Assuming she hadn't printed copies of the pictures, someone had taken them from her email. Someone she knew. Someone who, even after she was dead, disliked her enough to distribute naked photos of her. Photos she'd regretted. Could it be that this same person had hated Lacey enough to kill her? I looked at the time. I was already ten minutes late. I went downstairs. Sophie was working on her laptop, balanced on a pile of cushions on the floor. "I'm off," I told her, my hand already on the door latch.

"Have a great time," she said, looking up from her screen. I wanted to say more, to tell her that it was all going to be OK: our friendship, her and Tom. But the truth is, I didn't know if it was going to be OK. I closed the door gently and walked up the drive. The evening sun still had warmth left in it. I tilted my head toward the sky, letting the heat cover my face. As I approached the house, I saw that there were two cars parked outside. A navy-colored Range Rover and what looked like a new Audi convertible. I had a sinking feeling in my stomach. I wasn't the only one going to my parents' house for dinner tonight.

I slowed my pace as I made the last few steps to the front door. I peered in the window of the four-by-four as I passed it, looking for clues as to who it might be. As I pushed open the front door, I could hear people in the back garden. Distant conversation. I groaned. As I headed for the kitchen door, my mum entered the hallway from the living room. "Oh, darling, there you are! I was just wondering where you'd got to," Mum gushed. She took in my outfit and my damp hair. "Richard didn't tell you we had other guests, did he?" I bit my lip, shaking my head. "Bloody man," she said, laughing and rolling her eyes. "I'm so sorry, darling. This must seem like a bit of an ambush."

Mum was dressed in a fitted calf-length black dress. It was stylish and flattering. It complemented her figure perfectly. I looked down at my own slightly shabby outfit. Mum saw. "Katie, you look gorgeous. Don't worry. Come through and meet everyone... while I reprimand your father!" Mum had never referred to Richard as "father." That name had always been reserved for my real dad. Richard had always been known as "dad," a little thing but something that always defined their very different take on the role. The fact that she no longer flinched when she said the word *father* showed just how far she'd come these last few years.

Mum put her hand on my waist and guided me through to the kitchen. The worktop was covered in plates of food, canapés, salads, bottles of wine and champagne. There were vases of flowers everywhere, huge bouquets in the four corners of the room. The double doors to the patio were open. I could see figures standing around with drinks. I couldn't make out who they were through the white voile curtain that billowed lightly into the room on the breeze.

As we walked out into the sunshine, the chatter stopped abruptly. My mother stood close and made introductions. "Katie, you remember Claire and Michael Penhaligan, don't you?"

CHAPTER FORTY-ONE

I looked at their faces, polite smiles and stiff backs. I was paralyzed for a moment, standing here after all these years, in front of James's parents. I waited so long to answer that my mum gave me a light squeeze with her arm that was still wrapped around my middle.

"Yes, yes, of course." I swallowed, jerking back to life. Nobody said anything. My eyes dropped to my feet like a teenager. Mum rallied.

"And this..." She said it a fraction louder, trying to buoy everyone along. She introduced me to another couple that stood sipping wine. I didn't hear their names. All I could hear was the sound of my heart pounding in my ears.

The woman she introduced me to was plump and smiley. She looked like a drawing from a children's book, like someone who spent her days baking cakes. The man was short and wiry. He said nothing. He obviously had no desire to be here.

Richard stepped in, passing me a filled glass of champagne. I caught his eye, but he didn't seem to think that there was anything wrong. I gulped at the wine. Bubbles hit my throat like a thousand tiny wasp stings. I tried to gain control of my senses again.

"Are you still a radio presenter?" Claire interrupted, studying my face as she spoke, her clipped Chelsea accent giving a sharpened end to her words.

"Um... I'm a researcher... excuse me... Mum, do you want some help in the kitchen?" I locked eyes with her, and we walked silently back indoors.

"Why didn't you tell me?" I hissed when we were far enough away from the garden. I heard the hubbub of chat rise again.

"Darling, you know it really doesn't matter to me one bit what you're wearing..." She put a comforting arm on my sleeve.

"It's not about what I'm wearing," I whispered angrily. "Why are James's parents here?"

"I'm sorry, Katie." She flinched. "I had no idea that it would upset you like this." She looked hurt and confused.

"I'm not upset," I told her, frustrated that she couldn't see it. "I just don't understand."

"We've all been friends for a very long time." Mum spoke deliberately, trying to talk me down with each carefully articulated word. "We have dinner together every few months or so. It was our turn, that's all... I thought it might be nice." She tilted her head to the side, her face pleading for me to be calm. "I just wanted to show you off... I thought it might help you back into the fold... you know, if you decide to move back."

"Mum... I'm not moving back." I spoke gently. The fight had gone out of me. Tears filled her eyes, threatening to spill over. That's what she thought this was, a homecoming. The beginning of a new life for me in Cornwall. Is that why they'd decorated the cottage?

"Mum, I'm sorry..." I reached out my arm to touch her, but she took a step back.

"Oh, darling, no need to apologize. It's your life—but a mum can always hope." She laughed, but I knew she was still upset. "Will you stay... please?"

"One hour... maximum," I replied defeatedly.

"Thank you," she whispered as I headed back outside. Claire was standing by the patio doors. She accosted me immediately. Her slender fingers wrapped around my elbow as she steered me effortlessly toward the table of food. Away from the other guests. For a moment she said nothing. My mind worked quickly, desperately trying to fill the silence.

"How are you?" I asked, reaching over to pick up one of the large white dinner plates stacked on one side of the table.

Claire ignored my question. "James was very fond of you. He often talked about you." She spoke her words into the air without looking at me, as though she were talking to herself. I cast my eyes over the plates of food on the table, pretending that I was deliberating what to eat.

"I was fond of him too," I said, reaching for a spoon and selecting a vegetable and grain salad. I had no idea what I was putting on my plate.

"Why didn't you come to his funeral?" she asked, fixing me with a level stare. I was so shocked by the directness of her question that my head shot up. I looked at Claire properly for the first time. She was a lot thinner. Her once youthful face had become creased and her skin sallow. Aging disproportionately to the number of years that had passed. Her sunken eyes looked too big for her face, giving her a startled, fearful look.

"I... I'm... I didn't..." The words died in my mouth.

"Shhh, it's OK," she soothed, reaching out to me in the same way you might try to calm a wild animal. "I just wondered if there was ever something between you, whether there'd been a falling out." She spoke sweetly, but I could see something else there, just below the surface. I looked around me, desperate for an escape. Claire saw it and began backtracking. "I'm sorry. I've made you uncomfortable." She bit her lip, but she wasn't sorry at all.

"No, you haven't at all," I lied, staring at my plate, half filled with food I didn't want to eat. I needed to leave but didn't know how to. Claire was considering something.

"Your mum tells me you're doing a podcast." Her tone was a little sharper. I looked toward the door. Claire took a small step to her right. It was only a small shift, but it meant that I was trapped between her and the food table. I wasn't going anywhere. I rubbed my eye with my free hand. I wasn't sure if I could do this again. Lack of water and sleep over the last few days had left me drained and irritable. I decided not to answer. There was nothing to say. Claire waited, sipping on a glass of water with pursed lips.

"Well, if it isn't little Katie Chase!" It was Michael. He spoke in a loud, deep voice, sliding his large body slowly toward us. Claire moved her leg. Michael leaned in to kiss both my cheeks. His face was soft and doughy, moist with sweat.

"Hi." I tried to smile, but the muscles in my face were beginning to ache with the pretense of it all. Michael was bigger than I'd ever seen him. He wore a pink pinstriped shirt that only just covered his round protruding belly. The small white buttons gaped under the pressure. His face was red. Not just flushed, bright red. He panted between words as though he'd been running.

"I hear you're doing some radio thing about Lacey," he boomed. The glass of wine in his hand sloshed around as he spoke. "Terrible business all that..." he said, shaking his head. I looked at Claire. The corners of her mouth had turned down as she watched Michael speak. "It was never serious between her and James of course." He spoke loudly, his words joined together in a slur. "No, just a bit of fun... and who could blame him, eh?" He looked around for an audience as his brash laugh echoed around the walled garden. Talk behind him had stopped. Everyone was listening now.

"That girl ruined his life." Claire spat the words at Michael in an angry whisper. Her hands were shaking, and she looked close to tears. Michael completely ignored her, as if she hadn't even spoken.

"If you can't screw around when you're nineteen, when can you, eh?" His gravelly laugh descended into a hacking cough.

"Excuse me," I said, forcing my way past the two of them. I headed for the kitchen. Rage pulsed through my body. My fists were clenched so tightly my palms hurt. Richard caught up, walking alongside me, our shoulders nearly touching. As soon as we were inside the doors, he stopped me, putting both hands on my shoulders.

"Katie, I'm sorry." Richard looked devastated that Michael might have upset me.

"Why the hell is he here?" I asked loudly. Loudly enough for the people outside to hear me. I no longer cared. Richard spoke quietly, trying to lead me farther into the kitchen, away from the garden.

"In business, there are sometimes necessary evils. Unfortunately, Michael is one of those evils," he said sadly. He placed a weary hand on his thinning hair. He looked desperate. I thought back to the argument I'd overheard between James and Lacey. The argument about Michael.

"Did you know that Michael harassed Lacey at work?" I waited for his reaction.

"What do you mean harassed?" He looked confused.

"Groping, sexual suggestions..." I didn't know how to explain it, so it came out clumsily. "I heard James and Lacey talking about it once. She was really upset." Richard pressed his face into the palms of his hands, taking a long sharp breath in.

"No. No, I didn't realize that," he said with feeling.

"But you knew that it was something," I persisted. "I told you about it once... told you what I'd seen. Then there were the complaints." Richard looked stricken.

"I did know... I put Danny on the bar after you told me. I asked him to make sure none of the female bar staff were *ever* left on their own with him." He spoke with feeling.

"But you let him carry on drinking at the Carmen." I could see what this was doing to Richard, but he needed to hear this. He leaned against the worktop and nodded miserably.

"I thought I could control it. Control him. Michael is quite a powerful enemy to make in a small town like this. He oversaw planning, licensing. He was even in charge of the regional golfing committee. Their members spend thousands at the Carmen every year." The shame was starting to show as he spoke the words out loud. "As *soon* as the formal complaints were made, I spoke to him. Told him he couldn't drink in the bar anymore..." He held up his hands in defense. There was something in the way he worded it.

"Wait... did he still *go* to the Carmen?" I asked, shocked. Richard shifted uncomfortably, folding his arms high on his chest.

He spoke in a hushed voice, glancing furtively to the garden. "I used to let him and his friends drink in one of the suites. I made sure I was the *only* one who brought their drinks... They never had *any* contact with the women who worked there," he added hastily. I was appalled and he could see it.

"Katie, I'm sorry that you're... disappointed." He reached out and took my hand. I let him.

I wanted to tell him that it was OK, but it wasn't, and he knew it. "I'm tired. I'm going to head back..." I told him.

"Katie, please..." he begged.

"No, honestly, it's fine. I just need some sleep." I attempted a smile, but a bad taste lingered on the corners of my mouth. I didn't have the energy to make anyone feel better about their choices. Not tonight.

CHAPTER FORTY-TWO

"You know he didn't kill Lacey, don't you?" Richard asked. He trailed behind me as I walked toward the door.

"Do I?" I turned to face him, leaving the words suspended in the air between us.

"He might have been... inappropriate..." He looked so uncomfortable. "But he's not a murderer." I turned to walk away. Richard's eyes flickered anxiously toward the garden. "I would never have let him near you. You know that, don't you?" He pleaded. I didn't answer him. I pulled open the heavy glass door and breathed in the warm dusky night.

As I walked the long winding drive to the cottage, I heard the crunch of footsteps behind me. Claire was trotting unsteadily along the path. Her heels wobbled on the gravel as she tried to pull a smart navy jacket over her floral dress. I wasn't sure if she was walking toward me or to her car. I turned to leave.

Claire tugged at the end of her jacket, trying to compose herself. "I'm sorry if we upset you." Her apology was stiff and formal. I got the impression that this was not the real reason she'd followed me out here. "I know it doesn't seem like it, but in his own way, Michael is extremely upset about what happened. Everyone deals with things differently." Claire's tone was stern. I didn't speak. "Can I ask what your intentions are for this podcast?"

"My intentions?" I choked. "Mrs Penhaligan, Lacey was murdered. Somebody killed her, probably someone she knew, and everyone acted like... like it didn't matter. Like *she* didn't matter." My voice sounded unnaturally high. I could feel my throat swell with rage and repulsion. Angry with myself that I didn't have the courage to call her Claire.

"Don't be ridiculous. Of course, she mattered," Claire snapped back. "She mattered a damn sight more than my son did. He was a mess when he died. No job, a drinking problem, living in a *disgusting* caravan..." She drew the front of the blazer together, shuddering at the thought. "That's all anybody could say about him after he died." Her voice waivered. All the fight seemed to leave her. "Everybody forgot the kind, clever boy that he'd been. *My* little boy." She struggled to get the last words out. Tears poured down her cheeks. She made no attempt to wipe them away. I thought about the article in *The Times*. Maybe it hadn't been a PR job, a well-timed piece to coincide with the case against the police. Maybe Claire had just wanted everyone to remember the sweet bright child in the photo.

"We just want to find out the truth. The truth about Lacey *and* James," I said gently. "They deserve that. Everybody does after all this time." She nodded, unable to speak still. Paralyzed by the unhappiness that gripped her. With nothing else to say, I walked away. There was no comfort that I could possibly offer to Claire Penhaligan.

"Can I talk to you?" she called after me. Her words were urgent.

"Talk to me?" I was confused.

"On your podcast. I want to talk about James." I tried to think of a reply. A reason that she couldn't. I didn't think it was a good idea. Not for her sake or for the sake of the podcast. "Please, Katie?" She sounded desperate.

"I'll speak to Sophie," I said, pulling my phone out of my pocket and inputting a new contact. I handed it to her, inviting her to type her number in.

"Thank you." She wiped the tears from her cheeks with the palm of her hand, smearing a dark streak of mascara across her face. "I just want people to hear James's side. I want to tell his story." She started crying again. I nodded. Whatever Claire was going to say, I felt sure it wouldn't be James's story. I don't think they were ever close enough for her to know his story. I smiled sympathetically. My trainers slid into the gravel as I turned to leave. I was nearly at the cottage when my phone pinged through a message from Sophie. *Early listener figures are in— Katie, it's off the scale!!*

Sophie wasn't home when I got back to the cottage. She had probably gone to the pub with Tom to celebrate. I was tempted to walk down and join them, but I was exhausted. Every bit of my body felt tired, but I knew sleep wouldn't be coming anytime soon. My head was awash with unanswered questions. Untethered memories skipped between my thoughts, making it hard to focus.

Since we started this, there was an uncertainty that had niggled at me every day. Questions that had bothered me since we started this investigation. What if we don't find out who killed Lacey? What if nobody ever does? What if all this has been for nothing?

Tara would be here tomorrow to talk about Lacey. New information to add to the ever-growing pile. I climbed the stairs wired and agitated. It was still light outside, still early. Just as I reached the top step, I heard the click of the latch lifting on the front door. I looked down expecting to see Sophie. It was Tom. He hadn't noticed I was there. For a split second I considered edging unseen to my room.

"Hi," I said before I could change my mind. His head snapped up and he stood there, staring at me. "Where's Sophie?" I asked.

"Still at the pub. Do you want a drink?" He headed for the kitchen.

"Um... what here?" I wondered if he was suggesting going back to the pub. Tom didn't answer. I heard the fridge open and the clink of a glass bottle being placed on the worktop. I waited, unsure if I should go down.

"Katie?" he called. I went cautiously downstairs. Tom was pouring two glasses of white wine. He held one out to me. Our fingers touched for the briefest of moments as I took the drink, carefully avoiding eye contact. He returned to the living room. His own glass in one hand and the bottle of wine in the other. His face looked dark and troubled, like he had a lot on his mind. I followed him through. Perching awkwardly on the sofa opposite. We both concentrated on the contents of our glasses for a while. I rubbed my thumb backward and forward along the bottom edge, waiting for him to speak.

"Are you going to stay at the flat?" I asked. Tom nodded.

"I just wanted to check we have everything we need for the recording tomorrow." He dipped his head toward the pile of equipment in the corner of the room.

"Are you OK?" My voice was a little above a whisper. Tom was silent for a minute.

"We both saw it coming—it's not going to be a big dramatic breakup. Don't worry, we won't let it get in the way of the podcast."

"I'm sorry," I said, looking down at my glass. I could tell that he had lifted his head, watching me. We sat there in silence. The only sound was the occasional sips we took of our wine. It should have been uncomfortable, but it felt strangely familiar.

"What are you going to do?"

"I think it's already done," he said, giving me a wry smile.

I nodded. There was nothing to say.

Tom changed the subject. "Did you always *know*... about Jude?" he asked. For a moment I was taken aback by his question. It was obviously something that had been on his mind since we spoke the other night.

"About the cheating? I'm not sure. Probably." I tried to remember how it was at the beginning. "I used to tell myself that it didn't matter. That it didn't affect what we had... But it does matter. It chips away at you. It starts to destroy everything good."

"Would you do it differently if you had the chance?" He was genuinely interested.

"Probably not." We both laughed. Not much, but enough to take some of the pain out of it. Tom reached out and picked up the bottle of wine. He refilled his glass before offering it to me. I reached over and took it. We both drank for a moment. The silence began to feel heavier. I knew what was coming.

"Did you ever tell Jude about us?" I felt the blush creep up my neck. I liked that he used the word *us*. It made it sound like what happened had mattered. I shook my head, not able to look at him.

"Did you?" I asked, still staring at the blue and white striped rug.

"No. But I think he knew."

"We broke up the next day. The day that Lacey died," I reminded him.

"Was it because... because of what happened?" He looked like it was something he'd wanted to ask for a long time. I shook my head.

"Me and you... it was just one of many reasons me and Jude shouldn't have been together." Relief flooded his face. I willed him not to say it had been a mistake, that we shouldn't have done it. Of course, we shouldn't have done it. Jude was Tom's friend and my boyfriend. I still didn't want him to say that it had been a mistake.

The room had started to get dark. There were no lamps on, and the sun had disappeared quickly. Shadows began creeping across the floor as the light slunk away. I hadn't noticed until now. Tom leaned over to reach the bottle of wine by my feet. Our eyes locked. He froze, hand still holding the neck of the bottle. He was so close I could smell him, a familiar musky scent. My heart was pounding. He must have been able to hear it...

"I'm tired," I said suddenly. "I think I'm going to head up to bed." I stood up quickly and he returned to his seat. Tom looked surprised, but he didn't say anything. I finished my wine and took the empty glass to the kitchen. I said goodnight as I left the room.

"I'm sorry, Katie," Tom said softly. I stopped. My stomach twisted as an unexpected wave of emotion swept through me.

"I'm sorry too," I replied without turning around. My voice was a little above a whisper. I took my weary body up to my bedroom and quietly closed the door.

CHAPTER FORTY-THREE

The next morning, I woke up to the sound of raindrops hitting the windowsill outside. I opened the curtains before crawling back under the covers. The sky was a dark, moody shade of gray. Water spilled over the gutter above, cascading down the wall. I reached for my phone, scrolling mindlessly through my social media feed. One photo caught my eye. I paused the line of pictures sliding up the screen. It was a close-up of the wooden footbridge in the beach car park. An artistic shot. The color was almost sepia. The photo had been edited to deepen the grain lines of the weathered wooden posts, making it look aged and dramatic. Above it said @MostlySoph, Sophie's account. I read the caption: *The wooden footbridge, next to where Lacey's body was found. #pengully #smalltown #true-crime.* It was posted last night and already had over 32,000 likes.

I went onto Sophie's page and scrolled through her pictures. Over the last week she'd posted three photos promoting the launch of *Small Town*, something she'd never done with the podcast before. I searched the internet for information about the first episode release. To my surprise there were thousands of hits: forums, social media, news articles. At the top of the list was an article from the *Huffington Post*, added this morning: "New True Crime Podcast Set to Break UK Download Records." I read the short article.

> *Small Town is the work of social media royalty Sophie Miller and journalist Katie Chase. It delves into the narrow lives of the residents of a small Cornish town, a town that was shaken by the gruesome murder of nineteen-year-old Lacey Crew five years ago. Early indications suggest that* Small Town *is destined for big things. Overnight download figures show 262,000 listeners already and that number is rising fast...*

I read the figure three times before it sank in: 262,000 listeners. I closed the article on my phone. I didn't want to know any more. I felt dizzy when I thought of all the people that had heard us tell this story. "Narrow lives": Is that how we'd portrayed the people of Pengully? Not for the first time, I had a horrible sinking feeling that I'd done a terrible thing.

The first part of the morning passed quickly. Tom came over early and I made breakfast for us all. Sophie and Tom had seemed fine. Some of the awkwardness between them appeared to have lifted. At 10:30 a.m. there was a knock at the door. I opened it to an apprehensive-looking Tara. The rain was still coming down hard outside. She was soaked through. Tara shuffled in, looking awkward. She clung to her handbag with both hands, as though scared that someone would take it from her. Wet hair was stuck to both sides of her face and her mascara had run into a dark pool under her eyes.

"Did you walk up?" I asked. She nodded, her eyes darting nervously around the room.

"My husband had the car," she said glumly.

"You should have said. I would have come and picked you up..." She shook her head, small vigorous movements.

"I don't want my husband to know I'm doing this." I looked at Sophie. Neither of us wanted to remind her that once the podcast went out, it wouldn't just be her husband that would know. Everybody would know.

I offered to take her wet coat. She reluctantly slid it off her shoulders, moving her handbag from right to left so she didn't have to put it down. I hung it over the staircase. It had a damp mossy smell to it.

We'd already set the room up. Tom sat in his usual spot near the kitchen door, playing quietly with the mixing desk. He didn't acknowledge Tara's arrival, but she didn't seem bothered by it. "Do you have the money?" Tara asked rudely. Sophie wasn't fazed by her tone.

"The network's going to transfer it directly to your bank. Once we've got everything we need." There was a warning in Sophie's words. An expectation of what Tara would need to deliver in order to get her money.

"Shall we get started?" I asked brightly. Like a nurse gently coaxing their patient toward a procedure. Tara gave a tight expressionless nod, inching her way reluctantly into the room. Sophie indicated for her to sit down on the sofa. She perched close to the edge. Her old-fashioned bag sat in her lap.

"Tom is going to sort you out with some headphones and a mic... You'll get used to them really quickly. Just try to talk normally if you can," Sophie explained, as Tom came over with a headset for her. Tara placed it on top of her wet hair. Tom fiddled around with the attached microphone until it was positioned exactly right.

Tara fidgeted. Her soggy clothes clung to her wide frame. We sat down on the cushions we'd arranged on the floor, putting our own headsets on. "OK, Tara, Tom is going to run a few sound checks. We'll just chat so he can get the right levels."

I started. "Tara, how old are you?"

"Twenty-four," she answered sulkily after clearing her throat.

"OK. How long have you lived in Pengully?" I tried again, hoping for a longer answer.

"You know how long I've lived here for," she snapped.

I tried to keep the irritation out of my voice. "Are you married?" I remembered her pleasure in the shop when she'd shown me her ring. I hoped that this line of questioning would break her hostility.

"I am," she replied cautiously. "I got married last August in Pengully Church. We had our reception in the function room upstairs in the Bull." She was gathering pace. "We were going to have it at the Carmen... but to be honest, it was a bit of a rip-off. Just as good at the pub and saved us loads... no offense." I dismissed her apology with a brush of my hand, encouraging her to carry on. "Julia Humphries did the flowers. Do you remember Julia?" She didn't wait for my reply. "Anyway, they were amazing. Everyone said so... said it was the best wedding they'd *ever* been to." Tara spoke quickly, each word running into the next. "Anyway, the dress... I thought it was going to be a disaster, you see the..."

I let Tara talk on, her words just background noise. I caught Sophie's eye. Our faces remained expressionless, but there was an understanding between us. We'd let her finish her story, before starting the recording.

We waited for the tiniest of gaps in Tara's monolog before starting. "Welcome to *Small Town*," Sophie began. I looked up to see Tara recoil a little. The reality of what she was about to do striking her suddenly. I knew how she felt.

"Five years ago, Lacey Crew was murdered." Pause. "She was murdered in Cornwall, in a small town, by the beach." Pause. "Nobody was ever arrested, and no official charges were ever brought." Pause. "Lacey Crew was nineteen years old." We could have used the intro from the other episodes, but Sophie liked to record it from scratch each time. Authenticity was important to Sophie. "In this episode, we're speaking to one of Lacey's closest friends—Tara Haywood." Tara shrunk back into the sofa, trying to make herself disappear. "Can you tell us about Lacey?" Sophie asked her.

Tara hesitated, her jaw moved up and down, but no sound came out. I turned to look at her, smiling encouragement. "Lacey was my best friend," she croaked. Gone was her broad Cornish accent. She'd replaced it with something awkward and artificial. "We did everything together, ever since primary school. Lacey was beautiful. If she'd still been alive, she would have been one of my bridesmaids. I got married last year..." she explained to the listeners. I feared Tara was going to launch into more wedding stories. I quickly intervened.

"Is it true that Lacey had broken up with her boyfriend, James, the day she died?" I could feel Tom and Sophie's eyes on me. Tara stalled mid-sentence.

"She didn't... I'm not..." She gave up, slowly nodding at me. I made a circular motion with my hand, indicating that she needed to answer out loud. "Yes. Lacey broke up with James that day," she confirmed, glaring at me with undisguised contempt. For a moment, I thought she might leave.

"Do you know why?" I asked.

"No." I thought I was going to have to prompt her again, when she started to explain. "Lacey had met someone else. She wouldn't tell us who. I got the impression that, whoever it was, she liked them. Really liked them. I'd never seen her like that before," Tara said. Sophie's head shot up. This was brand-new information, information that not even the police knew.

CHAPTER FORTY-FOUR

"Do you know how long she'd been seeing this new man?"

Tara shook her head. I pointed to my own headphones, reminding her to speak her responses. "No, she never said, but I don't think it was long. Maybe two or three months?" Sophie's pen moved quickly across the page making notes.

"Did you tell the police about James and Lacey breaking up?" Tara would have no reason to protect James.

"No... I didn't." Tara looked trapped. She crossed and uncrossed her legs, looking down at her bag.

"Why, Tara? I don't understand..." I told her.

She squirmed uncomfortably in her chair. "Because they thought it was one of us." Her breathing was getting faster. Tara was starting to panic. "You saw what they did to James. We told the police as little as possible. We were all scared we'd be next..."

"OK, OK," I soothed. I needed to keep her calm, or we might lose her. "Tara? Can you tell us what happened that night? The night Lacey died?" I needed to see if her recollection matched Jude's version of events. She looked over at Sophie. I could tell she was deciding whether it was worth the money, whether she really needed to do this. Sophie's face was firm and unblinking. Tara took a deep breath and started. It was obviously worth the money.

"Me and Polly had gone to the beach early that day. We helped Danny set everything up. People started arriving at about 8 p.m., but me and Polly were there from the start..." she said proudly. "Lacey was working that night. She came down as soon as she finished..."

"Me and Polly left the beach around ten-thirty. They were in the car park—Lacey and James. They were arguing... Jude was trying to calm them down."

"What were they arguing about?" Sophie interjected.

"I don't know." Sophie raised her eyebrows in disbelief. "Honestly, I've no clue what they were arguing about. The breakup I guess." She looked like she was telling the truth.

"James was so angry, angrier than I'd ever seen him, but Lacey didn't care anymore. We left to go to the pub: me, James, Jude and Polly. Lacey wouldn't come. We tried to make her, but she just wouldn't." Tara's bottom lip quivered. "She just sat on the wall, looking at her phone. She didn't even say goodbye." Tara's bottom lip quivered. "A little while later Jude found her in the car park."

There was a whole section of her story missing.

"Did you and James leave the pub at the same time as Jude and Polly?" The color started to drain from her face. Her eyes flashed wildly around the room, looking for a way out.

Tara didn't answer. She sat there miserably, wringing her hands together. Sophie put her pen down. She looked at me, wondering where this was leading. Tara looked up, resigning herself to the inevitability of what was coming. I told her what I knew.

"Jude and Polly disappeared almost as soon as you got there, didn't they? When they came back into the bar a few minutes later, you and James were gone. They searched the pub, but there was no sign of either of you." I didn't want to corner her, but it needed to be said.

"Were you with James at the time Lacey was murdered?" She stared at her hands. "Tara, you're the only person that can tell us where he was." I spoke quietly, pleading with her to finally let it go.

"*Why?* What does it matter now? He's dead. They're both dead. Nothing I say is going to change that..." Tara was close to shouting. She pushed her face into her hands. Loud sobs shook her body. Nobody spoke. Tom caught Sophie's eye. Silently asking if they should stop the recording. Sophie shook her head and looked away.

I was about to try again when she spoke, her voice so low that Sophie had to ask her to speak up a little. She cleared her throat, and the words came back a little stronger.

"You don't get it... Lacey could be horrible to James. I know he had a temper, but she didn't care about him. Not really." She looked at me, like I might be the only person that would understand.

"About a year before she died, Lacey had an abortion." My head snapped up. I looked at Sophie who nodded calmly, urging her to go on. "I wasn't sure because she never said, but I got the impression that the baby wasn't James's. I know for a fact that she never told him about it." This was what she'd come here to tell us.

"Do you have any idea whose baby it might have been?" Sophie asked. I shifted uncomfortably on my cushion.

Tara shrugged. "I'm pretty sure she wasn't seeing anyone. No one special anyway. The new guy came much later. All I know is she couldn't get it done fast enough... See? She was *horrible* to him. She didn't deserve him. You of all people knew what she was like, Katie..." She was triumphant, expecting to find an ally in me.

I stared at her coldly. "Was she upset about the abortion?" I asked.

"I guess," she replied mildly, unaware of the change in atmosphere. "She was pretty weird about it for a while."

"Did you go with her, Tara? Did *anyone* go with her?" She shrugged. I placed my hands on the back of my neck, interlacing my fingers and exhaling loudly. I couldn't do this.

"Tom, we need to edit that out... We need to edit it *all* out." It was clumsy and aggressive, but I didn't care. Sophie was about to argue, but the look on my face made her bite back the words. The listeners didn't need to know about Lacey's abortion. They didn't need to know that she was all alone.

Acid rage was rising up from my stomach. I had to work to keep my voice even. "The abortion had nothing to do with that night, Tara..." I knew what she was trying to do.

Tara's cheeks flushed red. She hovered on the edge of the chair, like she might leave at any moment. Fingering her watch, one hand still held tightly to the top of her handbag. Sophie shot me a warning look, but I wasn't stopping, not now.

"James frightened her, didn't he? Jude said he had to *physically* pull him away from her that night in the car park." I was getting louder, emotion threatening to spill over. "You were her *friend*, Tara," I added more quietly. Tara screwed up her face like she might cry again. She thought that I would understand. Understand what it was like to be shut out by Lacey.

Moments passed and no one said anything. I thought it was over, but a minute later she spoke. But now her words were flat and her eyes stared dead ahead.

"When we got to the pub, Polly took Jude out the back. I knew she would. Me and James bought a drink... We left after about ten minutes."

"Why did you leave the pub, Tara?" I could tell from Sophie's tone that she was running out of patience.

Tara started to cry again, tears of self-pity. "Because... I wanted James. *I* wanted him. Lacey treated him like shit. He deserved to be happy," she wailed. "When we left the pub, we walked around the back of the dunes. We didn't even *go* to the car park..." She laughed, but it was a bitter hollow sound.

"Why? Why would you leave your friends and go wandering around the dunes at night... in the pouring rain?" Sophie was pushing hard.

"We had *sex*... OK?" she shouted. The room fell silent. Tara's anger seeped away the moment the words left her mouth. She sat frozen. The only sound was her slow, shallow breathing. I tried to speak, but I couldn't think of a single thing to say. Sophie took over.

"You and James had sex," she stated, letting the sentence hang in the air. "Was it up in the dunes?" Tara nodded mutely.

"Yes?" Sophie prompted.

"Yes," Tara added. "I told him how much I liked him... It just happened. Afterward, we walked back over the dunes to the party. We'd only been back a few minutes when Polly came back. You see? James *couldn't* have done it. He was with me the *whole* time." Her chest swelled as she tried to find a way out. She was unable or unwilling to grasp the magnitude of what she'd done.

"Why didn't you tell the police?" I spoke without feeling. I was going through the motions now. I no longer cared what Tara had to say.

"Me and James agreed. I begged him not to say anything. Can you imagine what people would have said?" Tom stood up. A look very close to hatred passed his face. His features were contorted with pain as he strode across the room, banging the front door closed as he left. Tara flinched at the noise.

"Did you not think about talking to the police later on... after James... killed himself?" Even Sophie was struggling to hide her frustration.

She shrugged. "What would have been the point?"

"*Tara*, everyone thought that James had *killed* her." I was breathless with shock. I couldn't hold it in anymore. How could she be so calm, knowing what they'd done? Or rather, what they hadn't done.

"OK..." Sophie raised the palms of her hands. "...I think we've got everything we need. Thank you." Sophie's words were clipped and final. Tara looked around, surprised that it was all over. She seemed almost disappointed. As Tara stood up to leave, Sophie went to get her coat that I'd hung on the banister at the bottom of the stairs. Underneath was a visible puddle of water from where it had dripped. As Tara climbed into her soggy jacket, Sophie remembered something.

"Did you know that Lacey had glamour photos taken a few months before she died?"

"God, I'd forgotten all about that." Tara giggled. "Yeah, she had them done in some studio near Broxley. I went with her. It wasn't that long after she'd had the abortion." Tara was blasé. "I've no idea why she wanted them. It was like she was trying to prove something. I don't know... prove that she could.

"It was weird. We got there and she was mad keen to do it. Took her clothes off straight away, like it was nothing. Ten minutes later, she completely freaked out. Got dressed and ran out of there as quickly as she could. I tried to talk to her about it afterward, but she wasn't interested." Tara was shuffling toward the door. Sophie blocked her way.

"One of those photos ended up in a national tabloid. Any idea how that might have happened?" Tara didn't seem to notice the accusation in Sophie's words.

"No idea. To be honest, I didn't even know she had copies of the photos." I joined them by the front door. "So, will I get the money?" Tara asked.

"You'll get your money," replied Sophie coldly.

"Do you want a lift home?" I asked her. It was the last thing I wanted to do, but the rain was coming down in sheets. Tara gave a stiff shake of her head. I leaned against the doorframe and watched her walk along the gravel drive in the rain. I breathed in the cool salty air for a moment, letting water drops from the brickwork fall gently on my arms. I turned to Sophie and closed the door.

"I don't understand. Why didn't *James* tell the police about Tara? He would have had an alibi. The police might have had a chance of catching the real killer," I told her. Sophie shook her head sadly. She looked tired.

"I thought James killed her. I really did," she replied.

"If James didn't kill Lacey, then who the hell did?"

CHAPTER FORTY-FIVE

After Tara left, me and Sophie talked through what we had: the timeline, the witnesses. If it was someone Lacey knew, someone that was at the party that night, the number of possibilities was decreasing rapidly. "Do you think we should tell Rebecca Rush about James's alibi?" I asked Sophie. She considered this for a moment.

"No. I hate to agree with Tara, but what would be the point? James was never convicted of the crime. There isn't anything to exonerate." Sophie spoke matter-of-factly, the gravity of what Tara had told us obviously lying more heavily on me. An hour later, Tom walked back through the door. He looked less angry, but his forehead was still creased in an anxious line. He seated himself on the sofa behind me.

"How much of that did you already know?" At first, I thought he was talking to Sophie, before I turned around to see him looking at me. I shrugged.

"I only knew what Jude told me. That James and Tara had left the pub together that night, right before Lacey's body was found." He nodded. It was clear that Tom knew nothing of this part of the night. I'm not even sure if he knew they'd been to the pub. It was hard to read his expression, but I think maybe it was disappointment.

"I saw James's parents the other night. My Mum and Dad invited them over for dinner." I'd been waiting for a good time to bring this up. "Claire Penhaligan wants to talk to us. She wants to tell James's side of the story."

Sophie was about to answer when Tom spoke. "Claire Penhaligan wouldn't know James's side of the story if it smacked her in the face." He echoed thoughts that I'd had. Sophie ignored him.

"Is she happy to be recorded?"

"I think so. She seemed pretty desperate to talk to us. Do you want me to arrange it?"

"Do you mind? A job has come up. It's just a couple of days, but I'll need to go back to London. I'm leaving on Sunday. I'll be back by Tuesday at the latest. We can record all the forensic stuff from the police later today. Then Tom can edit it along with episode four... which will be mainly Tara's story." She spoke like he wasn't in the room. Tom was behind me, so I couldn't see his face. I didn't need to. This was the first he'd heard about a job.

The weekend passed slowly. Me and Sophie moved around the cottage like ghosts, passing near to each other, hiding in our own corners, getting on with work as best we could. Tom stopped by for a few hours to work on the edits. We recorded episode three. Presenting the forensic evidence and the police view of what happened, or at least Rebecca Rush's view of what happened. The episode went well, a nice neat link from my version of the night to Tara's, which Tom would later edit.

On Sunday evening, a car came for Sophie, a silver executive-style sedan. She slipped quietly down the stairs, poking her head around the kitchen door. "I'm off now," she said.

"I hope it goes well," I replied. It all felt strangely formal and detached. We briefly hugged. She wore a blazer and baggy jeans; an expensive weekend bag was slung over her shoulder. They weren't clothes that I recognized.

There was a time when I knew everything she owned.

"I'll see you on Tuesday," she told us. Tom was finishing yesterday's edit. Hunched over a laptop on the coffee table. He lifted his hand briefly, before going back to his screen. Sophie closed the door behind her and I returned to my room. An hour or so later I heard Tom leave. He didn't say goodbye.

On Sunday night I received a message from Megan. *Do you fancy a coffee this week?* she asked. I replied quickly, surprised that I was looking forward to seeing her. *Would love to. Will message in a couple of days. x* I thought about telling her that I knew about Jude. But I realized it was no longer any of my business. The friendship was fledgling, but it had the beginnings of something good. Megan seemed interested in me, in what I had to say. I don't think it's something I've had for a while.

Me and Mum took the dogs to the beach in the morning. The heavy rain from the weekend had finally stopped and the low hazy cloud cover looked to be clearing. The sun would be back this afternoon. "I'm sorry about the other night... about the Penhaligans," Mum said as we strolled aimlessly along the edge of the shore.

"It's fine," I told her. It *was* fine. But I still felt troubled by the way that Richard had dealt with the accusations about Michael. I know it was just business. People often have another side to them. I just never thought that Richard did.

The spaniels bounded through the waves. Chasing each other in circles, leaving spirals of footprints across the wet sand. Morti occasionally walked beside me. His nose touching my hand to remind me he was there. "He really likes you." My Mum smiled, looking affectionately at the dog's wet curly head.

"I like him too." I laughed, tousling his hair.

"I was reading about *Small Town* today," she began carefully. "It sounds like it's been quite a hit. Katie, I know I wasn't exactly over the moon about you doing this, but... You do know how proud of you we are, don't you?"

"Of course." I smiled at her. Some of the worry on her face seemed to fall away and her shoulders lifted a little. As we wandered back up the beach, I realized how different I felt. The initial dread and fear I'd had about coming back had mostly passed. It hadn't been entirely replaced, but the longer I stayed, the more my uneasiness receded. It was beginning to feel like home again.

CHAPTER FORTY-SIX

Sophie had made me copies of her notes. In the afternoon, I took them up to my room, trawling through the handwritten pages for answers. They were incredibly thorough. Her bullet points gave shape to the thoughts floating aimlessly around my head. By early evening, I'd added to the notes with my own scrawls: A new timeline based on Tara and Jude's recollection of events. Key questions that needed addressing and a meagre list of potential suspects. I put my pen down and looked at what I'd achieved. Still no closer to finding out the truth, but I felt like I was moving forward, finally making a contribution.

It was early evening. The low sun prickled through the trees outside my window. I picked up my phone, scrolling through my contacts until I came to Claire Penhaligan's number. I carefully composed a text. *I've spoken to Sophie and we'd like to talk to you on the podcast. Let me know what times are good for you and we can arrange something.* After pressing send, I stared at my phone for a couple of minutes, awaiting a reply.

My stomach growled loudly with hunger. I crept downstairs in search of food. On the kitchen side was a half-eaten loaf of bread. I roughly cut off two slices and placed them in the toaster, before taking a cold bottle of chardonnay from the door of the fridge. "Can you pour me one?" I jumped at the sound of Tom's voice.

"Sorry, I did knock. I just need to grab a few bits... I should have texted."

"No, it's fine." I tried to return his smile. I retrieved two glasses from the overhead cupboard. We were so close in the small cottage kitchen he was almost touching. I placed the glasses in front of me and concentrated on the bottle. The sound of the long slow stream of wine seemed magnified in the tiny space. I pretended not to feel my hand shake or the presence of his body behind me. I turned, holding the filled glass out toward him. As he took it, I felt my breath catch in my chest.

"Kate, I need to..." he started, his voice was low and soft. A loud banging broke the tension and we both looked up in unison. Three slow firm raps on the front door. We each waited for the other to move. Finally, Tom went slowly toward the door. Before he got there, the knocking started again. This time it didn't stop. He moved quickly now, lifting the latch and swinging open the door. It was Danny. He was stood on the doorstep wearing an old stained gray T-shirt. His hair was disheveled, and his face gleamed with perspiration. A six-pack of beer hung by his side from his finger.

Danny walked into the cottage without saying a word. Tom closed the door behind him, watching, waiting for him to say something, but he didn't. His eyes slowly panned around the room, taking in his surroundings. He looked like he had no idea how he'd got here. I looked at Tom. He didn't know why Danny was here any more than I did. He sat down, placing the beer on the coffee table. He'd been drinking, but I don't think he was drunk. Not like he was the other night.

I quietly left the room, returning to the kitchen. I hoped leaving them alone would make it easier for Danny to talk, it seemed to be the reason he was here. I leaned against the kitchen side, clutching hold of my wineglass. I tilted my head toward the door, listening for conversation. "Are you OK, mate?" Tom asked eventually. I think he'd moved to the sofa opposite Danny. His voice sounded close. No answer. "Look, Danny, if there's something you want to..."

"I need to tell you something." Danny's voice was low and gravelly, like he'd not spoken in a while. "Tom, it's fucking awful... It's all my fault." He sniffed loudly. I think he was crying. Tom spoke calmly, but I could tell he was worried.

"Danny, what is it? Did you do something?" There was silence. I guessed Danny had answered with a nod or a shake of his head. A pause so long, I'd started moving toward the living room. Until Danny's words rooted me firmly to the spot.

"Lacey was raped." The air locked in my throat as I held my breath. I could hear him crying now. High-pitched grunts of sadness. Tom said nothing. The magnitude of what he'd just heard made him incapable of consoling Danny. I walked the last few paces into the room on trembling legs. Danny sobbed loudly into his hands, not noticing that I'd entered. Tom looked relieved to see me, his face searching mine in desperation.

"Can you tell us what happened?" I was hoping to coax him from his hands. Danny's head sprang up, looking wild and confused. He nodded but didn't say anything. Tom rose suddenly from the sofa.

"Katie, can I talk to you?" He nudged his head toward the kitchen. I followed him. "Do you think we should record this?" he asked in an urgent whisper. "If what he's saying is true, aren't we going to need it?" At that moment, Danny moved into the room, leaning his large body against the doorframe.

"I want to do your podcast... you know, speak on it. Everyone should know what he did." He looked like a child as he wiped his nose along his sleeve. His eyes drifting in and out of focus. I looked at Tom, thinking for a moment. I needed more time.

"Danny, I don't think we should record this." I spoke with more confidence than I felt. "Talk to us, of course, but once you've spoken about it on the podcast, you can't ever go back." He was too vulnerable. It would be wrong to expose him to thousands of listeners like that. Danny looked trustingly at Tom, waiting for his verdict.

"It's true, mate," he told him, placing a hand on his shoulder and guiding him back through to the living room. Tom gave me a look of gratitude before turning his attention back to Danny. This is not what Sophie would have done, but I would have to deal with that another day. I went upstairs to retrieve my notes and a pen. I wanted to make sure we got all the information, even if we didn't have a recording. I sat down next to Tom, our knees lightly touching.

"Danny, can you tell us how you know that Lacey was raped?" I started.

"I was there." We sat patiently, waiting until he was ready. "It was just over a year before she died. We were working at the Carmen. Lace had stopped glass collecting and had started doing shifts behind the bar. I hadn't been promoted to manager, not then. I was still working on the restaurant side, so I didn't see her much."

"Did you see a lot of her outside of work?" He nodded miserably. He looked so tired. The dark shadows under his eyes, against his pale complexion, gave him a haunted look.

"We saw each other a lot... She was my friend." His face scrunched up and the corners of his lips turned down as he began to cry again. "Nobody knew her like I did, not even James." Danny pressed the heels of his palms into his eyes, frustrated by his own tears. "She used to get a bit of hassle working behind the bar... you know, from blokes. Usually it was just banter, nothing she couldn't handle.

"One Friday night, we were closing everything down. All the customers had gone. I was wiping down tables, clearing glasses and stuff. Then I saw him. Coming out of the staff room, tucking his shirt into his trousers. His face was all red. He was actually panting he was so out of breath." Danny looked repulsed as he conjured the image in his head.

"Who was it, Danny?" I asked. I could hear a tremble in my voice, scared of what he might say.

"It was Michael Penhaligan."

CHAPTER FORTY-SEVEN

Suddenly it all made sense. "What happened, Danny?"

"I actually joked with him," he recalled bitterly. "I said, 'The toilets are back there, mate.' He was sorting himself out, you know? Straightening his clothes up. It was obvious he was pissed. Michael just laughed. Slapped me on the back as he walked past. When I'd finished up, I went to the staff room. I was locking up that night. I just assumed everyone had left—including Lacey. But she hadn't.

"When I opened the door, I saw her. She was in the corner on the floor, half hidden by one of the chairs. All I could see were her bare legs. I knew something was wrong straight away, before I even saw her face. I went over to her, she was curled up on her side, staring straight ahead. She wasn't even crying. There was a sort of blankness about her. I can't even explain it. Like someone had reached in and taken all the life out of her." Danny looked at the floor, picturing her face. A scene he must have played over and over in his mind.

"Did she tell you what had happened?" Tom asked him.

"Not that night. She couldn't talk, Tom. She couldn't do anything. I carried her to my car and drove her home. I was so worried, man. I'd never seen her like that. I thought she was having some kind of breakdown. When I got to her house, it was only her sister at home. Proper snide little cow she was. She took Lacey inside and told me to go. I bet she enjoyed seeing Lacey like that. Finally got her chance to be superior." He snarled. This wasn't a side of Megan I knew or had ever known.

Nobody spoke. "I should have done more. I should have protected her." He looked devastated. "I should have killed that evil bastard." His fists were clenched tightly. "A couple of days later I went to see her. That's when she told me.

"Lacey had been getting ready to go home that night. You know, getting her stuff together in the staff room. Michael had come in. She said he just joked with her at first. The usual shit he used to say to the female bar staff. Then he asked her for a kiss. Lacey told him no. Said she kept saying it, but he was insistent. She just wanted to go home. So she walked over and kissed his cheek. You know, harmless, just mucking around. That's when he grabbed her. He grabbed her so hard she had bruises all up her arms. She showed them to me.

"The next thing she knew, he was forcing himself on her. Lacey told me he didn't say a word when it was over. Just got up and left, like nothing had happened. She blamed herself. Kept saying all she'd wanted to do was go home. I tried to talk her into going to the police, convince her that it was the right thing, but Lacey wouldn't listen. Said she just wanted to put it behind her, move on with her life." Danny leaned back. A sort of calmness seemed to have enveloped him. A relief from the burden of keeping this secret for such a long time.

"Did James know what his dad had done?" I asked.

He shook his head. "No. Lacey told him his dad had tried it on, but she didn't tell him what had happened. Some of the bar staff had got together to make a formal complaint to your dad, you know, about Michael's behavior in the bar. Lacey told James about it. Said she was going to make a complaint too. The rape wasn't mentioned, but it was a start. If he'd just supported her... it might have given her the confidence she needed to take it to the police.

"James wouldn't listen. He begged her not to say anything. Spineless prick. Do you know the worst thing? James knew. He knew what an asshole his dad was. He knew what he was capable of, but he chose to protect himself." Danny reached over to the bottles of beer, ripping one away from its cardboard holder and looking around for something to open it with. Tom went to the kitchen to get him a bottle opener.

"Danny," I began cautiously. "Did you know that Lacey had an abortion? It would have been a couple of months after she was raped. Tara told us that Lacey was incredibly upset. That she couldn't be sure, but she got the impression that the baby wasn't James's." I looked at Danny's pitiful face. It was etched with the same pain I'd seen all those years ago, right after she died. It was then that I realized Danny hadn't just cared for Lacey as a friend. He'd been in love with her. Danny's bottom lip quivered as he shook his head. He hadn't known about the abortion. Tom returned with the bottle opener. He took the beer from Danny's limp, lifeless hands and opened it before giving it back to him.

"She didn't tell me... There was this time, after it happened, it was only a few weeks, but me and Lace weren't really talking." He looked like he didn't want to carry on. "It was my fault. I'd put pressure on her, you know, to go to the police. I was so angry, so fucking angry that I didn't know what to do with it. I ended up putting my shit on her. I think that's why she didn't tell me about the abortion. *She* was protecting *me*." His jaw was clenched in agony. "Lacey had to deal with being pregnant by her boyfriend's dad and all I did was throw my weight around."

He was consumed with guilt. "A few weeks later it had blown over between us. I apologized and we didn't talk about it again. Michael didn't drink in the bar anymore, after all the complaints. Lacey tried hard to go back to normal, but she was never the same. She did this glamour modeling thing a little while later. Got photos taken at a studio. She was excited, you know, trying to show me she was over it."

"What happened to the photos, Danny?" I asked.

"No idea." He looked confused. "I never saw them. I don't know if she ever planned on using them for anything." Danny obviously had no idea what had happened on the photo shoot.

"Did you ever speak to James about it?"

"Yeah." Danny shook his head in disbelief. "I told him what his dad had done, a few months after Lacey died. I told him everything. I knew he believed me. He didn't even seem that surprised. I tried to get him to have it out with his dad, but he wouldn't. He wouldn't do a single fucking thing. While the rest of us were destroyed by what happened to Lacey, he just carried on living his cushy life up in the big house..." It was an unfair thing to say. James was devastated by what happened to Lacey. I stayed silent. "I don't know how I stopped myself from beating the shit out of Michael. I used to see him about sometimes. He knew that I knew. I could tell by the way he looked at me."

Danny looked deflated, like he had nothing left. He drew the bottle of lager to his mouth and gulped hungrily until half of it was gone. The quiet had become uncomfortable, for me anyway. I remembered my notes. I tried to write words on the page, but my hand shook and I struggled to hold the pen.

Danny drank one more mouthful, before setting the bottle down on the coffee table and wiping his chin on the back of his hand. "A couple of weeks before she died, Lacey brought up the rape. I was shocked. I didn't think she'd ever talk about it again. She told me she was thinking about going to the police, reporting Michael. There was something different about her, she seemed stronger. I really think she would have done it." Me and Tom exchanged glances.

There was something I needed to ask him. "Who do you

think killed Lacey?" He sighed, running his hand through his hair.

"Ah, man, I don't know. One thing I do know, as much as I hated the guy, there was no way that James did that to her." Danny seemed reluctant to leave. He continued sipping from his bottle. A man quite used to drinking in silence.

"Why didn't you go to the police about Michael after Lacey died?" I asked quietly.

A tear slowly ran down Danny's cheek. "I nearly did. So many times. But it wasn't mine to tell. Keeping her secret felt like it was the last thing I could do for her."

CHAPTER FORTY-EIGHT

I nodded sadly at his misplaced loyalty. I was about to go upstairs, leave him and Tom to have some time. As soon as I left my seat, he stood up as though accepting his cue to go. He lurched toward the remaining bottles, picking them up with a gentle clang of glass. I led him toward the front door. He shuffled behind me, hunched by tiredness and emotion. His shoes barely left the floor. I said goodbye but he didn't hear me. He trudged out into the night, the same way he'd come in. Only this time, heading toward the beach. I watched him leave. "Do you think we should drive him home?" I asked Tom.

To my surprise Tom was right behind me. I turned around, not realizing how close he was. His face there, shadowed by the dim light. I took a small step back.

"What are we going to do? About... all this," I added hastily. My mouth felt dry. Tom didn't speak. His unblinking eyes didn't leave mine.

"If Michael knew that Lacey was going to the police about him, it gives him a motive to kill her. In fact, so far, he is the *only* person we've found with a motive to kill her." I tried to press on, ignoring the intensity of Tom's stare, how it was making me feel.

He leaned in. Our lips were so close they were nearly touching. I could feel his soft warm breath on my mouth. I pulled away, my heart racing. There didn't feel like there was enough air in my chest to breathe. I edged around his frame toward the stairs. Walking steadily up, step by step. Trying to move normally. I knew he was watching me. My legs felt so heavy, they were hard to lift. I didn't look back when I reached the top, just went to my room and closed the door behind me.

My hand paused on the handle as I rested the back of my head against the door. I couldn't do this. I wasn't sure if what was happening came from a place of lust or consolation or just nostalgia. Whatever it was, I couldn't do it.

I lay down on top of the bed, still fully clothed. I thought about Lacey. About her "perfect" life. For so long I thought she had everything. I wanted to cry when I thought about the pain she must have been in that last year. She had been let down by every single person in her life.

I turned onto my side and pulled my knees up to my chest. There had always been something between me and Tom, a sort of energy or connection between us. I suppose it had just been a teenage crush. He'd always been quiet. In a group of loud and confident characters I was drawn to his stillness. We had just started spending time together when Jude came along. Jude had consumed me. He had swallowed me up so entirely I barely knew who I was anymore. After that I stopped noticing Tom. Until the night I noticed him again.

The day before the beach party, I'd gone to the pub with Jude. It had been packed. Even with all the doors open it was hot. Sweaty bodies maneuvered around each other, trying to force their way to the bar. The beer garden was full. You couldn't see a single patch of grass. Picnic benches were covered in glasses, beer bottles and jugs, full and empty. The demand to clear was too much for the staff to keep up with.

People stood in small groups, iced drinks in hand, happily

pressed against one another. Jude hadn't stayed long. He'd left after about half an hour. I had no idea where he'd gone, I never did. There were lots of people from college in the garden that night. There had been no shortage of people to talk to. I circled the tables. Moving from person to person, catching up with friends. When I got to Tom's group, I stayed. He was there with James and some other guys I knew vaguely. Lacey and her friends were on the periphery, laughing and chatting. I stood next to him. Not really talking, not at first anyway. I'd glanced over a couple of times. We made eye contact and held on for longer than we should have. Goosebumps prickled up my arms like nettles.

It felt like nobody had noticed me in a really long time. For two years I'd played a supporting role to Jude. Just grateful for the part. For a little while that night, Tom had made me feel like I mattered, like I was important. Looking back, I'm not sure it really had anything to do with Jude *or* Tom. It was about me. The wine and the heat had given way to a giddy sort of hedonism. I'd felt it bubbling up inside of me. A dizzying feeling of freedom from myself and my insecurities.

As it got dark, fairy lights had turned on outside. Orange bulbs draped along the red brick wall that surrounded the garden. Everyone's face glowed from a day of sun and the reflection from the warm light. Music began playing. I didn't register the songs, just the low thud of the bass. I turned to Tom with my whole body. Shutting out the rest of the group from the conversation. We started talking in a way we hadn't done for a long time. Not like people who'd known each other their whole lives. He was confident. He'd made me laugh. I'd always thought he was quite shy, but he probably thought the same about me. Maybe this was who we really were. Or perhaps we both just got caught up in something that night, pretending we were other people.

Tom went to the bar to get me a drink. I'd waited for him in the garden, stood there alone in my strappy yellow sundress. Once or twice, I looked at the faces around me. Trying to see if Jude had returned. Just before Tom came back, I checked my phone. A text from him that simply read, *See you tomorrow. J x* I'd shown it to Tom, a look of understanding passed between us. The thought of Jude coming back to the pub that night had kept us apart. Kept us in check. The text message had freed us. It had felt like taking my seat belt off in a speeding car.

The group we'd been with had dispersed. Scattered across the crowded garden. It was just the two of us. We'd chatted and flirted, shared stories about ourselves that neither of us knew. We were pushed closer together as people had passed with drinks, looking for friends. Eventually, we'd moved to the outer edge of the garden, into the shadows. We pretended we were looking for space. But we both knew what it was. Occasionally our bare arms would touch. The tiny shivers down my spine made me pull away. Until the time that I didn't pull away. The time that I decided to let it happen.

CHAPTER FORTY-NINE

Tom had moved out of his parents' house a few weeks before. He wasn't going away to college like the rest of us. He was about to start his sound engineering course at a technical school just down the road. He'd rented a cheap studio apartment above one of the shops on the high street. I hadn't seen it, but I'd heard people talking about it. He was the first of the group to get his own place. We were coming to the end of our last drink. Taking half sips to make it last longer, unsure of what was next. Tom had leaned in and spoken. "Do you want to come back to mine?" He hadn't said "for a drink" or "to call a taxi." There was no pretense. I'd nodded, scared that my voice would give me away. That it would show just how much I wanted him.

We went back inside the pub and left through the side door. We both looked up and down the dark empty street, checking the two-minute walk up the hill was clear, that we wouldn't be seen. As soon as we set off, Tom took my hand. It felt big and warm and safe. We'd walked up the road in silence.

I shivered with anticipation. Tom stopped at a narrow door, hidden between two shops. The peeling blue paint was visible under the streetlights. He unlocked it as I stood behind him, following him inside to the dark thin hallway. There was a steep staircase that led to Tom's flat. It was covered in a threadbare olive-green carpet. The shop took up the ground floor, so the hallway wasn't shared with any other properties. Tom closed the door to the street, leaving us in darkness. A security light flickered on at the top of the stairs, creating a dim glow in the passageway. I could just see the outline of his face and the shape of his body.

I was about to walk toward the light when Tom gently took hold of my wrist. He eased me against the wall. The palms of my hands touched the wallpaper. I fingered the soft raised bumps of the pattern like Braille. Tom moved slowly toward me. I could smell sweet apple cider on his breath.

He seemed taller standing there so close to me. He stopped. His head angled down toward mine. I thought he'd changed his mind for a moment. But he was checking. Checking to see if I was OK, that it was something I wanted too. I reached up to kiss him, to show him. Lightly at first. I felt the plumpness of his bottom lip between mine. Suddenly, there was an urgency between us. His body pressed me deeper into the wall. I could feel the top of his thigh between my legs as our kisses became faster, more certain.

My hands were on his smooth back, sliding under his thin T-shirt. I pressed my fingers along each tight muscle, drawing him farther toward me. He stepped back, pulling his top over his head in one swift movement. He looked down at my body. He moved quickly to the buttons that ran down the front of my dress. He undid them, one at a time. I had a moment to think about what was happening, to change my mind. I kept waiting for the pangs of guilt, for the little voice in my head that would tell me to stop, but it never came. Three buttons down, it was clear to him that I wasn't wearing a bra. He drew the straps down over my shoulders and I felt the thin fabric of the dress fall to the floor.

We both took a sharp intake of breath as he pressed into me again. Kissing me so deeply, I thought my legs would give way. My whole body was shaking with desire. It seeped through every part of me. Nothing had ever felt like this before. He hooked his fingers under the sides of my knickers, before easing them down over my hips. That's when I felt him. The hardness of him, right before he slipped inside me. It felt so good I nearly cried out.

When it was over, we lay on the floor. Sweating and panting, not saying a word. For a few minutes I felt euphoric. Contentment washed over me. Tom ran his hand up and down the curve of my spine. For that brief time, I felt so close to him. "Let's go upstairs," he'd suggested. I felt around in the dark for my dress. Pulling it over my head and fastening the buttons as we walked up the stairs.

I was never sure whether it was coming into the stark light of Tom's flat, or my sweaty-faced reflection in the mirror on the way in that had brought me back to reality. The last trickle of desire had washed away, and I'd been left with a feeling of emptiness. I'd tried to push past it, accepting Tom's offer of a drink. Kissing him back when he came over to me, fondly stroking loose strands of my hair. But I couldn't stay.

I'd apologized. I kept saying sorry over and over. I nearly tripped going back down the stairs I was so desperate to get out. I could see that Tom didn't understand what he'd done, but there was nothing I could do. As I walked quickly down the street, my clammy skin frozen against the cool evening breeze, I felt it all. All the guilt and regret came crashing down on top of me. It hit so hard I thought I might fall under the weight of it.

I'd worn my goodness like a thick coat for so long: a good girlfriend, a good daughter, a good student. One stupid reckless night had ruined my perfect record.

The next day I could still smell him on me. The longing returned like a punch to the stomach. That morning I went to

Jude's house. "I can't do this anymore," I told him. He'd sat silently on the sofa, rubbing his hand slowly over his stubble. "Jude, are you listening to me?" I snapped. He looked up. It was as if he were seeing me for the first time. He said nothing. I turned to leave. I was almost at the door when he spoke.

"I thought this was it... you and me. I thought it was forever." I think I was hoping it would make amends, ease my guilt. It didn't. I felt more alone than ever.

I'd wanted to speak to Tom, to explain. I was hoping to see him at the party later that day. I'd tried to catch his eye when he'd finally arrived that night. But he never came over. I think that was one of the reasons I'd got so drunk. I remember watching him leave, his tall lean body striding down the beach. He didn't even look back.

After Lacey was murdered, everything changed. It had seemed disrespectful to dwell on trivial things. All conversations had to carry weight, to reflect the magnitude of what had happened in Pengully. I tried to get Tom on his own in the weeks before I moved to London. It was clear he was avoiding me. Whenever we were in the same place, he made sure he was surrounded by people. A part of me had never stopped wondering what would have happened if I'd stayed that night.

Three years later Tom got together with Sophie. She'd gone back to his flat after the New Year's Eve party. The next day I'd asked her if Tom knew she was my friend. Sophie had winked, said they hadn't done much talking.

I tried to smile, be happy for her, but I felt sick. My insides knotted together with jealousy, even after all that time. When Tom and Sophie became a couple, he made sure that I wasn't around. We barely ever spoke. I think Sophie always assumed that we were never really friends. He was civil to me. But too much had happened. Too much time had passed for me to tell him how much I'd cared.

CHAPTER FIFTY

I heard Tom gently close the front door as he left. I let my eyes fall closed. Faces filled the darkness in my head as I began to drift. Images came thick and fast: The lights in the beer garden and the taste of sweet rosé. Tom's fingers slipping under the thin straps of my dress, the hardness of his body. Dried blood around my foot and wet hair stuck to her face. The blue jumper is hanging down over her tiny hands, and she's laughing. I'm not sure what she's laughing at. Then I realize, it's me. She's laughing at me.

I sat bolt upright in bed, my eyes squinting in the dark room as they tried to adjust. It was then that it came into focus. A realization that hit me like a brick to the side of the head. I knew who had given Lacey's photos to the press.

I was tempted to phone Tom and tell him, but I knew that would be a mistake. I tried to sleep, but I couldn't relax. My mind flitted back and forth between memories, past and present. I thought about Lacey as I furiously twisted under the bed clothes, trying to find a spot comfortable enough so that sleep would be inevitable.

I thought about the last year of her life. The awful things

that had happened to her. I'd hated Lacey for such a long time, for what she'd done to me, for all the hurt and humiliation she'd put me through at school. Years that should have been the best of my life. Years that I'd never get back. Even when she was murdered, some of that hatred had lingered. I realized, as I lay there blinking into the darkness, that all those feelings had gone now. I felt only sadness for the girl down the road. The girl who never got any older.

I thought about what Jude had said, about people around here not moving on from that time. I understood. I'd run 300 miles away and I hadn't moved on.

I must have eventually fallen asleep. The last time I remember looking at the clock it was 3:18 a.m. I woke up in a tangle of limp sweaty covers. The time said 9:23 a.m. The sun had crept around the sides of the closed curtains and the seagulls clucked contentedly to one another. My eyes were so tired they hurt to be open. I wanted to go back to sleep, but I knew what I had to do. Sophie would be back later today. I wanted to do this on my own. If I was right about the person who'd given the photos of Lacey to the press, it wasn't something I wanted on the podcast.

I forced myself out of bed and into some clothes. I should have showered. It would have woken me up, but this was something I needed to do now.

I headed toward the steep trail that led down to the beach. The path that cut through the grass had become overgrown. In just a week, it had grown to nearly knee height. My legs swished through the dewy blades, still damp from last night. By the time I'd reached the gate, the water had already seeped through the front of my trainers, making my toes wet.

The day was warm and airless, even by the sea. A hazy mist hung over Pengully, blocking the sun's full force. Once that burned off in an hour or so, it was going to be hot. The sand on the top half of the beach was dry. Tiny twigs from the woody roots of the dunes were scattered in places. They were brittle, crunching underfoot, showing how long it had been since the tide had come up this far. I headed for the town, wishing I'd brought my sunglasses. My tired eyes strained against the sparkling glare bouncing off the still water. I felt less confident now about what I was doing. In the early hours of the morning, it had seemed simple. Today, the thought of confrontation made my stomach churn in fear.

The town end of the beach was starting to get busy. Families were grouped behind windbreaks, marking their spot in the sand. A little girl walked just ahead of me, holding on to her mum's hand. Her dad was ahead, carrying a baby in a bright sling across his chest. The girl wore a blue swimsuit covered in tiny cartoon ponies. Her long dark hair was plaited down her back. She chatted sweetly to her mum about what they were going to do that day. She told her it had been the best holiday she'd ever had. They looked at her with so much pride I felt a lump forming in my throat.

I wondered why Mum and Richard had never had a baby, a child that was theirs. Richard had been a wonderful stepfather, but he must have thought about them having a baby of their own.

By the time I reached the footbridge, I'd almost changed my mind. I paused on the wooden deck, my hand resting on the soft warm rail. I'd spent so much time trying to be a person that doesn't make ripples, hiding behind a polite composed exterior. Staying in the shadows, scared of showing my whole self. Not this time, I thought. I walked determinedly across the car park. Up the hill, toward the top of town.

When I stood at the end of the road, looking at the identical houses, I struggled to remember which one it was. There were four homes to choose from. All but one of them had perfectly mowed lawns and weed-free borders. The bushes were neatly clipped and the windows sparkled. The second one in stood out. I went to the top of the path. Layers of varnish on the dark wood-colored window frames had peeled off in streaks. Green algae and moss had built up over many years along the gutters and the big windows were dirty, covered in a coating of salt that the onshore winds blew around the town every winter, even as high up as this.

I walked slowly down the path, across cracked paving stones filled with clumps of dandelions. I knocked on the door. There was the sound of movement from inside, a faint banging like furniture being moved. I waited a few seconds. I didn't think that anybody was coming. I was about to knock again when the door slowly inched open. She looked awful. Her long thinning hair had turned mostly gray. It hung in greasy clumps down her shoulders. Her puffy lined face looked blank. There was a deadness to her pale eyes, like she couldn't see me. "Hello, Mrs. Crew. I'm not sure if you remember me?"

CHAPTER FIFTY-ONE

Her gaze was fixed on a spot the other side of the road. She didn't seem to hear what I'd said. I tried again. "Is Megan here?" Lonni Crew's eyes, vacant and confused, slid to my face.

"Hmm?" she muttered. I was about to apologize, leave before I upset her. Then I heard a baby giggling.

"Can I come in?" Lonni didn't say a word, she just turned and shuffled back into the hallway. I followed her through. The door to the living room was open and the curtains were closed. The house was dark and stuffy. A faint smell of incense hung in the airless room. Lonni dragged her slippered feet in front of me. She wore a long flowing skirt that jangled softly as she moved, as though tiny bells were attached to it.

The living room led through to the kitchen. I could see natural light trying to escape around the edges of the half-open door. Lonni dropped heavily onto an old brown sofa, grunting awkwardly as she landed. She stared at a piece of material she had in her hands. It looked like a hairband of some kind. She absently wound it around her wrist, before lifting it to her face and stroking it against her cheek.

I walked toward the kitchen and heard the baby gurgle again. As I nudged open the door, I saw Megan. She was on the phone, her back to me. She sounded like she was talking to a client, discussing the timeline for a project. Mia sat in a high-chair, the remnants of fruit and crackers scattered over the tray. She looked at me, throwing her biscuit-covered fists in the air. Megan turned around, dropping the phone from her ear for a moment. She raised her index finger, asking me to wait. The telephone conversation continued in the same way for several more minutes.

I looked around the cluttered room. A dresser covered in photos, some in frames and some just propped up against the shelf. Certificates and scraps of paper, alongside children's crayon drawings. On every available surface were piles of paper and folders. Material samples and pencil sketches. This was obviously where Megan worked when she wasn't at the shop. The baby began to get frustrated. Pulling at her straps and making a low humming whine.

Megan finished her call. She retrieved a packet of wipes from the side and began cleaning Mia's hands and face. She knew I wasn't here for a coffee. "Can I ask you something?" My voice sounded controlled, but my heart was pounding in my chest. She turned to me, unsmiling. "You told me you found photos on Lacey's computer, photos of us. Did you find glamour photos of Lacey as well?" Megan smiled, slowly shaking her head. I couldn't read her expression.

"Is that what you came to ask me about, Katie? About my sister's naked photos?" She looked angry. I could see her chest rising and falling quickly. For a second, I thought I'd got it wrong. I felt the beginnings of embarrassment as my mind worked quickly on how to backtrack. Then she spoke again. "Yes, I found them. I had no idea she'd had them done. We weren't exactly sisters that told each other things." Her voice had softened, but the annoyance was still there.

"A little while after she died, Polly and Tara contacted me. They wanted to have a memorial for Lacey—I guess they thought they hadn't milked her funeral enough, so they wanted to do another one," she added bitterly. "I don't know why I went along with it. For Mum, I suppose. Once the funeral was over, she really struggled. They wanted me to find photos. Ones they didn't have.

"I looked through Lacey's computer, through her albums. There were hundreds of them. I didn't look at them all, I could easily have missed them..." I shifted my weight onto my other leg. I could feel it twitching with nerves. "There were about ten of them. They were so tacky." Megan winced at the memory.

"Did you show them to anyone?" I wanted to be wrong. I wanted Megan to have given the photos to someone else. For it to have been *them* that betrayed Lacey.

"At the beginning, journalists were calling every day. Emailing, knocking on the door, offering us money. A few weeks in and all that stopped. It became just another unsolved murder. The press lost interest when they realized there was nothing new to write about. One of the journalists was this guy called Jamie. We'd gone out a couple of times for drinks while he was here investigating." Her confidence waivered and she looked away. "I'm not sure how much time had passed, but after he'd gone back to London I phoned him. I liked him. I thought it was something more than it was. It was so awkward. He was surprised to hear from me. I was embarrassed, so I pretended that the photos were the real reason I'd called.

"I told Jamie I had a story for him." Mia was getting restless. Megan handed her a bunch of keys, which she took straight to her open mouth. She stroked the front of her daughter's downy head sadly. "I told him about the photos I'd found. I emailed them over to him and he called me back almost immediately. Said he wanted to print them, that he'd give me money for them. I could have changed my mind, told him I didn't want the photos in the paper. He gave me the option. I told him he could have them, do what he wanted with them. I didn't want the money."

"Why did you do it?" I asked quietly.

"Why?" Her voice was raised, there was a tinge of hysteria. "Because I could. Because, for the first time in my life, I wanted to be in control. I didn't want to keep her dirty little secret. She didn't deserve it," Megan spat. "I kept waiting to feel bad about it. Even now, I sometimes think that I'll wake up one day and feel sorry for what I did. I'm glad I gave him those photos. I actually smile when I think about that photo being in the paper, there for everyone to see." She had a crazed look on her face, she was almost shouting. Mia began to cry. She looked at her with an empty expression. I thought for a second, that she was just going to leave her to cry. Something switched and she reached in, lifting Mia out of her chair, gently shushing her until she quieted.

"Megan... did you kill Lacey?" She stared at me, shaking her head, like I didn't understand.

"No. I didn't kill Lacey. Every single day I wish she were still here. Do you know why? Because however much Lacey was the center of everything when she was alive, it was nothing compared to when she died. Do you know what my Mum's in there clinging to?" Megan pointed toward the living room. "It's one of Lacey's hats from when she was a baby. That's just today. Tomorrow it might be a photo and the next, one of her dresses. That's a good day for her. A bad day is when she slaps me. Tells me she wishes it had been me and not Lacey. I'm trapped here, Katie, don't you see? If Lacey were still alive, I'd be long gone."

"I'm sorry, Megan. Is there no one that can..."

"Help?" she snapped. "No, Katie. No one can help. This town isn't interested in people like me and Mum." A silence fell between us. I moved toward the door. "Are you going to include this in the podcast?" she asked.

"No," I told her, shaking my head as I left the kitchen. I said goodbye to Lonni. She was still sitting on the sofa, holding the hat to her face. She didn't reply as I stepped out onto the bright cul-de-sac. I had an overwhelming feeling of sadness. I thought about how many lives had been ruined that night five years ago.

CHAPTER FIFTY-TWO

When I got back, the cottage was empty. I went through to the kitchen. There was no sign of Sophie.

I went upstairs and ran a bath. The water fell noisily from the wide tap, like a shiny pond feature. I sat on the cool stone floor, reaching out to slip my socks off. I thought about what Megan had told me. Was it so unimaginable that she might have killed Lacey? She said herself that she was jealous of her, that she'd never regretted handing those photos over. There was something in the way that she told me, that made me think that she was telling the truth. It was almost defiance. I think that if she had killed Lacey, nothing would have stopped her from standing in that kitchen today and telling me how she'd done it.

The bath felt good. The water was already hot, but I topped it up until my skin itched with the heat. I slid my shoulders down the curve of the porcelain and immersed my head fully underwater. I swished my hair from side to side, like I'd done when I was little, pretending to be a mermaid. For those few moments underwater, I felt light and free. After an hour my skin had cooled and the bubbles had mostly disappeared.

I heard a bang from outside. A door closing. I got dressed

and left the bathroom, rubbing the side of my hair with the towel. Sophie was back. I saw her bag at the bottom of the stairs and went down to see her. She looked lovely. The sort of healthy glow that someone has when they get back from holiday. We hugged. "Is Tom...?" she asked, biting her lip. I shook my head and she looked relieved. Neither of us spoke. For the first time in our friendship, I had to think about what I was going to say next.

"Danny came to the house last night." I rushed the words.

"What did he want?"

"He told us that Lacey was raped about a year before she died." Sophie's jaw dropped. "It was Michael Penhaligan. He attacked her one night at the Carmen."

"Did you record it?" I shook my head.

"There wasn't time," I lied. "If we'd waited, we would have lost him." Sophie looked disappointed.

"It was Megan that gave Lacey's photos to the press," I told her.

"What? Her own sister?" Sophie shook her head slowly in disbelief. I thought she would ask if I'd recorded it, but she didn't. Sophie was starting to see where the line was.

"Who do you think killed her?" she asked me.

"Michael Penhaligan," I replied. "He had motive and most likely opportunity..."

"Couldn't the same be said for someone who sold naked photos of her dead sister?" She was right, but I still didn't think that Megan had done it. My phone beeped. It was a message from Claire Penhaligan. I scanned the words quickly.

"James's mum has said she can talk to us tomorrow," I told her. "I'll let Tom know..." I started searching for his number when Sophie stopped me.

"We can do the recording ourselves, can't we? Like we used to?" She attempted a smile, but she looked upset.

"Of course. I'm sure we can figure it out between us." I

squeezed her arm and stood up. "Do you fancy a drink?" I asked, heading to the kitchen. I checked the fridge for wine. There was a bottle in the door, containing about half a glass. I checked the cupboards. Not only did we not have any more alcohol, but we were running low on food. I'd bought nothing since Sophie had been away. "Shall we go to the pub?" I suggested, guilty that I hadn't replenished supplies. Her face brightened.

"Great, give me five minutes to get changed." I looked down at my own jeans-and-T-shirt combination and decided it was fine for Tuesday night at the pub. It wouldn't be busy.

As we walked up the hill, I saw the blackboard outside the Bull: QUIZ NIGHT 8 P.M. "Shit," I muttered. I couldn't believe they were still doing the Tuesday night quiz. We used to go every week when we were at college. The quizmaster was hired for the night, a predictable red coat–style persona. He was deeply uncool, but he made it work.

The pub would be as busy as a Saturday night. There used to be about ten of us on a team, competing against the village elders, who took it far more seriously. Our table was always laden with drinks and as the quiz wore on our answers became louder and our heckling more raucous. It started with general knowledge and moved on to a music round. We were always terrible at that bit. The songs were mainly from the sixties and seventies, catering to the age of most of the drinkers.

When the answers came at the end, we'd usually never heard of the band. The final round was "name that celebrity." Four pages filled with grainy black-and-white photos were given to each of the tables. Poor resizing of the pictures meant that it was virtually impossible to guess who they were. By this stage of the night, we were all pissed. Those photos would sometimes make us laugh to the point of being asked to leave. They were some of the best nights. I hesitated. Stopping underneath the large wooden porch.

"Are you OK?" Sophie asked, taking in the words on the board.

"Uh-huh." I nodded brightly, grabbing hold of the brass handle and pressing my weight into the heavy door. As soon as my foot landed on the dirty red carpet, I changed my mind. The quiz was in full swing. The only noise was the DJ's singsong voice reading the questions like a bingo caller. The main room was filled with round wooden tables and chairs so close to each other that there was almost no room to move around. The only way to the bar was to cut between the quizmaster and the audience. As we squeezed around the table nearest the door, the DJ abandoned his question.

"What time do you call this, ladies?" He laughed down the microphone. Everyone looked up from their quiz sheets. I didn't take in all the faces that were there, but I took in enough. Claire and Michael Penhaligan, on the right-hand side, sat at a table with two similarly dressed couples. Megan was at the back. Sitting opposite her were Jude, Danny and another woman that I didn't recognize. There was Tara, Polly and few others. All eyes were on us. I could feel the blush creeping up the back of my neck like a cobweb. We were the only ones at the bar. On quiz night, you order drinks only between rounds. I turned my back on the tables, pretending to be engaged in deciding what to drink. I could see from the corner of my eye that Sophie was watching me. The barman came over and asked her what she wanted.

"Can we get two bottles of wine, please... to go."

"Are you sure...? I really don't mind staying..." I tried to assure her.

"Let's go home." A smile of understanding passed between us. An understanding that hadn't been there for a long time. I paid. I insisted. The barman looked at me like he had only just noticed I was there. Sophie had that effect on people. We took a bottle each and headed toward the door. I kept my head down.

Focusing on the little black circles on the carpet, old chewing gum stains and burn holes. As we stepped onto the pavement outside, we heard the DJ call after us.

"Was it something we said, ladies?"

"Yes, it was," Sophie said. We clutched each other laughing, a sort of hysteria from the relief of getting out. We strolled back down the hill. The evening sun was half sunk behind the trees, making the leaves around the top look like they were on fire. When we got as far as the car park, we stopped, deciding which way to go. "Shall we sit on the beach for a bit?" Sophie asked. I nodded; we made our way slowly across the concrete flat, heading for the wooden footbridge.

Neither of us said anything. The sun was nearly behind us now. The clouds were lined with bright ribbons of color: yellows, pinks, reds. A few people were leaving the beach. Families with empty fish and chip wrappers and couples back from a sunset walk. We stopped on the bridge, resting our arms on the dented wooden handrail, still warm from the day's sun. I looked at a spot on the concrete a few feet away.

"It's hard to believe that she died there."

"Hard to believe that there's nothing here to mark it, to remember her. It's like it never happened." Sophie had thought it too.

CHAPTER FIFTY-THREE

We walked on. A peaceful silence had settled between us. "I never liked Lacey," I confessed. Even now, I was scared of saying it out loud. Sophie looked over at me as we sat down on the warm pale sand. "She wasn't very nice, not to me anyway. I never did find out why. I hated her for such a long time that even when she died I couldn't let it go. Coming here, doing this... it's put a lot of things to rest, things that needed to be."

"I'm glad." Sophie drew circles in the sand with her finger.

"God, Soph, she was nineteen. *Nineteen.*" I shook my head, thinking about how young she was. How young we all were when it happened. Sophie nodded, but she looked consumed with something else.

"Did you talk to Tom?" I asked her. I could tell from her profile that she was trying to stop herself from crying.

"He called when I was away. Told me he thinks we should end things." Her voice wobbled. She cleared her throat, quickly composing herself. "I know it's for the best. We haven't been getting on for a while now. I'm tired of trying to make it work. I think we both are. We were never very well suited." I shuffled a little closer. Her body was rigid, eyes fixed on a point far out at sea. I placed my arm around her, pulling her gently into the hug. For a second, she resisted. Keeping her back tensed and in position. I didn't move. Slowly, Sophie sank into the embrace. Her head dropped down to my shoulder. I felt her body shudder as she finally gave way to the emotional tide she'd been keeping at bay.

The tears that she'd been holding back now ran freely down her cheeks. We sat there like that until the sun had almost disappeared. We walked home the quick way, wandering up the hill, past Red Rock House. Our arms almost touched as they swung by our sides in unison. We said very little on the way back. It was comfortable. Things weren't perfect, but it suddenly struck me that they didn't need to be. We weren't kids anymore. Life had changed. I knew in that moment, that whatever shape our new friendship took, that it was going to be OK.

The next day was hot. I'd slept badly, thrashing around in a knot of sheets, trying to get cool. The heat had disturbed my dreams. Images of Lacey lying on the floor. Instead of the wet glossy tarmac reflecting under the streetlight, she was lying on grass. Bright, green grass. It wasn't dark wherever she was. The sun had come up. Lacey looked like she'd been there all night.

I was trying to stop people that walked by from looking at her. I couldn't see their faces. Everyone was just staring. I kept calling out to them, asking them why they wouldn't help her, why they'd just left her there all alone. Nobody answered.

The text notification sounded on my phone. I lifted it from the bedside table, struggling to see the words on the screen against the bright light that shone through the window. It was from Claire Penhaligan, received at 1:24 a.m. The jumble of words made almost no sense but seemed to suggest she would be here midmorning. The arrangement of the sentences was confusing, littered with odd words. Claire had obviously not been sober when she'd sent the message.

I got up and threw some clothes on. I really wanted to have

a shower. To wash away the sweaty tiredness and confusion, but there wasn't time. I opened the window. A faint cool wind blew through the room, touching my face and passing through my thin pajama top. I pulled my hair into a high topknot, enjoying the feeling of air on my neck.

I got dressed and went downstairs. The curtains were still closed. The coffee table was strewn with the remnants of last night: an empty bottle of wine, our notes. There were untidy scrawls in the margins, added to as we spoke late into the night. There was a leftover bowl of cereal, dregs of milk with little pieces of muesli floating on the surface. Sophie had obviously eaten and left. Probably for a run. I put the kettle on and spent the next half an hour sorting the room out, clearing away dishes, pushing the sofas back and gathering up our papers. I moved my attention to the sound equipment. Without Tom here today, me and Sophie would be on our own with the recording.

The setup we used before was much more basic than this. I went to the mixing desk and tried following the cables that ran from the back of the black box, looking to see if they were connected to anything. I had no idea what I was doing. There was equipment here that I couldn't even name, never mind operate. I felt guilty playing around with Tom's things. It felt like we were cutting him out of the project.

Sophie got back, red-faced and out of breath after her run. She went to the kitchen to get a glass of water. I heard her struggling to breathe evenly, as though she'd pushed herself too hard. Between us, we managed to get the sound working. We bypassed a few things and stripped it back, so it was what we were used to.

Sophie went upstairs to shower, while I arranged the cushions and made tea. Claire would be here any minute. I was strangely nervous. She was an intimidating character, pushy and self-assured. She rarely went without what she wanted. I thought about what it must have been like for James, growing up in a big empty house with Claire and Michael as his parents. I knew the loneliness of it. I'd grown up in my own big empty house, no siblings and working parents. But it was different for me. Mum, Richard and me, we'd been a team, a unit. James didn't have that kind of closeness.

The morning came and went. We watched the clock, wishing we could be outside in the blazing sunshine. We'd opened the small living room window, but it didn't relieve much of the stuffiness. Several flies came in, vibrating loudly around the room, adding to Sophie's irritation. Eventually, there was a soft knocking on the door, so quiet we were unsure if we'd imagined it. I opened the door. Claire Penhaligan was overdressed for the temperature. She wore a red and black skirt suit. It looked expensive and thick, like it was made of wool. The collar of a silk shirt sat perfectly pressed on the neck of the jacket, revealing a narrow line of pearls around her creased neck. She looked dressed for a business meeting.

Under one arm, she carried a leather manuscript holder and in the other was her mobile phone and her car keys. Her gray hair was neatly cropped and styled. As I welcomed her in, she lifted the corners of her mouth into a half smile, but there was no attempt at sincerity. Claire moved brusquely. Her smart black heels tapped across the floor. Her eyes didn't venture around the room. She had no interest in taking in her surroundings. This was work. She had a job to do.

Claire perched herself on the edge of the sofa without being asked. It was clear that there would be no apology for her lateness. She tucked her knees in primly to the side and smoothed down her jacket with the palms of her hands. She looked like she was preparing to be filmed. It occurred to me how well she must have fit in at all the political events she attended in Westminster. Michael Penhaligan's wife, the solicitor. Sophie was barely hiding her annoyance. She'd said nothing to Claire when she arrived. Busying herself with headphones, I could see her watching out of the corner of her eye, trying to get the measure of Claire as she settled on the sofa.

"Right then, Claire. Let's get you mic'd up." Sophie moved confidently toward her. Claire said nothing, but she looked at the headset with displeasure. Her thin painted lips pressed into a line. Sophie placed it on her head, pulling it down over her ears. It had a flattening effect. Claire kept lightly touching the earpieces, fussing imaginary strands of hair back into place. Me and Sophie took our usual place among the pillow nests on the floor. We ran some quick sound checks, altering the levels a little so that our voices came through clearly. We were ready. Sophie nodded. She would be taking the lead on the interview. I could see her lips twitching in anticipation.

After the usual introduction, she started. "Today we're joined by Claire Penhaligan. Claire was mother to James Penhal..."

"I still am," Claire interrupted.

"Sorry?" Sophie looked at her, confused.

"I'm *still* his mother," she snapped.

CHAPTER FIFTY-FOUR

"Of course." It had thrown her. I could see Sophie trying to get back on course. "Claire is mother to James Penhaligan. James had been Lacey's boyfriend for the last two years of her life. Three years ago, James died in an apparent suicide. The police took the unusual step of suggesting that he had been their prime suspect and that they would no longer be looking for anyone else in connection with her death."

Claire's eyes bored into Sophie's head as she read from her notes. "Can you tell us about James?" Claire looked disappointed, like she'd been expecting something more challenging.

"He was, well... He was incredibly bright. He could have gone to any college he'd wanted. It wasn't just the law he had a flare for. He was an incredibly gifted mathematician, writer, sportsman..."

"But what was he *like?*" Sophie pressed. Claire's forehead creased, unsure of what she was being asked.

"He played rugby and cricket for the county. His A-level marine biology project was selected for a Young Scientist award and he'd *finally* began to concentrate on languages." She said the last part with a mixture of triumph and relief. As though it had been a source of conflict between them. Sophie gnawed on the inside of her cheek, dragging her thumbnail across her forehead impatiently.

"*Other* than academic achievements, can you tell me what James was like as a person?" Sophie was struggling to keep the annoyance from her voice.

"Well, he was polite, conscientious, he was..."

"Claire..." Sophie interrupted her. Her voice thick with frustration. She pulled her fingers slowly down her face and sighed. I thought she was going to stop the recording. I braced myself for Claire's response. She was visibly crumbling. Her bold confidence was seeping away. The deep bags under her eyes lifted into a grimace, like a screwed-up ball of paper. Sophie watched her, full of remorse.

"I was going to say kind... He was kind." Her bottom lip quivered and her voice was gravelly as the emotion gathered in her throat. Sophie flinched. She waited for the tension to settle.

"How did you feel about Lacey?"

Claire considered her answer. "I didn't like her. Neither of us did." I assumed she was talking about Michael when she said "us."

"Why?"

"Lacey Crew was an empty-headed vain little..." Claire tumbled over her words, stopping herself just in time. "She wasn't right for James. Everybody knew it," she added primly. Sophie's eyes narrowed.

"Did your husband have any interest in Lacey?" Sophie was looking carefully at the paper in front of her.

"My husband? Why on earth would my husband be interested in a nineteen-year-old girl?" she spat. Sophie raised her eyebrows.

"We've heard, from a number of sources, that your husband was *very* interested in nineteen-year-olds." She watched Claire's reaction carefully.

"Nonsense. It was all just town gossip. Jealousy most likely..." Her hands gestured in agitation, but I could see them shaking. She looked wildly around the room. Her eyes rested on the recording equipment.

"So, you didn't know that a number of female staff had made complaints about Michael's behavior at the Carmen?" Claire pressed her lips together several times, like she was blotting her lipstick. She seemed to be unaware that she was doing it.

"What do you want from me?" she snapped, clipping the end of each word as she spoke. "Do you want me to say that I knew Michael used to flirt with the girls up at the bar? Fine. I knew. I'm not stupid. I've seen how he is with young women when he's had a drink. I fail to see what any of this has to do with what happened to James, or Lacey for that matter." Her eyes blazed. The momentary show of vulnerability was gone.

"Do you know Danny?" Sophie asked. "He was a friend of James's. He used to manage the bar at the Carmen a few years ago." Sophie had lowered her voice, approaching her from a new direction. Claire nodded cautiously, worried about where this might be leading. "Well, Danny came to see us. He told us that one night, when he and Lacey were closing up, Michael went to the staff room and attacked her. Danny saw him leave, so there is no question that he was there. A few days later, Danny went to her house to ask her what had happened. Claire... Lacey told him that Michael raped her that night."

We waited for her to talk, but she just sat there. Her eyes on the coffee table. The rapid rise and fall of her chest was the only movement. It must have been the shock. Sophie watched, staring intently at her face.

"Claire... did you know that Michael had raped Lacey?" Claire looked up, an injured animal too weak to move away from its predator. "Oh, God, you knew?" Sophie's face crinkled into a look of disgust. I looked wildly from Claire to Sophie, waiting for an answer, the full horror of what I was hearing barely sinking in. Claire's eyes were unfocused, she blinked slowly, as though she was falling asleep. *"Claire,"* Sophie shouted.

"Yes... I knew."

CHAPTER FIFTY-FIVE

"How long have you known?" Sophie struggled to keep the revulsion from her voice. Claire didn't seem to notice. Her head was bowed again. She spoke to the floor. "James told me, the day he died." She cleared her throat, but her voice was still weak and unsteady. "He came to the house that night. God, he was so angry. He was shouting, asking for his dad..." She shook her head, remembering. Tears streamed down her cheeks. "I told James that Michael wasn't home, but he didn't believe me. He pushed his way into the house and went upstairs. I waited in the kitchen for him. I tried to be calm, I really did... but he was just so *angry*." Her words were fading as she was caught up in the images that played in her mind.

"Claire?" I spoke gently. She looked up, surprised to see me.

"He came into the kitchen. He looked wild. Not like James at all. I could tell he'd been drinking. He told me what Michael had done to Lacey. I didn't believe him at first. I laughed. It all sounded so preposterous. But as he told me the whole story, he was so filled with hatred that I knew he was telling the truth. James told me that he was going to go to the police. I begged him... I was virtually on my hands and knees, pleading with him

not to do it. It would have ruined us. All of us." She looked to
Sophie and then to me, trying to make us understand. "James
refused to listen. He left, taking a full bottle of bourbon with
him. That was the last time I ever saw him alive. The last time I
would ever see my son alive, and when he closed that front
door, do you know what I felt? Relief. I was glad he was gone."
She looked upward and closed her eyes, like she was praying for
forgiveness.

"What happened next?" Sophie asked.

She hesitated. "I went to bed. Michael wasn't due home
that night and I was tired. At about 4 a.m. I woke up. I hadn't
slept properly. I had this terrible feeling that something was
wrong..." Sophie was about to say something, but I shot her a
warning look and she stopped. "I went to the bathroom." She
moved her hand in a side-to-side motion, retracing the steps in
her mind. "I opened the cupboard to take one of my pills... and
the box was open. All the blister packs were gone. All of
them..." she whispered.

"Did James take the pills?" Sophie asked, loudly enough to
snap her out of her daze. She nodded. "That's when I knew. I
looked out of the window, toward the woods at the back of the
house. It was still dark. I ran outside. I got as far as the lane
before I had to turn back and get a flashlight I couldn't see
anything.

"Every step I took toward those woods I said a prayer,
hoping it wasn't true, but I knew. I saw the rope first. The flashlight picked up the cord high in the tree and I followed it with
the light to the ground. I was so relieved when James wasn't
there. I only moved another couple of feet when I saw him. I
checked his breathing, his pulse, but his skin felt cold. I knew it
was too late." Fresh tears ran down her face.

"The benzodiazepine that James took, they were yours?" I
asked. She nodded as she blew her nose on a tissue she'd pulled
out of her jacket pocket. "Why didn't you tell the police?"

"For the same reason I didn't tell them about what Michael did. It would have ruined us. Those pills were prescribed to me for anxiety... for alcohol issues I suffered a *long* time ago. I'm a solicitor." She jutted her chin out haughtily. "I couldn't have everyone knowing our business." Her eyes flashed at Sophie. "You can give me that look all you want, but you have no idea what it was like. I'd lost my son. I wasn't about to lose my husband and my career as well." Neither of us said anything. Something occurred to me.

"Claire, how did you know that James had gone to the woods?"

She sighed. "As soon as I saw that the pills were missing, I thought he might try to hurt himself. I knew straight away where he'd be... the pigeons." We looked at her, confused. "The dovecote he built when he was a child. It had been attached to that same tree in the woods. He loved the sound of those bloody birds." Claire Penhaligan fell apart. Her body racked with noisy sobs. It was impossible not to feel pity for her.

"You know that we can't keep this information to ourselves, Claire, don't you?" Sophie asked her. She nodded, still crying loudly into her tissue. The woman was so damaged with regret that I don't think she cared what happened. We couldn't ask her any more. She was broken. Not even Sophie would attempt to question her further.

After a few minutes, her sobbing came to a stop. Only the sound of her stuttering breaths could be heard. I walked Claire to the door. All the strident confidence she'd entered the cottage with earlier had gone. Her hunched body limped lifelessly across the room. I offered to drive her home. "I drove," she replied blankly. Before I could say anything, she was gone. Neither of us said goodbye.

Sophie was checking the recording, making sure that we'd got it all. I leaned against the cottage wall outside, basking in the heat. I tried to piece together what we'd just heard. If Lacey really was planning on going to the police about the rape, Michael and Claire would have stood to lose everything. They were so concerned with protecting their careers and their standing in the community that they let their own son go to his grave suspected of murder.

I understood now why they'd pursued a case against the police: a chance to shift some of the blame. "Do you think Claire and Michael were *both* involved in Lacey's murder?" I asked Sophie. She thought for a moment.

"If Claire is telling the truth, she didn't know about the rape until after Lacey died... she didn't have a motive. Not back then." I nodded, trying to piece together the evidence in my mind.

I thought about the necklace. Lacey's necklace that was placed on the bridge months later. "Maybe Claire found out that Michael had killed her. Maybe she found the necklace... returned it to the scene out of some sort of guilt or reparation." Sophie nodded, but her thoughts were elsewhere. I wanted more than anything to believe that it was Michael that killed her. But there was something not quite right about it, something that wasn't connecting in my head. It was as though the string that pulled this whole thing together had slipped loose. Sometimes, I felt no closer to the truth than when we started all this.

Sophie was sending a text. She looked animated, already working on the different ways that we might present Michael as the killer. "Well... I think we did it!" she said triumphantly.

"Do you really think it was Michael?" I was doubtful. Sophie was taken aback.

"How can you not? He raped her, Katie; she was going to the police. For Christ's sake... him and his wife covered up their involvement in their own *son's* death. They even tried to deflect that guilt by blaming the police." She sounded exasperated. There was no question in Sophie's mind that Michael had done it, or that Claire had in some way tried to cover it up.

"You're probably right," I conceded. I had no tangible reason to discard what was the most likely theory, other than just a feeling. Sophie looked dubious but left it at that. The rest of the afternoon passed slowly. We ate from the meager selection of food that was left in the cupboards. Sophie did another Ocado order. I offered to pay, but she brushed it aside, said it would be gifted as part of a deal she had with them.

The cottage didn't have a garden, just the grassy area at the front. We took blankets and cushions outside. Laying on our backs, wearing the swimsuits I'd got for us at the Carmen. I felt on edge. A restless anxiety had taken hold and I couldn't shake it. I tried reading and listening to music, but I couldn't settle on anything. By the early evening I was almost vibrating with agitation.

I brought our notes outside. Trying to see if there was something that I'd missed. I struggled with every sentence. The words lost meaning as my mind drifted. I gave up when I realized I was getting nowhere. Sophie's phone rang. She took it back into the house and was gone for a while. I lay on my back, my eyes hidden from the sun in the crook of my arm. When Sophie came back, I was almost asleep.

"That was the agency," she explained. "They have another job for me. It's only for a couple of nights, but it will mean going back to London today..." Sophie waited for my reaction. She looked apologetic.

Sudden anger began to rise in me. "I didn't want this," I told her. Sophie was confused. "The podcast, coming back here." I raised my arm in the direction of Pengully. My voice had got louder. "This was *your* project, Sophie... You *made* me come back... and now I'm left to finish it alone." I chocked on the last words as tears came fast.

"Kate... I'm so sorry." Sophie reached for me, shocked by my outburst. We sat like that for a while. Sophie held me tight. The wave of sadness and despair that I'd felt for days finally spilling over.

Slowly, my breathing returned to normal, and I lifted my head from Sophie's shoulder.

"I'll cancel the job," she promised.

"No, don't," I replied.

Sophie tilted her head to one side, watching me. "Are you sure?" she asked gently.

"Yes. You should go. This is something I need to do. Something I should have faced a long time ago."

CHAPTER FIFTY-SIX

Sophie packed quickly and we said our goodbyes. Although she was going for only a couple of days, it felt strangely emotional. I was a little lost after she'd left. The sun was beginning to lose some of its heat as the sky turned a burnt orange.

I walked up to the main house, but neither Mum nor Richard was there. I let myself in through the garage and found both spaniels home alone. Morti jumped up immediately. His tail wagged furiously as he wiggled over to me. Perno didn't leave his bed. He simply opened one eye and lazily turned his head to see who it was.

I decided to head to the beach. I needed to walk off the feeling of restlessness. I went to the wine cooler next to the fridge and grabbed a bottle. Mum wouldn't mind. I rummaged in the cupboard looking for a plastic cup to take with me, but there were only expensive glasses. As I reached the door, bottle in hand, Morti followed me. His head dipped and his big brown eyes looked at me pleadingly. I laughed. "Fine, you can come." I quickly scribbled Mum a note and headed back to the cottage.

I grabbed my backpack and a towel from upstairs, wedging

the cold bottle of wine down the side of the bag. I pulled the door closed and set off down the hill with Morti in tow. The sea and cliffs looked as beautiful as I had ever seen them. I could feel the air become lighter as a gentle onshore breeze whispered against my skin, fanning the jumbled thoughts that floated around my head.

As I trudged down the path I started to think more clearly. I slipped my shoes off when I got to the beach. I hadn't planned on going to the spot of the beach party, but as I rounded the corner of the dunes, I heard the music. The faint sound of voices up ahead. I watched as the thin wispy trail of smoke rose skyward from a bonfire. There were about twenty people standing around, beer bottles and plastic glasses in their hands. They looked so young. How could it have been only five years ago that I was standing here? It seemed like a lifetime.

Nobody noticed me as I approached. I climbed the slope of the dunes just behind the fire and sat down on the edge of the tall grasses. I pulled the cold bottle of wine from my bag and unscrewed the cap, drinking straight from the bottle.

I watched them. The looks they gave one another, the way they moved around. Groups melting into other groups, people breaking off. We must have looked just like that. I searched their young carefree faces and wondered if they had secrets too. Secrets that they hadn't even told each other.

My heels dug into the sand. I could feel the spiky roots of the dune grass pressing into my feet. I watched the few boats that were anchored close to the shore. Expensive sail boats. A man and woman moved around the deck of the one closest to the beach. They were too far away to tell what they were doing. I tried to imagine who they were. What life might be like for them on their big white yacht.

The wine tasted good, sharp and crisp. The condensation trickled over my fingers as I drew the bottle to my mouth again.

My eyes were focused on the horizon, so I didn't notice him at first. He was a third of the way up the sandy slope before I saw him. It was Danny. My heart sank as I registered who it was. He saw and looked apologetic.

"Do you mind if I sit down?" He looked better, a lot better than the last two times I'd seen him. His eyes were brighter and his skin looked clearer. I offered him the bottle. Danny shook his head.

"I'm trying to knock it on the head for a bit," he said, acknowledging what everyone else already knew: that he had a problem, that he wasn't OK. We sat quietly, watching the party down below. I wondered if Danny saw himself there too.

"I didn't tell you everything the other night," Danny told me. I fingered the mouth of the bottle, avoiding his eye. "The night James died, I saw him in the pub. He was there drinking on his own. I'd been at him for weeks, trying to get him to confront his dad. I really goaded him, wouldn't let it go. I told him he was gutless, that he'd let Lacey down. I reminded him over and over that his dad had raped her... that he might even have been the one that killed her. I could tell it was breaking him, but I just carried on, you know?" I nodded. "James left the pub."

"Did he say where he was going?" I asked. Danny shrugged.

"Back to the caravan, I guessed. I was so fucking angry I didn't care where he was going. A couple of hours later, he sent me a text. It just said that he was sorry for everything. I replied, asked him where he was, and he just said 'home.'

"I felt scared, man. I knew something wasn't right, you know? I left the pub and walked up to his parents' house. When I got there, all the lights were off. I just had this feeling. This fucking awful feeling... I walked down the side lane to the woods. It was so dark. I only had the light from my phone. I was pointing it at the ground so I wouldn't trip over. When I turned the corner, I waved the light around. That's when I saw him. He was hanging from the tree. I managed to get him down. I've no idea how. I was so scared, Kate." I looked at his profile and saw a lump form in his throat as he swallowed. "He was dead. I've played it over in my mind a hundred times and I'm sure he was dead. I kept checking."

"Dan, he was... He must have been," I tried to reassure him.

"I left him there. I ran as quickly as I could out of the woods and went home. I should have called the police. As soon as I woke up the next day, I knew I'd done something terrible. I was off my head. Everyone in the pub had seen us argue that night. I thought that if I stayed, the police would think that I'd done it. I didn't know it would be his Mum that found him." Danny's voice cracked. He bowed his head, pinching the bridge of his nose with his thumb and forefinger as he tried to compose himself.

I waited for him to carry on. "Do you know the joke of it all? All that time after Lacey died, I could have gone to the police and told them what Michael had done to her. But I didn't. I was too weak to do it myself, so I turned it all on James.

"When someone dies, someone that you care about, you have all this love still and there's nowhere for it to go. It destroys you. I was so consumed with my own grief that I didn't see that James felt the same way." A calmness had come over Danny as he stared out to sea. "I'm going to meet with a police officer that worked on the case. I spoke to her this morning."

"DC Rush?" I asked.

Danny nodded. "I'm going to tell her everything: about James, what happened to Lacey, the whole thing. He shuffled in the sand, getting ready to leave. I wanted to wish him luck, tell him that what he was doing was brave. Nothing sounded right, so I just squeezed his arm. He nodded at me in gratitude and stood up to leave.

"Danny, can I ask you something? That night, the night of your party on the beach, why was Lacey working the evening shift at the Carmen?"

Danny paused for a moment. He dipped his head and rubbed the back of his neck. "Because she wanted to. I tried to get her to swap shifts, come to the party earlier, but she wouldn't." He looked troubled. "The man she was seeing... it was someone from work. She said she had something she needed to sort out with him that night."

"Who else was working on the bar that night?" I felt an uncomfortable stirring in my stomach.

"We'd all asked for the night off. The only other person working on the bar that night was... your dad."

I lifted my head to look at him, but Danny was staring at his feet. "Richard?" The word sounded like an echo ricocheting around my head. I felt the color drain away from my face. Danny turned to me, watching my reaction. "Richard...?" I rocked my body slowly, backward and forward, as though if I moved it enough, I might be able to shake the thought from my head.

"Katie... I'm sorry." He placed a hand on my shoulder. I pulled my knees toward my chest and lowered my head. I felt like I was going to be sick.

"Did you know? Did everyone know?" I felt detached, like I was watching myself from a long way away. My voice sounded muffled, drowned out by the sound of blood rushing in my ears.

"No one knew. I didn't know. It was only afterward that I put it all together."

"Why didn't you..." My words tailed off.

"...say something?" He finished the sentence for me. "Who would I have told. You? James? The police? What good would it have done? Lacey was dead. I know you don't want to hear this... but Richard is a good man."

I wanted to argue with him, but I felt weak.

"I'm sorry you found out like this, Katie, really I am. But I can't do it anymore." I lifted my head and our eyes met.

"What?" I asked in a frail voice.

"The secrets, Kate. They're killing me."

Danny stood up and left without a word.

CHAPTER FIFTY-SEVEN

Lacey and Richard were having an affair.

I sat on the beach, a strange swell rising up inside of me. My mind began reaching for the loose thread. I could almost touch it, but I was scared to grab hold. I closed my eyes, lifting the wine to my lips, letting the liquid pour freely into my mouth.

Someone was playing a guitar. The smoke from the bonfire shifted on the breeze, cloaking me in smoke. I breathed in the acrid cloud, tasting burning wood and lighter fuel on my tongue. I could see Lacey's face. She'd walked over to me. I didn't see her at first as I'd been looking down at the bottle of vodka. "Ahh, little Katie Chase," she said. I can't remember if I replied, but she'd laughed. She just kept on laughing.

"What's so funny?" I'd asked her. She'd reached into her bag and got out the blue jumper, pulled it over her body. I remember looking up and seeing tiny flyaway blond hairs lifted by the static. They framed her head like a halo in the glow of the firelight. I was so drunk. I just wanted her to leave. I was struggling to sit up and it was getting hard to focus.

· · ·

I couldn't lift my head to meet her face. My eyes were level with her feet. Scarlet-painted toes. One foot pointed toward the ground, burrowing mindlessly into the sand as she spoke. My head was spinning. I placed the palms of my hands on the ground, trying to stop the floor from shifting. I concentrated on her tiny tanned feet as my eyes began to close.

She must have walked away. I couldn't hear her voice anymore. My cheek was pressed into the dry sand, face sunk so deep that I could feel the fine grains touch my lashes when I blinked. I still had my phone in my hand. I'd squinted at the screen, clumsily pushing at buttons. That must have been when I called home.

The next thing I remember was waking up, soaked through after the rainstorm, to the sound of Polly's screams.

I looked around for Morti, but I couldn't see him. The sun was disappearing. The party below was getting busier. Flames from the fire licked at new wood that had been added to the pile. The music had been turned up.

I needed to leave. I needed to speak to Mum. I left the half-drunk bottle of wine protruding from the sand and stumbled down the slope to the beach. I tried to walk quickly, but the soft ground swallowed my feet with every step. I was out of breath after only a few yards. I stared at the red cliffs ahead of me. I stared so hard that my eyes watered, and I had to force myself to blink.

My racing thoughts were making me feel out of control. I wanted to believe it wasn't true. I wanted to believe that Danny was wrong, that he was lying or mistaken.

I remembered moments that now made sense, small inconsequential things that now slotted perfectly into place. Why Richard hadn't wanted me to come on the staff weekend away. The late nights at work, even after he'd put managers in place.

I reached the bottom of the footpath. The hard ground was steadier to walk on but the dusty tree roots that snaked about the floor hurt my feet. Richard was having an affair with Lacey. Had he been planning on leaving Mum for her? As the anger built up in my body, I could feel the adrenaline lifting me, pushing me faster and faster.

I focused on my footsteps, striding up the hill. A steady pulse, like a clock pendulum ticking. My thoughts contorted as I tried to move the puzzle pieces around in my head. I pictured Lacey that night. The way she'd laughed at me. The way the blue jumper hung down over her hands as she pushed blond hair from her face. How her fingers gripped the ends of the knitted cuffs. The blue jumper... It was one of Richard's.

I stopped on the path. A wave of nausea swept over me so fast I thought my legs would give way. I leaned over, swaying toward the verge. My sleeve attached itself to the thorns that wound their way around the hedge. As I pulled away, I heard ripping. The sound made me retch.

I placed my hands on my knees. Hunched, trying to steady myself. It was then that I heard it. Footsteps behind me, running so fast I had only seconds to react before they reached me. The impact was instant. A blow to the back of my legs, knocking me off my feet. I lay on the hard ground, my face scratched by brambles, my breathing labored in panic.

I lay there for a moment, waiting for another blow. I looked up to see the tail of a spaniel speeding off into the distance. Morti. I was too scared to even feel relief. I lifted my body slowly from the floor and continued walking, my legs limp with fear.

As I reached the cottage, dusk was turning to night. I could only just make out the shape of the dog, waiting for me by the front door. There was no sound. The air would usually be filled with the noise of gulls, their familiar bedtime cawing. Tonight there was nothing. My feet crunched along the familiar gravel path. The pulse of my footsteps had slowed. All the anger and determination that had driven me earlier had seeped away.

I couldn't see any lights on in the main house. I decided to go through the garage. As I slid the heavy door back, I saw Richard's car. His E-Type Jaguar. His pride and joy. I'd always thought the car was beautiful. Not tonight. Tonight it looked brash and garish under the artificial garage lights. I wondered if he'd taken Lacey for a drive in it. I had an overwhelming urge to throw something at it, to scar the perfect body work. Chip the glossy red paint like cheap nail varnish.

My hand was shaking as I opened the door to the kitchen. Mum was standing there with her back to me, looking through to the living room. As she turned, my heart almost stopped with sadness for what I was about to do. She wore a fluffy purple dressing gown, pulled tightly across her middle. She was wearing her glasses and had a steaming mug of tea in her hands.

Mum jumped when she saw me, letting out a squeal of shock. Tea dripped from the bottom of the mug onto the tiled floor. "Mum, I'm sorry," I said, going to her. I took the tea from her hands and placed it on the worktop. I wanted to hold her. Mum's shock turned to fear when she saw my face.

CHAPTER FIFTY-EIGHT

"Katie, what happened... Are you OK...? Richard... *Richard!*"
She'd called out to him before I had a chance to stop her. I
touched my cheek. The cuts from the brambles stung. As I
pulled my hand away, I could see blood on my fingers. "Katie..."
There was panic in her voice.

"I'm fine, honestly. It's just some scratches." Mum looked so
confused. There was relief on her face when Richard rushed
into the kitchen. He was wearing his dressing gown too. They
were on their way to bed.

"Wendy, what's the... Katie?" Richard instinctively reached
up to touch my cheek. I flinched, recoiling my head in horror.
Mum and Richard stood there, stunned by my reaction.

"Mum," I said taking her hand. "Can I speak to you
upstairs, please?" I tried to guide her out of the room, but she
resisted.

"Katie, you're scaring me. Tell me what's happened," she
pleaded. Richard put his arm around Mum's shoulder. I
snapped.

"Get *away* from her," I hissed through gritted teeth.

"Katie, I don't know what's going on, but..." He was trying

to be calm.

"You don't know what's going on?" A hollow bitter-sounding laugh escaped my chest. Mum's face was full of concern. She'd never seen me like this before.

"Look, Katie... Can we all just sit down and talk about whatever this is?" Richard tried again, pointing to the living room. I attempted to pull Mum away again, taking her toward the hall, away from him.

"Stop it, Katie. That's enough." Mum was angry now. She snatched her hand away, face twisted with hurt and confusion.

"Mum." I lowered my voice, trying to be gentle. "Richard... Richard was having an affair with Lacey. Mum, he was going to leave you." I spoke like he wasn't in the room. Her hand shot to her face. She tried to speak, but it was as though she couldn't process the words.

Richard stumbled backward until his body hit the kitchen island. He held on to the sides of his head, his eyes wide with terror. Any doubts I may have had vanished in that moment.

I turned to Richard. "It was Danny that told me. He worked it out after Lacey died. He said the secrets were *killing* him. *Your* secret, Richard. Do you know what he said to me tonight? He told me you're a 'good man,'" I sneered. My bottom lip curled with disgust.

"There was something I'd been trying to remember for so long and it came to me tonight: the jumper. The jumper that she wore that night. It was yours. I thought I was going mad... but it just *kept* coming back to me." As I spoke, something else connected in my head. I looked at Richard. My voice was thick with fear.

"She nearly told me about your affair that night. I'm sure of it. That was why she put your jumper on... to show me. It was only because I was so drunk that she didn't. Had Lacey threatened you?" I asked him. I didn't wait for a reply.

"The jumper... she was wearing it when she left the beach.

She was wearing it when Jude saw her in the car park. The police never found it. Why would the killer take *your* jumper?" Richard said nothing. He stared at the floor shaking his head. "*Richard?*" I screamed.

Mum was silent. She gripped the front of her dressing gown, watching me. "Oh my God... you killed her, didn't you?" My voice was quieter, almost a whisper. I felt breathless under the weight of the horror I was uncovering.

Richard held up his hands in panic. He looked terrified. His eyes pleaded with me to stop. "Katie, it's not what you think. Please, I can explain..." I started backing away, but he took hold of my arm.

"Get *off*," I shouted, flailing my arm and twisting myself free.

"I'm sorry... I'm sorry." He was desperate. "Yes, I had an affair with Lacey. It lasted three or four months. It didn't *mean* anything. Not to me anyway. It all got too much. She'd started turning up at the house. Saying she loved me, that she wanted me to leave you. I never, *ever* thought for one minute about breaking up our family." He turned to Mum. "Wendy, I'm so sorry. I never meant for it to happen." His eyes filled with tears; his voice choked with emotion. "You have to believe me. I *didn't* kill her." He looked hopelessly to Mum and then to me.

"Mum... we need to go. You need to come with me." Her face was glazed. There was a blankness to it. It was like she couldn't hear me. "*Mum.*" I tried to pull her toward the door. Her face came into focus and her eyes flashed.

"No." She spoke softly, her voice was eerily calm. I dropped my hold on her arm in surprise.

"Mum?" I said more quietly.

"Your dad didn't kill her."

"I know you don't want to believe that he..."

Mum was firm. "I know your dad didn't kill her... because I did."

CHAPTER FIFTY-NINE

The room fell silent. "Mum, you don't need to do this. You don't need to protect him," I told her. But a different sort of fear began to creep up the back of my neck. Mum was composed. She didn't look scared or upset. Her face looked relaxed, sort of peaceful.

A new feeling of nausea rose up from the pit of my stomach. Richard watched Mum. He looked disorientated. His body swayed a little as he tried to focus on her words. It was like he was looking at a stranger in his house.

"I knew about the affair. I knew almost from the start, I think." Mum pulled one of the stools out from under the breakfast bar. She carefully sat herself down and took a sip of her tea.

"It was little things at first: the way you dressed, your smell when you came home. I checked the messages on your phone. You were so useless at adultery you didn't even delete them." She spoke almost fondly, a half-smile on her face. Me and Richard looked at each other, a building realization between us. "I saw her outside the house a couple of times, when she thought no one was home."

"Why didn't you say something?" Richard was overcome.

"What, and force you to end your little fling?" Mum shook her head. "If I'd done that, I might have lost you for good. No, I wanted to let it run its course and for you to come back to me. Not because I'd made you, because you wanted to. It didn't work out like that in the end." Mum turned to me. "You called me from the beach. You left a message on the answering machine. You were so drunk, *so* upset." Her eyes filled with tears. "It was hard to make out what you were saying, but you mentioned Lacey. I was scared that she'd told you.

"I was so angry. That *girl* was not only trying to destroy my marriage, I thought she was going to destroy *you*. I paced around the house, trying to think of a way that I could make it better for you. Before I knew what I was doing, I'd walked through the garage and got into my car. I needed to find you." She pointed at the door I'd just entered through. "I drove down the hill to the beach car park. The rain was so heavy, I could hardly see the road. Water was running down the sides of the lane like a river.

"When I got to the car park, she was there, sitting on the wall by herself. If I hadn't seen her, I'm not sure what I would have done. I probably would have found you, and we would have gone home.

"I stopped the car in front of her and she looked up. As soon as she saw me, she knew. She even smiled. Can you believe that? I got out of the car. I was soaked in seconds. Lacey was too, but she didn't seem to care. I asked her why. Why she was intent on ruining my family? I thought she would apologize or deny it, but she didn't. She just stood there and laughed. Told me that my cushy life would be coming to an end.

"I was so shocked that a girl, a nineteen-year-old girl—the same age as you—would speak to me like that. I was too shocked to even answer her. She turned her back on me and walked toward the footbridge. I don't know what happened, I really don't. Something broke in me." Mum looked at me, willing me to understand. My body felt cold, like ice water was coursing through my veins.

"I went up behind her and grabbed her shoulders. I didn't want to hurt her. I just wanted her to be sorry for what she'd done to us. I felt disconnected, like I had no control over my body. My hands went to her throat and I started squeezing. I didn't let go. I couldn't. It felt like my arms were locked. I was only holding her for a few seconds. Honestly, that's all it felt like. I realized what I was doing, and I let go. She fell to the floor. Her eyes were open. I could see her lips under the street-light... They were blue. There was nothing I could do. I knew it was too late. I took her mobile phone from her hand and put it in my pocket. That's when I saw she was wearing Richard's jumper. I don't know why I didn't notice it before.

"I knew I needed to take it. I couldn't leave anything behind that could lead back to us." There was that word again, *us*. Like we'd all played a part in it. "I pulled the jumper from her body. As it came off, her head hit the concrete. The noise was so sickening I nearly phoned the police myself." For the first time since starting her story, her face showed traces of remorse.

"I put the jumper in the boot, got into the car and left. I never really expected to get away with it. As I drove out of the car park and turned around in the road, I saw Jude and that Polly girl walking around the corner. I was sure that in the days after, they would remember the car they'd seen. Work out that it was me driving.

"I drove around for a while. Eventually the rain stopped. All I could think about was you, Katie, alone and drunk on the beach. I knew I had to go back and get you. When I pulled into the car park again, everyone was there: the police, you, your friends. Jude brought you over to the car. I felt sure he would remember seeing me then. You looked so pale. Your wet clothes clinging to your shivering body." A tear rolled slowly down Mum's cheek as she remembered.

"You got into the car and turned the light on to look at the cut on your foot. I thought you would notice how wet I was, that you would wonder why. But you were so traumatized you didn't see anything," she said sadly.

"What about the necklace?" I couldn't believe that I was able to ask her, that I could even say the words out loud.

"A few days later, I went to get the jumper and phone from my car. As I unfolded it, something fell to the floor. It was the necklace. I was going to throw it away with the rest of her things, but I opened the locket. It was a photo of Lacey with her grandad. I got rid of the jumper and phone, but I couldn't bring myself to get rid of the necklace. I walked around with it in my pocket for weeks. Then one day I saw Lonni in town. She was pacing up and down, making a nuisance of herself. I'd not thought about it before, not even at the funeral, but it hit me that day just what that woman had lost.

"I wanted her to have the locket. One night, I went back to the car park and hung the necklace on the end of the bridge." Mum nodded her head slowly, as if returning the locket had restored order.

Richard was staring at her, like he had no idea who she was or what she was saying. He held on to his stomach with clenched fists and slid to the floor. A low agonizing moan escaped his throat. Mum didn't even look at him. "The only person I was thinking of was *you*, Katie. I couldn't let her do it. I couldn't have our perfect family broken up, not after last time. I saw how much you lost when your father left. How everyone in town looked at us, pitied us."

"Is that what you were worried about? What people thought of us?" I felt like I was going to be sick. I searched her face in desperation, for any semblance of the mum I knew.

"I'm sorry." She was so calm, so measured, as though she was apologizing for forgetting my birthday or speaking out of turn. Richard sobbed loudly on the floor. Mum acted as though she couldn't hear him.

"Mum, you killed her. She was nineteen years old and you killed her..." My voice sounded small, as if I were rehearsing lines. I needed to say the words out loud to make them real, to make *this* real. I stumbled backward toward the door. She watched me, the tears from earlier now dry.

"Katie..." Richard whimpered. "Please, don't go." I closed the door quietly behind me as I left. Staggering toward the cottage, I felt like I was walking in a fog. My speed increased with every step, until I was running. Scrabbling across the gravel, my feet twisting and sliding on the stones in my panic. As I lifted the latch on the door, I noticed that Morti was by my side.

CHAPTER SIXTY

The cottage was silent and dark. Just the light from the moon shining through the windows and the sound of my heartbeat.

I paced the dark room for what felt like hours. A repetitive route back and forth across the stone floor. I replayed Mum's story over and over in my mind. Her face, her demeanor, I tried to cling onto parts of her that I recognized. The Mum that I knew. The kind, caring woman. The one that walked me to school, read me stories, cried with happiness for me when I got into college. The woman who put her own hurt and anguish aside when my dad had left, focusing only on my happiness. That woman was not standing in the kitchen tonight.

I climbed onto the sofa and lay curled on my side. Morti slunk onto the end, groaning quietly as he dropped to sleeping position. I reached behind me for one of the blankets, draped across the back of the cushions. I pulled the soft, fine wool throw to my face, a throw carefully chosen by Megan when she renovated the cottage. Megan. That was why Mum had befriended her. Why she'd got Richard to find her clients, let her design the Carmen suites. Guilt. Guilt that she'd killed her sister. That what she'd done had meant Megan was trapped in Pengully forever, caring for her grief-stricken mother.

It was why she hadn't wanted me to do the podcast. Why she'd asked Megan to talk me out of doing it. She wasn't concerned about us reigniting all the pain people had suffered. She was only concerned about being found out.

I lay there and closed my eyes. The cottage was hot and stuffy, but my skin felt cold. My limbs trembled as the last drops of adrenaline juddered through my body. Mum wasn't a monster. She was full of remorse, I reasoned. She'd felt guilt about taking Lonni's daughter from her, for what she'd done to Megan.

But there was one thing she felt no guilt about. Even after all these years, she hadn't been crushed under the weight of it. Lacey. She felt no guilt about what she'd done to Lacey, taking her life away from her.

CHAPTER SIXTY-ONE

I was alone in the cottage for three days with no one to talk to but the dog. I turned my phone off and didn't speak to anyone. Every few hours I would let Morti out for a run. I never ventured farther than the front door. Each time he left, I felt sure that he would return to the main house, but he never did.

On the third day, I woke up and knew what I had to do. I'd known all along; I just didn't have the courage to do it. I found Rebecca Rush's business card, tucked into the back pocket of my purse.

That morning, I called and told her everything. I'd barely said hello before I told her. "It was my mum, Rebecca... sorry, DC Rush," I corrected myself.

"Rebecca is fine," she replied gently. "What did your mum do?" she asked.

"She murdered Lacey. Richard, my stepdad, was having an affair with Lacey... so she killed her." I felt sick saying the words out loud.

"Are you at their house now?" she asked calmly.

"No, I'm at the cottage next door." I could hear the wobble in my voice as I tried to control my emotions.

"OK. What I'm going to do is send some officers over to their house. Stay where you are. I'll be with you as soon as I can." She spoke slowly and kindly, like she was speaking to a child. It made me feel safe for the first time in days. I was about to put the phone down when she spoke again. "Katie? You did the right thing."

Two police cars had arrived in minutes. I put my trainers on, tying the laces and slowly double-knotting them. I walked up the driveway and stood a little way from the house, watching the scene unfold outside my childhood home.

Rebecca Rush wasn't there. She'd arrived later with a warrant to search the house. A young police constable was talking to my parents. I wasn't close enough to hear what was being said. They both looked resigned to the inevitability of their arrest. I caught Richard's eye. A look of gratitude crossed his face. Thankful that I'd finally brought this to an end. Mum called out to me, "Darling—please take care of the dogs." I nodded. She'd looked at me proudly. As though, in amongst all the horror, she could cling to the fact that her daughter had done the right thing, that she'd raised me properly.

Sophie came back the next day. The police had stopped her as she came down the drive. They let her pass when she explained who she was, but they wouldn't tell her anything. She burst through the door, pale and scared. "Katie, what happened? I was so worried... you wouldn't answer your phone, then I saw the police." She pointed toward Red Rock House where officers were still stationed in the driveway. She ran to me, crying in panic and relief.

As we held each other, I cried too. A mixture of loneliness and regret and loss. "It was Mum." I spoke into her hair through the tears. "Mum killed Lacey." Sophie had buried her deep shock quickly.

"Oh, Katie." She held me tight until the sound of my sobs subsided.

The next day I spoke to her about the podcast. "Will the network make us finish it?" It was a question that I'd been too terrified to ask yesterday.

"I've spoken to them. It's fine. They won't make us finish it." She hugged me. Sophie would never tell me the full story of what she had worked out with the network. I'm sure they weren't happy. But it was something she wanted to protect me from. I would always be grateful for what Sophie did for me in those days after it happened.

For weeks afterward, journalists and photographers camped out on the driveway of Red Rock. It would have been a story even without the overnight success of the podcast. The investigator's mother turning out to be the murderer had made it irresistible. The press interviewed as many people as they could in Pengully. Most people refused to talk to them. I'm not sure if they were protecting us or protecting the town. It didn't matter. We'd seen it before when Lacey was murdered. We knew they'd be gone soon.

A week after it happened, Tom came to the cottage. I was pleased to see him. He was kind, the stillness of him made me feel safe. He asked me what my plans were, but I didn't know. Just getting through the day was about all that I had the capacity for. I'd started writing again. Not much, but it helped make me feel more like myself, more connected to who I am, or at least who I was.

When Tom left, he'd kissed me. Just gently on the lips, but I'd felt a stirring. A sense of hope that the numbness might be temporary. That my feelings weren't lost forever.

CHAPTER SIXTY-TWO

I've been living in Red Rock Cottage for five months since it happened. In some ways it feels like Sophie was never here. I miss her. We'd spoken a few times on the phone and had texted, but it was sometimes hard to know what to say. I felt guilty about losing her the podcast, denting her career. She felt bad about bringing me back to do it in the first place. I often think about how things would have been if we hadn't come here. If we'd covered another murder, in another small town.

I wondered if I'd known what was going to happen, would I still have come?

Mum had been calm as they lowered her into the back of the police car. She'd been expecting it for five years. Richard had moved out of Red Rock House and into one of the rooms at the Carmen. Morti and Perno lived with me now. It wasn't something that was ever discussed. They just became my dogs. I loved having them around.

It looked like Richard was standing by her. His own guilt for the part he'd played had left him with little choice. Richard had engaged the services of an expensive London solicitor to work on Mum's case. It meant that he was having to sell the main house.

Most days brought a parade of couples being shown around the property. Shiny four-by-fours and expensive clothes, all looking to buy into their very own luxury seaside dream. Richard was keeping the cottage for now. I'd started paying rent. I'd insisted. I hadn't seen him since the day of their arrest. Despite the odd text message, to sort out practicalities, we'd never met up.

I didn't blame him for what Mum did. How could I? It didn't make me hate him any less. Some offenses aren't punishable by law. That doesn't mean that they should go unpunished. The loss of Red Rock, of me, of Mum. The fact that Lacey would still be alive if he hadn't started an affair with her. All of it had broken him.

Mum had pleaded not guilty to the charges and was awaiting trial. She called me once a week from prison when she was first arrested. The judge felt that the severity of her crime, combined with her having the financial means to disappear, made it too high risk to grant her bail.

Her calls had come every Thursday for the first few weeks. I dreaded them. Every time I prepared to speak to her, I hoped that this time she'd make me understand. This time she'd help me to see why she'd killed Lacey. She never did.

We might have been able to forge something in the aftermath. I might have been able to feel some level of sorrow for her. If not understanding, then a kind of empathy for what she'd been through with my father and with Richard. Her lack of remorse made it impossible. It was as if she felt imprisonment was a substitute for feelings of guilt. If she'd ever felt bad about what she'd done to Lacey, it had been alleviated by her arrest.

I saw Megan around from time to time. We spoke a little, but we'd never be friends, we both knew it. Megan did an interview with the *Mail on Sunday* in the weeks after Mum's arrest.

It had been a big double-page spread. There was no mention of the photos or how she really felt about Lacey. I'm sure it paid well.

I could easily judge her for the choices she'd made, but none of us had come out of this blameless. I began to see her with Jude more and more. They looked like they were trying to make it work as a family. I was pleased for them. Me and Jude avoided each other whenever we could. We still spoke occasionally, but it was polite, distant. We both needed to move on, and we couldn't do that together. Not even as friends.

Danny had gone to the police about the rape. Michael Penhaligan was arrested. Other women had come forward with allegations and it was enough to hold him until the trial. His face had been plastered over the papers for days. Whether he was found guilty or not, Michael had lost everything.

The town was shocked by the revelations. A collective shame hung over the town, but I wondered if some were more shocked than others.

Claire continued to live at the rectory. I'd seen her a couple of times in town. We never spoke. If it hadn't been for me, her life in Pengully would have carried on as normal. Nobody would have found out what her husband had done. The pretense could have continued for years.

I'd sublet my flat in London to a friend of a friend called Daisy. She seemed nice. I never really got to know her, but she's easygoing and taking care of everything.

I've been doing some freelance writing work. Regular pieces for the local paper and the occasional national. It doesn't pay a lot, but I don't need much living here. I'd tried to hand my notice in at the paper, but Chris, my boss, wouldn't hear of it. I told him what had happened, and he was very kind. He told me I could take unpaid leave for as long as I needed to. He was much nicer than I'd realized. I've noticed that a lot recently. People turning out to be much nicer than I thought they were.

I've been wondering if maybe it's me. I'm much more open with people these days.

I saw quite a lot of Tom. He'd moved to a little village, about ten miles from Pengully. We sometimes meet for a drink in his local pub. Nobody knows us there, so it's easier. On a Friday, he often stops by with a couple of beers and Chinese food after work. He doesn't stay. We both know it's too soon, but I'm looking forward to a time when it isn't.

Last week I went to visit Lacey's grave. It's not really a grave, but a plaque. A place where people can leave flowers up at the crematorium. I've been trying to go there for a while now, since Mum was arrested.

I drove there one windy October day. I walked down the main path from the car park. Holding the edges of my thin coat to my neck, guarding against the cold. To the right of the grounds was a walled garden with a hidden entranceway tucked into the corner. I pushed on the old wooden door.

Years of Cornish weather had left the blue paint peeling and the hinges rusted. The garden was beautiful, not organized manicured beauty, but the sort of garden you know is loved. Burnt reds and oranges highlighted against dark evergreens. There was an old wooden bench in the far corner surrounded by lavender. The woody remnants of the flowers still visible. I walked along the path that skirted the many plaques arranged around the middle. Some were fixed to logs and big joints of driftwood. Others were attached to large rocks, acting as a sort of rustic headstone.

I read the names as I passed by them, calculating the age they would have been when they died. None were as young as Lacey. After a few minutes I found her. The stone was more formal than the others in the garden, a square-cut piece of polished marble. Her name and date of birth were carved in calligraphy. It read, DAUGHTER, SISTER, FRIEND. GONE BUT NEVER FORGOTTEN.

Some flowers had been planted in front of the stone. There was a small cuddly brown bear, wet and muddy, almost hidden among the long blades of grass. A rainbow-colored butterfly on a stick protruded from the soil. It bounced idly on the wind, strangely mesmerizing. I ran my hand over the smooth cold polished stone and thought about Lacey.

Reaching into my pocket, I pulled out a handful of shells that I'd collected from the beach. Each one made a gentle plink as I laid it on top of the stone. "I'm so sorry this happened to you," I said out loud, emotion tugging at my throat. I gave the garden one last look, before stuffing my hands deep into my pockets and heading back home.

A LETTER FROM AMY

Thank you so much for choosing *The Beach Party*. I hope you enjoyed reading it as much as I enjoyed writing it.

If you want to keep up to date with all my latest releases, just sign up at the following link. Your email address will never be shared, and you can unsubscribe at any time.

www.bookouture.com/amy-sheppard

I grew up in Cornwall before moving away for many years in my early twenties. At the point I wrote *The Beach Party*, I'd been living back in Cornwall for two years and madly in love with it again! I'm not sure I could write a novel based anywhere else, even if I wanted to. Cornwall is the heart of all my stories.

I love hearing what you think of the characters, the plot—Pengully! I always appreciate reviews, or you can get in touch with me via Instagram or Facebook.

Amy x

facebook.com/amysheppardfood

instagram.com/amysheppardfood

ACKNOWLEDGMENTS

I just wanted to say thank you to the people that have not only made this book possible, but have made the journey that much more lovely...

To Paul and our boys, Elliot and Sam, I'm so lucky to have you. Thank you for supporting every single one of my ideas. Not all of them work out—I'm so happy this is one that did.

Thank you to my mum and dad for your love and kindness. To my mum, this book wouldn't have happened without you. Every week you cheer me on and I'm so grateful.

Thanks to my friends and family for all your support. To Amy Cassidy, for everything that you do. I'm so thankful to have you in my life.

I've been with my agent Clare for six years. Clare has been such a huge source of encouragement and has (many times!) given me the confidence to press on when I thought about giving up on writing.

I want to thank my editor, Lydia. I knew within five minutes of talking to Lydia that I wanted her to edit my books! Thank you for "getting it" straight away—the characters, the plot—and helping to shape this into the story I wanted to tell.

I want to thank the whole team at Bookouture for your passion and enthusiasm for *The Beach Party* and for bringing it to life the way you have.

Finally, I'd like to thank my followers on social media. What a weird and wonderful journey these last six years have been!

Thank you so much for all your messages and words of encouragement. I'm so excited that I get to share this next bit with you.

Amy x

Printed in Great Britain
by Amazon

85696100R00171